Something Happened to Ali Greenleaf

Something Happened to Ali Greenleaf

HAYLEY KRISCHER

RAZORBILL

Author's Note on Content:

This book contains intense scenes depicting sexual assault and drug abuse.

RAZORBILL

An imprint of Penguin Random House LLC, New York

First published in the United States of America by Razorbill,
an imprint of Penguin Random House LLC, 2020

LIBRARY OF CONGRESS CATALOGING-IN-PUBLICATION DATA
Names: Krischer, Hayley, author.
Title: Something happened to Ali Greenleaf / Hayley Krischer. Description: New York :
Razorbill, 2020. | Audience: Ages 14+. | Summary: Told from two viewpoints, Blythe promises
to fix things after her best friend rapes naive Ali at a party, drawing her into the ruthless
popular crowd while Ali is still reeling. Includes a list of resources for victims of assault.
Identifiers: LCCN 2020020354 | ISBN 9780593114117 (hardcover) |
ISBN 9780593114124 (ebook)
Subjects: CYAC: Rape—Fiction. | Friendship—Fiction. | High schools—Fiction. |
Schools—Fiction. Classification: LCC PZ7.1.K748 Som 2020 | DDC [Fic]—dc23
LC record available at https://lccn.loc.gov/2020020354

Printed in the United States of America

1 3 5 7 9 10 8 6 4 2

Interior design by Samira Iravani
Text set in Walbaum MT Std

To Jake and Elke

Something Happened to Ali Greenleaf

If there was somebody who would've said, listen, I don't know what's going on, but this thing happened to me. And if you are experiencing it, you're not alone. You're not nasty. You're not bad, and it's not your fault. If there was somebody who would've just interjected that, I think it would've changed the trajectory of my life.

—TARANA BURKE, FOUNDER OF THE #METOO MOVEMENT

1

BLYTHE

Some nights it seems like the world has its arms wide open, that the future sizzles with possibility. White streetlights glare in your eyes like disco balls as you whiz down the road. Stars glitter in the black sky. Your favorite song bursts out, and the bass shimmies the car under you as you and your friends chant along.

This is not one of those nights.

We get to Sophie Miller's house and right away my boyfriend, Devon, and his best friend, Sean, leave me alone inside so they can smoke cigars with the rest of the soccer team. "Cigars are for old men," I say to Dev as he kisses me.

"I promise to chew some gum before we make out," he says. Another kiss and he's off.

Sean, the beatific Sean Nessel, is the reason we're here. Sean has a thing for a junior girl—Ali Greenleaf. She's tonight's focus. "She stares at me a lot," he said earlier, back at Dev's house. "Who doesn't stare at you a lot, Nessel?" I wanted to say, but it would have come out awkward.

Sean and Dev are still close—I hear them and the other guys roaring about their win yesterday. State Champs, all because of Sean's winning goal. In the school paper since day one. Front page every day. Like they don't get enough attention since the football team disbanded last year. Now the football moms and the entire town have put all their attention on the soccer boys. Their groveling attention. Outside, the guys are chanting a primal call. DE-FEAT. DE-FEAT. It makes me uncomfortable, all that male animalistic bonding with their claps and their stomps. Everyone at the party is tuned in to it; you can tell by their heads turned toward the windows where the sounds are coming from. Even when they're not in the room, the boys' growls take over.

My crew of girls—we're known as the Core Four: me, Donnie Alperstein, Suki Fields, and Cate Sandoval—should be here by now, but they're not. People aren't used to seeing me alone. I bury my head in my phone and text Cate.

Where are you

Be there in 2

"Oh my God, Blythe Jensen!" A girl I don't know hops in front of me. This happens a lot. When people get drunk, they introduce themselves to me. I nod politely.

"We're in chemistry together," she says.

"Where's the keg?"

She stumbles over directions. She's actually *describing to me* where the keg is. So I stop her before it gets too irritating.

"You would be so useful if you could just find the keg and get me a beer," I say.

"Oh! Sure!"

Ali Greenleaf, the girl Sean wants to hook up with tonight, walks in the door about a minute later. She's with Cherie Mizner, Raj Patel, and another girl, who I think is Cherie's sister. Ali is a scrawny chicken. A goose neck. A pasty-faced pumpkin. Full lips. Like a baby. Her hair with a loose curl. Bangs, which aren't easy to pull off. She has nice hair. Some cute freckles. Wearing a bunch of bracelets up her arm. I like the bracelets. I'll give her that.

Chemistry Girl is standing right in front of me again, twitching. She says "thank you" when she hands me the beer.

But I want to watch Ali. I want to see what Sean sees in her. She turns to her friend, her face glowing in that innocent way a face does. She's the kind of girl who doesn't realize how pretty she is. I can see it in her eyes. That scared look. One more oblivious girl who has no idea what's coming to her. Because I've been through this many times with Sean. Ali will come crying to me, wanting to know what happened between them. *I know you thought he liked you so much, and he does like you, sweetie, except Sean just isn't the commitment type.* It'll happen a few days from now. A week from now. This is textbook Sean. And these stupid girls, forever thinking they're the one he's going to be different with.

I text Dev: *Nessel's girl is here. Better come back in.*

Cate marches in with Suki and Donnie following. She pushes through the crowd to get to me, and the other girls follow. No one says a word about being pushed by them. They just step out of the way.

"So, so, so sorry it took us so long to get here. My mother was giving me a hard time," Cate says.

"Oh, *mothers*," I say, my words dripping.

Cate's mother is originally from Puerto Rico. She still

makes Cate's lunch every morning. Feeds us when we eat at her house. Pours us wine. Wants to fatten us up.

My mother is not this way. I wish I didn't have to help my mother sort her pills or deal with fielding my father's phone calls because he's so worried about her, but that is how it is at my house.

"Plus it took Donnie forever to leave," Suki says to Donnie, who is wobbling a little already. She's been stealing her sister's Vicodin lately, left over from a running injury. And maybe she took too much. She's wearing an oversize army jacket with a short white shirt showing off her brown belly and black skinny jeans. Her tight black curls are wild tonight—the bottom half is a washed-out blue.

Donnie twists around and trips over her foot. I catch her elbow.

"You gonna be okay, Don?"

"B, I'm sooo good." She licks her lips, wiping her hair away from her eyes. She pulls a blue strand out of her mouth.

ALI

Sammi, Raj, and I sit in a little circle drinking beer and smoking Raj's Lucky Strike cigarettes, which are destroying the back of my throat. These Lucky Strikes are Raj's grandfather's. The old man has emphysema and Lucky Strikes aren't easy to find, so he has Raj Google tobacco shops where they sell them. The two of them make a monthly pilgrimage, his grandfather with his portable oxygen tank. His grandpa stockpiles them. As long as Raj keeps it a secret, he'll throw Raj a pack or two.

Raj has been on varsity soccer since he was a sophomore. Which means he's friends with Sean Nessel, which means he's often in *close proximity* to Sean Nessel.

We play the Who Has Had Sex? game and focus on Blythe Jensen. Sometimes I wonder what it's like to be her. In the hallway at school, she's always staring straight ahead, like there's a light at the end of the hall, or a camera, or something else, much further away and superior. As if she's looking anywhere other than here.

"I don't think it's a question of *if* Blythe Jensen's had sex," I say. "She's been going out with Devon Strong forever. It's *how much* sex."

"Actually, the discussion is whether she's got a whip and handcuffs," Sammi says. "She looks like a punisher."

"Okay, Raj, your turn. What about him?" I point to a super-thin hockey player whose shoulders are bigger than his feet.

"I don't even know why we play this game," Raj says. "Half of this room has had sex."

Raj has wavy brown hair; it's soft and puffy and kind of hangs over one eye. All that softness, plus those brilliant green eyes and his skin, a mellow brown from his father's side, whose family is from India, goes against this intense glare, his eyes squinty, even behind his black-rimmed glasses, like he's angry, or thinking too much. "I'm just perpetually skeptical," he told me once when I asked him about it.

Then Sean Nessel glides past a window. Sean Nessel and his silky blond hair to his shoulders. I'm just going to say it: Everything in my life revolves around Sean Nessel. This is no secret. Raj and Sammi understand the full weight of my Sean Nessel obsession.

Even this stupid game. It's just a diversion. We're here at this party for a reason. The three of us, waiting here for something to happen. Because Sean Nessel came up to me and Raj on Friday in the hallway.

To

My

Locker.

It's why Cherie, Sammi's older sister, who is home from college for the weekend, helped us sneak out. It's why we lied to their mom and dad. And Sammi never lies to her parents. It's why I told my father I'd be sleeping at Sammi's and wouldn't be going anywhere. It's why we're at this party. Because Sean Nessel told us to come to this party. He told me. Well, actually, first he told Raj. And then he turned to me, his voice radiating in my brain. And his finger strayed, so that he pointed right at my face.

You should go.

Sean Nessel said this to me. To my face. *You should go.*

In the collages I make, Sean Nessel is my little doll. I turn his pupils into heart eyes in a blip. I wash him in a hazy pink. I meld him with rainbows and hearts.

Sean Nessel. With the cheekbones and the blond hair

swept to the side. The shoulders. Biceps coming out from under his T-shirt. And how does a guy have such perfect skin?

I shake my head, coming out of my cloud as Sean Nessel walks through the front door like a magical freaking unicorn.

BLYTHE

Sean and Dev stroll through the door, laughing after their cigar smoke-out. *Hoot. Hoot. Hoot.* The whole place shoots up two decibels. I sip my drink and give Suki a side-eye.

Behind the noise I hear Sophie Miller crying, "You guys, *you guys.*" Whining.

"What did you think was going to happen when you invite the school to your house, honey?" Donnie says, slurring.

"You think we'd take it easy? Nooooo," I say.

No one takes it easy on anyone.

ALI

People are hooting. They all want Sean Nessel's attention. I take a big gulp of my beer. Stare at him until my eyes water.

I'm going to hypnotize you, Sean Nessel. I stare at him. Stare at him, stare at him. Until my powers get him to stare back at me. His hands. His arms. His faded turquoise T-shirt tight over his chest. His flushed cheeks, like a sunset. He's a sunset. And I'm the beach. I stare away because I'm feeling so hot and I can hardly breathe. I duck my head into Sammi's shoulder.

"You're shaking," she says.

I'm shaking. I have to lift my head back up. Just look one more time. Didn't he want me here? He wanted me here. So I'm here. I did so much to get here! Look at me, Sean Nessel. Look at me.

And then it happens. Sean Nessel looks back at me. Once. Twice. It's like a stream between us, a narrow and sweaty tunnel of love where everyone else in the room floats away.

Deep breath. If I can breathe. I can hardly breathe.

I'm going to be sick.

Sammi pinches me on the side of my leg, and I swat her.

With his eyes still on me, Sean nods his head to the left, over in the direction of a side door. An abundance of Jedi mind tricks have preceded this night. *I am the girl you've been looking for.*

BLYTHE

I watch Sean talking to Ali. Stupid girl. She's so predictable, like the other girls. It'll start innocently. He'll go jogging with someone. Or he'll get the hall pass with someone. Or he'll hook up with some girl from another team at a soccer match like he did the first night of State Champs just a few weeks ago. But I think back to the Nationals in South Carolina last year, when Sean told Dev that after the game he went back to the hotel room with two girls. *Two girls?* Sounds like a porn, I told Dev. But then I couldn't stop thinking about it, and every time I thought about it, there was that rush of heat between my thighs.

Dev's nothing like Sean. Dev's concerned when I talk about my mother. Dev actually listens. The way he treats everything I say like it's the weight of the world.

If Dev is a Golden Retriever, Sean is a Siberian Husky, fierce and maybe on the edge of the wild.

Cate is trying to show me a picture of herself in a dress she wants to wear to the dance, which is two months away. It's a washed-out lavender dress. Halter top with cutouts in the middle and back and a high-waist cigarette skirt. The skirt part is so tight that you'd have to peel it off her. I'm thinking about my own thighs and how I have some cellulite and how my mother called me out on it at the pool this summer. My mother is going to want to go dress shopping with me for the dance too. It's our thing together. I say *thing* lightly.

"So what do you think about the dress, B?"

Donnie jumps in: "I think there's entirely too much cleavage. It's messy."

Donnie's the only person I don't mind being less pretty than.

I pull the phone from Cate's hand. The dress is awful. And I hate her for bringing it up and making me think about my mom, who I'm going to have to eventually go dress shopping with.

"I can't help that I have boobs," Cate says to Donnie, looking down at her chest. Her breasts have been that way since she was ten. It's a sore spot.

"I thought you were going to try that leotard? To flatten you out?" Suki says, rubbing her hands across her chest. Suki is practically a pencil with her black leggings and big T-shirts. She calls herself a proud Jewish Chinese American. Celebrates the New Year three times: Rosh Hashanah, the Chinese New Year, and with the rest of the idiots on December 31st.

"You don't flatten out a dress like that."

"Go back on that no-carb diet. Last time you were on that, your boobs totally shrank," I say.

"Or maybe she should try eating cotton balls filled with orange juice again," Donnie says. Her quips are designed to kill.

"Wait, you really ate those cotton balls with the orange juice? I thought that was a joke. I thought you were just watching those girls on YouTube?" I say.

"You're basically making fun of that time I had an eating disorder, and I don't appreciate it," Cate says. She's serious now.

"Hold up. That *time* you had an eating disorder?" Suki says.

Donnie and I stare at each other with wide-open eyes. Oh, when Suki goes after Cate, it's bad. We jump up and down, raising our hands in the air.

"It's onnnnnn!"

But Suki is not having this. "Calm down, people. It is not

on." She pleads with me, then grits her teeth. She turns to Cate. Those two are tight. Like Donnie and I are tight. You don't go over that line about eating disorders; you keep that shit silent, buried deep—but Suki did. "Cate, *you know* it is not on."

Donnie makes fun of Suki, drawing out her words, teasing her. "There is nothing ON about this."

"It is so clearly off. It's like, 'lights out, bitch,'" I say.

Cate's eyes get big and teary. She lights a cigarette. Deep inhale. Cate with her big burly stance, her gold hoop earrings with her name blazing through them—CATE—it's all a show. She's the easiest to tease.

"I'm not laughing," Cate says. Even though she's smiling. She knows if she doesn't laugh, the teasing will never end. Laugh it off, Cate. Just laugh it off.

"Grow up, Heather. Bulimia is so '87," I say, and give her the *end it* signal—one quick hand swipe in front of my neck.

Cate flicks her ashes hard at me and Donnie, which we probably deserve. I twist my head away from the flying embers, and that's when I see Sean leading Ali into another room.

ALI

"Heyyyyy, Greenleaf," Sean Nessel says, with a drawl. He might be drunk. "I want to show you something." He leads me into the kitchen. His hand is softer than I had imagined and moist.

"So what kind of last name is Greenleaf?"

I tell Sean Nessel the whole story about my grandfather coming over from Germany to Ellis Island and how the immigration officer couldn't pronounce Grunblatt—he had trouble with the "u" inflection. "Greenleaf" is the English translation for Grunblatt. My grandfather really didn't want to be called Greenleaf because that didn't seem like a real American last name, but that's where he ended up.

I completely overtalk it. I can't shut up. Shut up, Ali. Shut up.

Sean Nessel just stares at me like I'm insane.

"I used to get teased as a kid about my last name too. You know, Nessel. People called me Nestle chocolate. Hershey's kisses. Nestle chocolate face."

"Wait, you got teased?"

"Yeah. Doesn't everyone get teased about something?"

"I can't see you getting teased about anything," I say. My heart eyes are about to explode, and I realize I'm not wearing a T-shirt bra, as in the padded kind. My headlights are about to blind Sean Nessel. I cross my arms over my breasts.

He arranges a row of three small vodka bottles on the counter, the kind you get on an airplane. I really don't need to drink. I finished a beer and am already feeling silly and surly. But he opens the first one, takes a sip, and hands it to me.

"So cute," I say. "Little bottles. Just tiny things."

"Drink it."

"You're like the Mad Hatter," I tease. "'Drink it. This one will make you big.'"

"Isn't that what you want? To be big?"

"I want to get buzzed."

STOP.

Did I just say that? I'm being too forward. Too cocky. Anyway, I'm already buzzed. What am I doing?

"Well, I don't mean buzzed," I say. But these are never the kinds of declarations you can take back.

"Nah, it's okay," he says, laughing. "You're funny." But I don't feel funny. I feel too grown up. My hair is down and long. It's wild from the fall winds. I shake it around, getting it to hang over one eye. And then I do what any sensible person would do in the presence of a god like Sean Nessel. I take a hearty sip.

My mouth is on fire. I choke in a coughing fit.

"Take another sip. It'll take the edge off the first one," he says.

"It burns."

"It's supposed to."

I sip again, and the vodka gushes into my mouth. I glimpse Sammi and Raj still comfy with their beers sitting with some other friends. Finally, my dream is here, but I feel out of control, too hurried, like one of those weird car commercials where the lights are streaking through a dark desert road.

He hands me a hard seltzer and tells me to drink it as a chaser. One at a time. Small and easy, he says. So I listen because I am drinking vodka with Sean Nessel. If nothing else happens to me this year, this moment sipping vodka from small airplane bottles will be enough.

His hand is at the back of my head now, and he rustles my hair. "What a cute girl you are, Ali," he says. "I like the way you look at me in the hall. You have cute hair. I'm so glad you came here tonight. That's why I'm here, you know?"

My eyes widen and I smile. My hands shake. I'm breathless. My mouth is numb when he slips his tongue inside it. I want to kiss him back, but my head is hot and his tongue is so big in my mouth, all I can do is move my neck. It doesn't take long for my mouth to feel raw from kissing and for my face to get sweaty. I'm fuzzy, probably need to sit down, but when Sean Nessel asks me to go upstairs, I say yes.

I know what upstairs means. Upstairs means *clothes off.*

BLYTHE

Cherie is sitting on the couch ledge right behind me. She doesn't notice me until I poke her.

"Oh, Blythe. Heyyy," she says.

Cherie used to be one of the most popular girls in school until she became a raging feminist when she was a senior. Just dumped all her friends. Wouldn't talk to anyone except two girls from the drama club who are here at this party.

"Your girl has disappeared into the smoky den of iniquity," I say. I'm so happy to torment Cherie.

"What's that supposed to mean?" she says. "What girl?"

"Ali Greenleaf," I say. "She's your girl, isn't she?"

"More like my sister's girl."

16

I shrug. I'm now drinking Jack and Coke, courtesy of Donnie. It burns as it goes down. Donnie locks her arm in mine.

"These boys take what they want, you know that," Donnie says to Cherie.

Cherie looks away, her face in a worried pinch.

I've lost track of time. I finish my Jack and Coke. It's time to go. I kiss Dev and stroke his neck. I want to go back to his house. His mother will make us grilled cheese sandwiches. Because Dev's mother is one of those mothers who grills you a sandwich at midnight. Dev's mother makes him her priority. My mother is incapable of functioning the same way. This is what happens when you have a mother with bipolar. You don't get sandwiches at midnight. You get worry instead.

I shake it from my mind and think about Dev's mom and how she'll linger in the kitchen. How I'll sit on his lap sipping whole milk as she asks us about the party. How she'll call me *sweetheart*. That look of his that he'll give me. Those eyes holding on to me like that. Squeezing me. We'll go back in his room and get naked in his bed.

"Let's go," I say, and nibble on his ear.

"Nessel," he says. "We have to wait for Nessel."

2

ALI

Sean Nessel pushes open a bedroom door. His hands fall across my hips as he glides us forward. It's so easy; I could be on ice skates. We sit down on the floor and kiss more, but soft, not with saliva and spit everywhere. He lays me down, slips his jacket off, rubs my breasts over my shirt, then under my shirt over my bra, and then under my bra.

I want to whisper something, but if I open my mouth, something stupid will spill out like, "I've never done this before." And I want him touching me. I want to be here, drunk and making out with Sean Nessel, even if I'm not the greatest kisser and even if my breasts aren't huge, and even if no one has ever, really, gone under my bra before.

Then his hands are inside my jeans, and I let him do that too, because I am so warm and his hands feel so good on the inside of my thighs. We kiss like this for what seems like a while. My body buzzes. I'm for sure drunk.

You want a different take, don't you? That I'm scared. Or that it doesn't feel good. But it does. It feels frightening and amazing all at once.

The music from downstairs vibrates through the floor—there's this song that's not really slow, but it's intense and moody. My body rocks along with Sean Nessel's and I feel him. You know what I'm saying? *Feel him.* My mind goes to such a crazy place filled with roses and flowers and all the rainbows and feathers I've ever decorated his face with in my collage book. I'm turned on. I've kissed other boys before, and nothing has ever felt like this.

He starts pulling down my underpants and I am breathing so heavy, and then he stands up and I lie on the floor with my knees touching and my underpants dangling from one leg, and he is trying to kick off his shoes with the heel of his foot and laughing because he can't get them off. He does this funny dance, or maybe he's just stumbling. Either way, I'm laughing.

He's unzipping his pants. Why is he unzipping his pants?

I hear the party going on below us, the song still blaring through the floor.

"Wait," I say.

But he just sort of moans like this: *uh-huh.*

"Wait."

And in three seconds, he's on top of me. His body feels like deadweight. The rough carpet and his wool soccer jacket scratch across my back and thighs. My hand fights against his shoulder, shoving him away, but he's not paying attention. My T-shirt is riding up, but I'm naked down below and his penis jabs at my inner thigh and then closer to my vagina.

"Sean, I don't—"

"Shhh, relax," he says.

"You have to stop."

He forces his penis into me, and I feel like I'm ripping open, literally tearing. It hurts so bad, and he's grunting, shoving himself in. Then there's a wet, heavy rush between my thighs. He grinds his hips into my bony pelvis, and I push his face away with one hand.

"You're hurting me," I say. I cannot believe this is happening. Doesn't he hear me?

My body is too lazy from the alcohol, and though I fight him off, pressing into his chest, the pain is like this crazy lightning bolt, so I groan out, and he muzzles my mouth with his hand. Pins my shoulder to the ground and grinds himself deeper into me. I pound on his back with my fist.

I can't move.

I cannot move.

When I scream again, it's a low holler this time; I only hear my voice inside my head.

As his body bangs into me, a low-level ringing goes off in my head. The ringing carries through my ears, then across to my nose and down my throat.

He gets up and reaches for the light, and I'm crying and my knees are shaking, and the lights are on. Blood covers the inside of my thighs and his jacket.

I'm hysterical, hardly able to catch my breath, and Sean Nessel seethes. "Holy shit, what the hell is this? Your period?"

"No," I cry, shocked at my own blood. My words buckle. "I didn't know." I wipe the snot from my face.

He curses and paces, telling me how he ripped up his dick and now there was blood all over his soccer jacket. "How are we gonna clean all this shit up?" he says. He paces the room with his pants off and with me still crying and his penis has blood on it, and he finally finds a tissue and wipes the blood off.

He throws the bloodied tissue in the garbage and then throws the box of tissues at me and tells me to wipe myself off. So I do. I'm doing everything he says. I can't even do it myself first. I've never been so paralyzed in my life.

"Okay, okay," he keeps repeating, pacing around the room and putting his pants back on. "I'll get your friend, so just stay here and stop crying or something. You're going to be fine."

I've never been this drunk before. But am I though? Am I that drunk at all? Don't I know exactly what just went on? Wasn't I right there? He looks at me again as if I'm not the girl he brought upstairs. My mouth is numb. I am dizzy and for certain at least very buzzed, very confused. All I can think is that my father is going to find out. The whole school is going to find out.

I run over to the trash basket where all the bloody tissues are and puke. Vomit rages out of my mouth burning everything.

I wipe the snot and puke off my face with my sweatshirt and turn to him.

"I told you to stop," I say, and then tears erupt. Miles and miles of tears.

He's blank, looking confused. He rubs his hands in his hair and paces more. That hair. My first dream about Sean Nessel was me kissing him, stroking him at the back of his head like a sweet puppy.

I flap my arms because I look like a duck when I cry. The room felt big in the dark, but with the lights on, it's tiny. There are dirty socks on the floor, and I pour what is left of the hard seltzer onto one of the socks and wipe the rest of the blood off my inner thighs and my ankle.

He just stands there, shaking his head.

Downstairs. Faces flash in weird disco lights, and I have no idea where Sammi is. I barrel my way through to the front door. It feels like it takes hours to get there and more people cram into the hall.

My shoulder burns. I can't see the door. I just want to see the door before I cry. Before I can't make it out of here without puking, or screaming, or falling to my knees.

Hopefully, when Sean Nessel goes to clean his jacket, all evidence of me will come off. Hopefully, when school comes on Monday, Sean Nessel won't even look at me. I hope he can just smile and keep walking.

3

BLYTHE

I wrap my finger around Suki's pinkie and lead her to the bathroom, which is near the stairs. I can't believe we have to wait for Nessel. For Sean. Mr. Perfect, who is somewhere seducing a junior he'll never talk to again. I need something that'll stop me from falling asleep, and Suki has a fresh bottle of Ritalin prescribed from her doctor. We crush it on the sink and snort it. It goes up quick, and I get a jolt. Just the right amount of energy that'll help me drive these guys home. Just a tiny bump. But I'm shaky. She's shaky. We see it in each other. More sips of beer to mellow out the high. That's all.

"Where's Sean?" Suki says.

"He's upstairs with some junior."

"Oh, that," she says. Her eyes glaze over. Jaw clenches.

"Yeah, that."

Suki's been down the Sean road. She looks tiny every time I tell her Sean is with some girl, which is often. I might just lie to her next time because it feels cruel.

It's been at least six months since they were together. One day she was about to have his babies—that's what a guy like Sean will do to you. And it lasted for a week, the two of them. Then I find out he's having sex with Jen Tucker in her car and going down Blake Sawyer's pants behind the gym. I never said she was my girlfriend, Sean said when I asked him.

Her hands shake on the sink counter. "Sukes, your hands. They're shaking," I say.

She points down at mine. My hands are shaking too.

Something is off tonight. Something isn't right.

Out of the bathroom, Ali practically runs me over. Her face is manic and teary. Eyes popping out of her skull. Racing nowhere. Her head spinning back and forth looking for an exit. I'm standing right there in front of her, and she doesn't even notice me.

So I just say anything, just because I want to know. I want to see her eyes.

"Leaving so soon?" I say.

She turns to me, and her eyes widen even more with desperation. Her face looks broken, vacant.

Jesus, what did he do to her?

Across the room I see Sean talking to Dev. He's shaking his head, telling him something. Something's wrong. Something happened.

Ali's face is melting almost.

And then she lets out this excruciating cry. Like someone's dead.

"What's wrong with you?" I say. "Calm down."

But something happened. She's rambling, babbling, not making any sense.

And in a way, it reminds me of me.

Stupid girl. Stupid, stupid girl! Playing with the big boys.

This is what it looks like. When you're small and unnecessary. I know this feeling. I know it well.

I make my way over to Dev, pushing bodies aside.

"Nessel just told me something about blood being on his jacket," Dev whispers. "I'm like, 'bro, what the hell are you talking about?' He's not bleeding anywhere."

"He was with that girl Ali upstairs," I say.

Dev stares at me funny. He can't put it together.

"Do I need to explain it to you, Dev? Really?" I say, snapping. So much Nessel love. So much empathy for everyone. I love Dev for this and it's what also drives me insane. "He went upstairs with her. Suki and I saw him."

"So you and Suki are keeping tabs on Nessel? That's kind of creepy, no?"

"It's not like that, Dev—" I look to the front door to see where Ali went, but she's gone.

"We have to get him out of here," Dev says.

Sean, Dev, and I walk out; Sean's head is down and he doesn't say a word until we get in the car.

"Can you drive, B? Can you drive? You're the only one who can drive, B. All we have left is you," Sean says.

"I'm okay," I say. But I'm totally not. We should call an Uber, but too much has gone on. I just want to get out of here.

"That girl made a mess of my jacket," Sean says. I peek in the rearview mirror at a stop sign and see that he's got his big varsity soccer jacket rolled up in a ball.

"Why do you keep saying that, bro?" Dev asks. "You said that earlier."

"She had her period, dude. She bled, like, everywhere."

But I wonder if it was her period at all. I wonder if it was more like her first time.

Sean's garbly wasted. Talking things that half make sense. He says she was crying and that he didn't even realize that she was crying until after.

"How am I supposed to know these things? Do you know how many girls hit on me? Do you? What did she think we were going to do up there? And she's looking at me all sexy. What did she think was going to happen?"

"Aww, all the girls love Nessel, and they're just crying over you, dude. They love you." Dev's smiling, but I can tell it's not real. He winces when he says it. "She's young. She's just freaked out probably. She'll be fine."

I'm staring at the black of the road in front of me and thinking about why a girl might cry after she has sex. I think it doesn't have to do so much with love. I think it has a lot to do with regret.

When I pull up at Sean's house about ten minutes later, he spits on the curb, saying he's going to puke. Dev's already asleep. His hair is muddled up against the window.

Sean puts his head inside my window.

"You have to help me, B."

"Help you into the house?"

"No. Come on, B. Think. Think!" He raises his voice. He can't even get his words out. To see a god fall. Have you ever seen a god fall? I don't want to see it. I can't bear to look. I nod; it's a painful blow.

"We've been friends for so long, B. You know I would never hurt anyone. But she said I hurt her. And maybe, I don't know. Maybe I was too intense. You know I wouldn't do anything to anyone." Sean's crying now. He's a hurricane of emotions. He's quivering. He's mumbling about school and how he'll get kicked out and how he'll never get into college.

"Sean. Sean. You have to calm down." I stroke his hair. It's silk. You know it had to be that way. Silk.

"Of course you didn't hurt anyone." The words slip out of me. Somehow, it's all so clear and I know exactly what to say. Maybe it's the Ritalin finally working. "Don't worry. I'll talk to her. I'll tell her it's going to be fine. She'll understand. I'll fix it for you."

He cowers in the window, his head now resting on the inside of the door. I stroke his cheek down to his chin. I promise him it's going to be fine.

4

ALI

I get to my front door, and it's weird because all the lights are off except for this glow near the kitchen. I'm nervous to walk inside, sweaty. I wonder if this is my life. If this is happening to me.

Maybe it's not. Maybe I'm dead.

The buzzing in my back pocket jolts me. It's Sammi looking for me. I know it's awful, but I shut off my phone, shut her out—I just want to get into my house. I know I'm going to have to talk to her.

And then I hear a low humming, a woman's voice. Is it music that's playing? Billie Holiday? Some kind of jazz. Then a laughing, a cackle. I walk in farther, and my stomach drops at the sight of flesh.

There is a woman in my living room. She has a T-shirt on and is lying on her back. I can't see her face, not that I'd know her. Underwear. White granny panties.

The man's face resting next to her face is for sure . . . for certain . . . *my father*. With no shirt on. The two of them, whispering and kissing.

Then the woman opens her eyes and screams—and her voice crashes around me and I flinch, because for a second, I think, *What now? Did something else horrible happen?* And then I realize, no, she's screaming because of me. Because I walked in. And I look away because, God, it's my father in some weird postcoital position.

My father, in the fastest move I've ever seen in my life, whips his head around to face the doorway toward me, then rolls her away from him, away from my view.

"Holy shit—" my father says, and scrambles for his T-shirt. "You weren't supposed to be home tonight!"

The woman scurries to the bathroom, tugging her jeans on as she moves.

"Who is *she*?" I say, my voice garbled. She is no one I've ever met before. Not that there have been many. There was one ex-girlfriend that enlightened me, let's say, and that's a nice way to put it. If you want to consider enlightenment showing me how to use tampons. My mother was not happy about this. "You could have waited until you saw me so I could teach you," she had said to me, utterly wounded. "Well, maybe if you hadn't run away to live in some hippie town, you'd be around when some idiot boy decides to have a pool party two days after I get my period so that you can show me how to use a tampon," I said and hung up on her.

The woman walks out of the bathroom, jeans on now. She swings her long, curly, blond hair away from her face. Her lips are pink and raw looking.

"Ali, this is Sheila."

"I'm going to my room. I'm pretending like this isn't happening."

I storm off to the steps, but my thighs ache as I walk. My head spins. I'm still drunk.

"Alistair! Stop right there." My father rarely screams. But his voice bellows now.

"Explain to me what is going on. You were supposed to be sleeping at Sammi's."

"I wanted to come home," I say. "Is that so bad?" My voice is quivering now. I'm going to cry, explode all over the place. It's all settling in. The vodka. My head pounding. The soreness between my legs.

"Where are your shoes?"

"Who cares about my shoes, Dad? Shoes are so unimportant right now. Trust me. Shoes are so, like, the last thing that any of us should be thinking about."

"Did you and Sammi get into a fight or something?"

"I don't want to talk to you about anything," I say and face the wall because I could break into tears so easily. I could drift right into it. This is the night I need my father most. Sometimes a girl just needs to sit and cry with her dad on the couch. Except tonight, that's out of the question, because Sheila the She Woman is here. I suck the damp air of the den in through my nostrils and close my eyes.

"Ali, are you drunk?"

"John, I don't mind leaving," I hear Sheila the She Woman say. She's got a super-low voice, like a weird old cow.

"No, no. Just hold on a sec."

I'm dying to turn around to get another glimpse of her, except I don't want my father to study my face. I've still got traces of eyeliner smudges, I'm sure. There are other things he might notice too. That I've been crying. That I've been kissed—hard. That a boy strapped his hand across my mouth. My dad is perceptive that way. He's clued in to my emotions.

I want to blab about the whole night, but what would I say? *Hey, Dad. I got drunk. Oh, and Sean Nessel popped my cherry. We were swigging straight vodka from airplane bottles because I'm absolutely stupid. We lied to Sammi's parents. And Sammi—she doesn't even know where I am! Use protection? Ha! What protection?*

All those years of my father and his excruciatingly painful monologues about how important it is to protect yourself from HIV, herpes, pregnancy . . . all out the window in one traumatic night with Sean Nessel.

Oh, I'm totally going straight to hell on a roller coaster. I'm, like, on the Space Mountain express to the earth's flaming pit.

"Can I just please, *please*, go upstairs and go to bed if I promise to talk to you in the morning?" I say. "It's been the worst night, and I feel like I'm going to throw up."

Fine, he tells me. But he's not letting me off the hook, he says. He wants to know what's going on. He wants to know why I smell like a brewery. Oh, and he makes me apologize to Sheila the She Woman. I oblige.

In my room, I crawl into bed. My legs are sore and my inner thighs hurt as I pull my knees up to my chest. No matter how badly I want to, I can't take a shower now. Besides my father questioning why I'm taking a shower at eleven o'clock at night, any residue on my body is the only evidence that this night happened. I want my body to feel this experience.

Feel the cracked blood around my vagina, feel my sore back, feel the imprint of Sean Nessel's hand on my shoulder. This is what being an adult is, right? This is how people become mature. They suffer and move on.

I'll make a conscious effort not to look different or walk funny in the morning. Because, after tonight, I plan to erase this.

I try to imagine my mother, playing with my hair or tickling my back. But tonight my mother is far away in New Mexico, under the stars, because that's where she decided to move when I was twelve years old to clean up her act. To sober up. To live in a little low-pressure community in the desert. To take life One Day at a Time, her favorite sober catchphrase, as she always reminds me before we hang up the phone. Little does she know what happened to her baby girl tonight.

I wish she was here to rub the knot out of my spine. Do X Marks the Spot. What would she have said?

Nothing. Nothing that my father can't say.

That is, if I'd bother to tell him.

And I don't even know where to begin.

So I curl up in bed, hold my legs tight, and scrunch the cool sheet between my thighs. Alone. I know I'll stop crying once this night is over. I know I'll be stronger once I can pull myself together. But in this moment, I want my mother.

5

BLYTHE

After we drop Sean off, after all those tears that he spilled as we practically carried him to his front steps, Dev and I drive home in silence.

"Do you believe him? I think he's just beyond wasted," I say when we park.

But I don't want to know.

Dev and Sean have been tied together since kindergarten. Dev's always been Sean's head cheerleader. His hype man. The guy who makes Sean look better than he actually is. Because Dev truly sees Sean as a sweet, vulnerable guy, who, despite the rotation of girls, can still get his heart broken. A guy who still wants to know how to act. Sometimes he asks Dev about sex. What it's like between us.

"Are her legs supposed to shake like that after?" Sean asked him just two weeks ago.

"Oh my God, what did you tell him?" I said.

"I told him the truth because he looks up to us, B," Dev said. "'Yeah, bro, they should shake.'"

It seemed sweet. Like he cared.

I'm no one's hype man. I have my own team to do that for me. The Core Four. They would lay everything on the line for me. Have I talked to girls for Sean, reassured them, coddled them? Sure. What kind of monster would I be if I just left these girls crying after he decided they weren't worth his time? But for Sean to beg me to talk to someone like he did tonight? This is new.

Dev places his hand on my thigh, nothing more. He's as stupefied as I am.

The truth is that I have no memories of my life before Sean Nessel was in it. There was my father always commenting how he handled the soccer ball. We'd watch him from the top of my street when he lived near me, before his parents got divorced. My father would say things like, "Kid has a natural talent." Or "Kid has a great foot." We'd walk up there—this was in fourth grade—just so my dad could talk to Mr. Nessel. Just to compliment him on his son's foot.

Before that, Sean Nessel was the kid who chased me around the playground during recess. I'd be out of breath, hiding from him under the slide, but he'd always come for me. Even when the other boys, boys like Dev, would be throwing a tennis ball against the school wall. They wanted to play Pegs. Sean wanted to chase me. And I let him chase me for at least the first half of recess. I loved it. I loved the thrill of being wanted by him, even though I couldn't explain that in my little silver leggings and my pink T-shirts and my boots or my high-tops with all the studs on them.

"I'm gonna get you tomorrow, Jensen," Sean would yell to me with a huge smile, his face streaked with red before he went over to join his friends at the wall.

I didn't meet Donnie until sixth grade when we got to middle school. Back then it was just me, Cate, and Suki. Cate would say to me, "I can stop him, B. I'm bigger than him." And she *was* bigger than him for a while—her round body didn't get muscular until we got to middle school and all stretched out. Sean was wiry then, lean with popping muscles, but not a monster, before he shot up to whatever tall height he's at now.

Did I want him to stop chasing me? I *lived* for him to chase me. But I didn't know how to say that to Cate. To anyone. So I went home that night and demanded that my father take me to the mall to get running sneakers.

"You have sneakers," he said, looking down at my high-tops. With their gold glitter laces.

"Not ones like these. Sneakers that'll make me run fast."

"Okay, but is there a reason?"

"Because I need to outrun someone."

My father was concerned. He looked at me, serious. "A bully?"

"Bully, no! Sean Nessel is chasing me all over during recess."

My father's face. Like a proud papa. Sean Nessel, the kid with the foot, chasing his baby girl.

"You know what it means when a boy chases a girl, don't you, Blythe? It means that he likes you."

When I went to school the next day, I hid my new sneakers in my backpack like a secret weapon. I didn't want Sean to know what I had. It would be a surprise. A sneak attack. A sneak-*ers* attack.

In class, during a small break, he walked by my desk on his way to the water fountain. He bent down, whispering to me, "I'm going to get you today, Jensen."

I gazed up at his face. No hesitation. "I'll be waiting," I said.

He smiled so big that I thought his face would explode. I couldn't even sit in my seat right, I was so excited. Cate turned around, her pudgy face desperate. "What's going on?" she mouthed.

I shrugged. It was my thing with Sean. Our game of chase. I didn't want her or anyone else part of it.

Later, when the bell rang, I told Suki and Cate not to wait for me because I had to go to the bathroom. I ran over there, sat in the stall, and changed into my new sneakers. Teal and purple. Shoved my boots in my backpack. Hung it up in my locker, then walked to the school door. My heart racing. My body pounding. I opened the door and stood at the top of the steps, searching for Sean until I found him playing Pegs at the wall.

I strode over slowly, so out of breath already, my body throbbing. I wanted to scream his name, holler for him. *Come and get me.* But I didn't have to. Because he spotted me through everyone. His face beamed. Then he looked down at my feet, and his mouth dropped open wide. He laughed, rested his hands on his hips, nodded, and without any warning, rocketed toward me.

I pivoted and ran, faster than I ever had before, zooming between kids, not stopping for a second. I could hear him catching up, behind me, grunting. Then I just felt him all of a sudden, his body tackling me into the mulch near the tire swing. My face skidded across the wood chips and then a thud of both our bodies, together and then hitting the ground. There was a moment or two that the air completely escaped me and maybe the same happened to Sean because he rolled off me and we both wriggled on the ground, gasping.

That's when the recess teacher sprinted over, grabbed Sean by the hand, and hauled his body up to stand. "I saw you, Sean," she yelled. "I saw you leap on top of Blythe. I saw you chase her. I saw you attack her. What on earth were you thinking?"

I couldn't even gulp a breath of air to defend him in the moment. My leggings were torn up at the knee, my face dirty and full of mulch. A bunch of girls, including Suki and Cate, lifted me up. Suki frantically saying over and over in my ear, "Are you okay, B? Are you okay?"

The recess teacher, I can't even remember her name now, dragged Sean away. His face never left mine until she brought him inside.

Later the principal asked me, "Was this a game you were playing, Blythe? Did you want to be chased by Sean?"

"Yes," I told her. Yes. Was there any other answer?

6

ALI

You know when you've exercised a lot at the gym, or run a few miles or so, or played an intense game of some sport and you're sore the next day? Everything hurts. Even when you're not moving, it hurts. Like all your muscles have been crunched between two metal clamps. Well, that's what I feel like. My vagina, as in my *actual vagina*, hurts. As if someone tore something out of it. There are muscles, tissue inside there, and it's shredded.

I slide my T-shirt over my shoulder, where he pressed me down. I can't even think about it without shaking, without that lightning bolt shivering up through my ribs. Piercing me. There's a big black mark there. A bruise, a wide bruise that wants to come through. It'll get more purple. More yellowish. Until it taunts me, reminding me every day what a fraud he turned out to be and how stupid in love I was.

Cute bangs, he had said to me at my locker.

I shake my head. Stupid bangs. I hate these bangs. I yank them. Want to tear them from my skull.

I grab scissors off my desk and cut my hair, shearing my bangs so they look like an awful version of Bettie Page. They're straggling, and the hairs flick down over my forehead like razor-sharp dental instruments.

I'm nauseous now. My rumbling, sickened belly. That bitter taste in my mouth.

Now I have to destroy my Sean Nessel collage book. It's just a composition book, the cover, a picture of Sean Nessel from the school newspaper, his hair behind his ears, looking to the left at something in the distance. Hearts and flowers near his eye. Roses and peonies and lilacs and hydrangeas. Purple hearts on his sleeves, hearts and hearts and more hearts, as if they're growing from his face like some magical creature. Inside the book, more of the same. My obsession with Sean Nessel layered over streaks of a pink and orange sunset, sweeping behind him as he kicks the ball or runs down the field or smiles for the camera, all the colors, bleeding around him, so sweet and infectious. So innocent.

What a joke. A sick, demented joke.

I gag a few times.

I'm so angry. I followed that idiot Sean Nessel up those stairs, into that dark bedroom, and took off my jeans. I'm so angry, so mad at myself. He spoke to me all of one time before the party. Once. With Raj, standing there watching me at my locker. And it somehow was enough to make me believe he wanted what I wanted. Some diluted fantasy. Now, Sean Nessel knows even less about me, except that his dick was buried inside me.

I rip a few of the pages—whatever I can get my hands on—my sweet pasted-on collage of little hearts and cutout flowers, all the tiny petals that I layered with such care, I tear them apart—out of the book. Pages fall to the ground.

My father beats on my door like a jail cell warden. "I hope you're up. You need to get downstairs. *Now.*" He clomps away.

The clock says after ten. I bury what's left of my collage book under my bed. Look at me. I was such a child with my stupid flowers and hearts.

I turn on my phone. A million texts from Sammi. From Raj. A message this morning from my mother. How would that conversation go? Her voice, pressing me from so far away. *How are you, honey? Your voice sounds shaky. What's wrong?* I can't call her back. Not now.

In the bathroom, I stare into the mirror at myself. Deep breath, Ali. Take a deep breath. I brush my teeth. I scrub my face. Who knows how I smell. I want to get into the shower, but I consider what happened last night.

Was I raped?

This might be the strangest question I'll ever have to ask myself.

If I say yes, then it means Sean Nessel didn't listen when I said stop. It means I lost my virginity to Sean Nessel this way.

I think of the TV shows that I've seen on rape victims. I know the first thing I'd have to do is go to the police, or have someone professionally check me. Anyone who's watched *SVU* knows this. But I don't want any remains of him on me anymore. There's a crackly feeling between my legs. I'm dirty and I want it off.

So I force myself into the shower. The hot water and beating pellets of the special massage shower head that my dad just installed numb my back and arms. My shoulder. My bruised shoulder. I can't even turn it into the shower, it burns if I do. How am I going to cover up this shoulder?

I turn into the stream with my face. It beats down on my cheeks. My skin hurts. It burns. And I turn the heat higher. And higher again.

7

BLYTHE

Some friendships are about loyalty. Some friendships are built on secrets. Some friendships are built on mutual infatuation. Donnie and I are all of these.

That's why the next morning I shower—I get all that party off me, and those awful conversations, my promises, my icky, icky promises—and haul my ass over to Donnie's house. I look in the mirror, the steam clouding my view. I hate myself today.

Donnie is my other side. My emotional side. The side who falls apart. The side who has nothing to hide. She's got the together family. The rocket-scientist mother. The minivan. The massive house. The beautiful working parents. The sisters and their Instagram accounts, where they post pictures of each other all day long in bathing suits and stringy leather outfits (her one older sister is a fashion designer) lounging over each other like melting bodies.

Donnie has no one to take care of.

She has no self-loathing.

If only.

I'm the hard side. The calculated side. The side that holds it all in. The controlled one.

Donnie's house is on a block of palatial mansions. She calls it "fake mansion-ing." It's very typical Donnie to underplay everything.

I walk up the stairs and Donnie is still in bed. She's wearing an eye mask, and she's snoring. Her dark hair circles the pillow.

Donnie's mother is black—dark-skinned black—and her father is Jewish with an olive tone.

Me, one side is straight from the *shtetl*, as my mother likes to say. Her family is a mix of Eastern European Jews. Great-grandparents from very poor villages. Poland. Czechoslovakia (before it was divided up into two different countries). Lithuania. Austria. A little of this, a little of that. Then to the Lower East Side of Manhattan, where all the other Jews went when they escaped the Nazis. My father's family, Swedish royalty.

People comment on the two of us together. On the color of our skin. Our hair. Me, a blond. Donnie, with the black curls. Last year, a few assholes at a frat party Donnie's sister dragged us to screamed, "I want to Oreo Cookie the two of you girls in bed." Racist and drunk.

I pull off my boots and toss them over by the door—hoping they clunk against the wall so she'll wake up. But no. They just hit her thick, white shag carpet, practically bouncing as they land.

I crawl into bed and inch next to her, wrapping my arm around her waist. She's wearing a loose white T-shirt, her thin gold chains pooling at her neck and shoulder crease. Her silver cuff around her wrist. I whisper in her ear, "Donnieeeee . . ."

She flips her head around. Whips off her eye mask.

"Your wake-up call, lover," I say to her.

"Jensen? What the fuck are you doing here?"

I smell it as she speaks. Her breath is rancid.

"Seriously, I had two hours of sleep. Was puking all night."

"Ugh," I turn away. "I can smell it. I beg you to brush."

She winces and hops out of bed to the bathroom, where I hear her brushing her teeth.

I wiggle my jeans off so I can feel the silky sheets across my thighs.

Donnie climbs into bed next to me. She pets my hair, scratching at my scalp a little. Caressing me how I like it.

"Stop petting me like a dog, Don." I squeeze a pillow between my knees. "Something happened last night. Something big. Like, too much."

"*Something big.* Ooooh? Why so cryptic, Jensen? It's not like you."

So I tell her about Sean. I tell her about how I was glad to see Ali terrified outside of the bathroom, because I knew that look. I was all too familiar with that look.

"Part of me wanted her to be hurt. Isn't that just awful? Aren't I awful?"

She rubs her eyes, scratches her head a few times.

"No, it just makes you human. Because you'll always be in love with Sean, and you'll always be jealous of whoever he's with."

"Get out of here. I'm not in love with Sean. I spend a lot of time with him because of Dev."

Of course she's right. Of course I *like* Sean. I like his aura. Of course I feel special around him. That I'm the girl he goes to for advice. When the other girls get tossed, I'm there in the wings. I'm his steady best friend, along with Dev. And it feels good to have that power. It has nothing to do with lust. But Donnie. She stirs shit up. She's been on this kick for a while. My secret crush on Nessel, she says.

"Changing the subject," I say. "I feel sorry for Ali. She doesn't know what happened to her. I'm sure of that." Ali. Her face a deer in headlights.

"But you seem to know." Donnie widens her eyes.

I don't want to say too much. Especially after Sean broke down last night. I have loyalty toward Sean, even though Donnie, I know, would never pass this on to anyone.

"He was whimpering in the car about me needing to help him."

"So he really hurt her, then?"

"His jacket was rolled up in a ball. Blood was all over it, he said." I shudder.

"Did you see the jacket?"

I shake my head.

"Broken cherry."

"You can't go back after you split that cherry. That's forever."

"I don't know why you feel so bad for Sean," Donnie says, and turns away. She's not wrong—but Donnie doesn't understand.

I think about last night and how he was crying on my shoulder—I've never seen a guy cry before like that. And I just wanted to hold him and fix it for him.

I tell Donnie about my plan to become friends with Ali Greenleaf. That I'm going to just manage the whole thing. Make sure she's okay.

"Sean wants me to look out for her. You have to give him credit for that."

"I sense a social media assassination," Donnie says, and pulls the covers over her head. Then she wraps her arms around my shoulders and spoons me, nudging my hips so they lock in with hers. I'm safe in this cocoon of Donnie's silk sheets.

And I'll show empathy for Ali. Help her get over those shitty feelings. I can relate. I'll tell her how it hurts for a while. How you keep playing the same scene over and over again in your mind.

That's how it was for me, at least, after the Initiation.

The Initiation is an unspoken tradition in my school. You get chosen for it as a freshman girl. And once you're chosen, you're expected to follow through. A senior girl walks you through the part that's *To Be Expected*. My senior was Amanda Shire.

"At some point in high school, you're going to give a blow job," she said. "You do it with a guy you think is down with you. But then he spreads the word. It goes viral. You feel used. You're tagged a slut. But in this situation, you're protected. You're not going to get any shame. You're going to do it and it'll be callous. It's not about pleasure; it's not about bonding. This is about your *future*. It's about your *safety*. The girls who set this up, before you even came into this world, before you even bothered to ask your mother if you could shave your nasty leg hair—they set it up because girls were getting raped. Girls were getting pushed into this without controlling it. Now there's no curiosity. Now there's no shame. You do it on *them*. They're your practice and then it's over."

This is what Amanda Shire told us.

I could have said no. But no one says no. Donnie and I got on our knees that night. Suki and Cate weren't asked. We held hands for the first half, which the guys liked. They're not supposed to talk. But ours did. They whispered. Things I couldn't hear. There were soft moans. Amanda Shire told us to expect this. "They're just human," she said.

I kept my eyes closed. Otherwise you risk looking at their hairy, thick thighs. I sang a song in my head. To this day I can't even listen to that song without hating myself.

They don't expect you to swallow; they tell you to pull back. But some gets on your face. It drips on the floor. I'll give Amanda Shire this: It's a robotic experience. Except for their faces after. Their smiles. The way I had to wipe my mouth and then look at them, look at the guy I was paired with. Alex Kramer. After, still sitting on that cold floor as the guys filed out, wanting to cry. Donnie saw my hatred, how I was about to weep or puke or both. "Keep it together, Jensen. Don't fold, Jensen," she said, whispering.

After the Initiation, you're invited to all the senior parties. All the parties that mean anything. You made it through *that*—so guys don't fuck with you. They accept you. At least that's the concept. I don't know anymore what I believe.

When I was a freshman, before the Initiation, you'd hear

rumors about guys slipping a roofie in someone's drink. A few guys recording someone going down a girl's pants, a girl who was wasted, and then putting it on Twitter. But you didn't have to go through something so traumatic to be put through hell. You just had to jerk off a guy at a party. Let someone finger you behind a pool house. I've seen girls go through hell for the most innocent acts, especially early on, because *I put them through hell.*

So to be in this exclusive group where your reputation is always protected—how could anyone not want that?

Except after, I didn't feel like I did it for myself. I felt like I was doing it for them. Those needy boys. Those boys who take.

That's when I met Dev. Well, I always knew him, that cute, shy boy in my AP class. The guy who always hung out with Sean Nessel. We were at a party down the shore. Drinking jungle juice from a garbage can. Dev was there, and Cate wanted to hook up with him. I was sent over to lasso him. To talk up Cate. Then it was an hour later, and Dev and I were still talking. Cate sneering at me from the corner. I shrugged. She had no chance with him anyway.

I latched on to Dev, and he made me feel protected. I told him about my mother. About my father. He hung on to my words and understood me. He didn't want to play any games. And he wanted me with him all the time. Then it was the three of us. Me, him, and Sean. Fingers overlapping each other.

Dev's the only other person besides Donnie who knows how I feel about the Initiation. He thinks it's bullshit. That it was always bullshit. That it was some made-up thing concocted by some demented senior. Some girl who wanted to shame everyone.

"How could it be bullshit if I did it then, Dev?" I said. "Then what happens to me? Am I bullshit? Have I been used?"

I couldn't believe that. I can't believe that. Maybe it does work. No girls have been sexually assaulted since that time, none that I've heard of. So maybe it did work to a certain extent. Maybe the Initiation serves its purpose. Acts as a deterrent.

That doesn't mean it doesn't scar you. That you never forget it. That I didn't feel taken. That I still don't.

That's how I'll approach Ali. I'll explain to her that we've been in the same position. That everyone has to have some kind of initiation, even if it's not organized like mine was. I'll be empathetic, sure. I'll tell her maybe Sean was wasted, that he pushed things a little too far, and it was uncomfortable for her. That it might really mess with her head. But then I'll explain that Sean is a great guy. He couldn't . . . he couldn't help himself or something. That the whole night he was talking about how cute she was. He was so excited to be around her. He couldn't stop himself. If she could have seen him that night crying. His silky hair falling in his face. Have you ever seen a god fall?

8

A L I

My father is waiting at the kitchen table wearing his Phish shirt because that's what he always wears on weekends.

"What did you do to your hair?"

"I—" I touch my bangs. How do I say it? That I'm still drunk? That I'm in shock?

"Forget it, I don't want to know." He shakes his head. More disgusted than I'd ever thought he'd be. "You want me to ask questions or should I just let you talk?" he says.

"The way I see it is that you have some explaining to do too," I say, hoping that his making out with his date Sheila the She Woman in the living room deflects whatever trouble I'm in.

"Yeah, well, I'm an adult, so I don't actually have any explaining to do," he says. And he looks at me like *start talking.*

"I didn't sleep at Sammi's."

"Yes, I know that."

My father sees right through all the bullshit, because the downside to having a cool dad is that he's already done it all, and according to him, he's done even more than anything I even know about. Whatever that means. Plus, I've recently learned about bands like Phish—specifically *what people do* when they're seeing a band like Phish. As in they take a lot of acid, mushrooms, and whippits. My father's been around.

"Cherie drove us to a party. But I'm not going to tell you whose house we were at, so you shouldn't ask me that."

"Oh. Okay. I'll make sure not to ask you." He rolls his eyes. "What else?"

"There was a beer keg."

"And?"

"And then . . . Sean Nessel. He walks into the party."

"Hold up. Sean Nessel, from your collage book? With all the roses and the hearts, the kid in the school newspaper, Sean Nessel?"

"That one."

Buzz in my back pocket. A text from Sammi.

Just want to know if you're alive or dead

Can't right now. Talking to my dad.

"And you're not going to like this next part. At all. So close your eyes or something."

"I've always told you that you'll never—"

"*I know,* Dad . . . I'll never get in trouble for telling you the truth, but that was before, when I had nothing to tell you. Except for things like I didn't brush my teeth. Or I didn't do my homework. But what I'm about to tell you is *not* like that."

He rubs his eyes, weary.

"I need you to shut your eyes."

"What? Ali—"

"Please, Dad. I can't look at you."

So he shuts them. "I'm ready."

I tell him about how Sean Nessel started opening those little airplane bottles of vodka.

"Wait a second—" My father clears his throat and shifts in his chair. "Go ahead."

"I thought I could tell you the truth— Why are you getting all uncomfortable like I'm going to be in trouble?"

"You can," he says, "but it doesn't mean I'm not going to react strongly. You're not in trouble. Whatever you tell me, you're not in trouble. But drinking vodka? You're not in trouble—but I'm upset."

"Well, there's more," I say. I focus on the furrow between my dad's eyebrows that's been there for the past couple of years. I don't remember seeing it before then—it wasn't in pictures. It's something that grew out of worry. Fear. First with my mother. Now it's going to deepen like a valley after I tell him this. I wring my hands and surrender my head to the table.

"You can tell me anything, Ali," he says, his eyelids squinting open.

"I don't want to say it," I wail. "And I want you to shut your eyes!"

"You want to write it?" he says, and rummages for paper in the junk drawer, coming up with a pink Post-it Note and a pencil.

So I look at the paper. I squeeze my hands together.

This is what I write:

SEX

I push the paper close to him.

"Can I open my eyes?"

But when he opens his eyes, I'm going to be a different girl.

I want to warn him. I'm not your daughter anymore. I used to be. Until last night.

"Ali—I'm opening my eyes." And he does. He sees the note. Sighs. Rubs his fingers over his face. No matter how hard you rub, Dad, this isn't going to go away. I feel bad for him actually. I want to hug him, apologize. Explain more.

He trails his finger over the paper and then flips it over. That word *SEX* is gone.

"Do you love this boy?"

I can't talk now because I just told my father my biggest secret ever. And he's a man. I can't imagine what he thinks. My stomach knots up.

I shake my head. No.

"Does he love you?"

I laugh, tears spilling down my face. My body erupts into a crying fit, and I cover my eyes with my hands. I'm so ashamed. It was such a mistake. Such a stupid, stupid mistake. And now I'm going to pay for it forever.

My father comes around the table and kneels on the floor, wrapping his solid arm over my back as I grunt and snort.

"Is that why you mangled your bangs like that?"

"Yeah, sure," I say. Because it's as good of a reason as any.

"It's okay, honey. It's okay."

"It's not okay," I scream. My face fires up, my whole body full of angry heat. But I can't say any more. I'm not ready to. Because this is what it would sound like if I spoke: *I didn't want to have sex with him.*

He cups my face in his hands like I'm a little girl again and I'm choking on something awful.

"Look at me, Ali," he says. I stare at his furrow. "Are you telling me everything?"

"He's never going to call me. He used me," I say, stuttering. "That's what I'm telling you. And now all the girls who drool over him are going to start bashing me on social media. I'm going to be the school slut, and you're probably going to have to homeschool me."

The TV is on in the other room. A breakfast cereal commercial. All the vitamins you need to live a healthy life.

Sammi texts again: *Now?*

No. Later. 🖤

I pray that my father doesn't think I'm disgusting.

My father is processing this. This is what he tells me: "Of all the talks we had about sex. Of letting the first time be with someone you love and who loves you back. About drinking. I'm so open about all of it. And this is how it goes down?" he says. But he's not asking me. This is a rhetorical rant to the teenage gods.

He needs to shut off the TV. He needs to process more. He's not mad at me, he promises. I didn't do anything wrong—though I beg to differ, because according to the laws in this country, I was drinking, like, a shitload. And though I have no problem admitting that yes, I will most likely drink again at some point soon before I reach the legal age of twenty-one (though never again around a boy I'm obsessed with), it was most certainly illegal.

He keeps telling me that it's okay. But I've broken my father's heart.

My father calms down. Apologizes for making me feel bad. But I know what it is. It's not like he expected me to lose my virginity when I'm married or anything ridiculous like that. But he expected me to lose it to someone I at least had a relationship with. He expected something better for me than this. He holds me tighter and I snuggle into his armpit. He's all soft under there.

Later, in my bed, Sammi's texts firing away, wanting details, wanting information, and every text I get from her, there's a part of me that expects it to be Sean Nessel. Isn't that crazy? That every time my phone buzzes, I think it's going to be him saying, "I'm sorry." Or "I was really drunk." Or something. Anything.

I know this isn't good. I know that I shouldn't be having these thoughts.

Because he held me down. He put his hand over my mouth. I shouldn't want this person to be in my thoughts. Rainbows, sunsets, roses. I stretch my arms at the sky. Why do I still see forever in his stupid eyes? I have to see gray. I have to see black.

Sammi texts me again because this is Sammi: impatient and persistent.

What the fuck? You're freaking me out. Just come over.

"I'm going to Sammi's house," I yell to my father, and

before he can say anything, I'm out the door, on my bike. Riding into the wind.

Sammi's mother is making lasagna when I get there because it's Sunday, and this is what mothers do when they live in your house and are not having a nervous breakdown in the desert. Speaking of mothers, I still have to call mine back.

We sit on Sammi's bed staring at each other. Neither of us saying anything. Her eyes bugging out. Too wide and scared.

"What did you do to your hair?"

I cover my forehead with my hands, flinching. "I don't want to talk about it."

But Sammi pushes and pushes, her eyes flaring. She wants to know about my bangs. Wants to know what happened last night. She's relentless.

I crawl under her sheet. Hold it over my head.

"Holding a sheet over your head isn't going to stop me from harassing you."

"I can't say it, otherwise," I say from under the sheet.

I crunch the sheet in my hand. But it's not enough. I want to suffocate under here. I shove the pillow to my face and scream.

"Ali? What the hell?" Sammi practically climbs on top of me. "What's going on?"

"I sort of had sex with him." I'm still under the sheet.

We had this whole plan about how we were going to talk to each other about when we lost our virginity. That we'd call or text even if we were, like, lying romantically in front of a fire with the guy, the imaginary boyfriend. That was the plan, and now I feel so bad that I fucked it up. Because I was so eager to go upstairs with Sean Nessel. I was so eager to give him everything.

"Wait, what? I knew you went upstairs with him, but sex? Actual sex? Is that why you ran out?"

Cherie busts into Sammi's bedroom. I can see her shadow in the door.

"Why are you screaming like that?"

"It's Ali. She's under the covers."

"Ali? We can see you under there," Cherie says. "What the hell happened to you last night?"

I whip the sheet off my head, wrap it around my shoulders.

"She had sex."

Cherie sits on the bed. "Nessel?"

I nod my head.

"Don't question her, Cherie."

"Sean Nessel is freakishly good looking, but the guy has a shit reputation," Cherie says. "Everyone knows it. I'm sorry I didn't tell you. I should have warned you."

"I already knew about him. Nothing would have changed my mind. I followed him up there like an idiot."

I wish I was just the girl who had sex with Sean Nessel. Rather than the girl who was . . . I can't say it. I can't say it because if I say it, it'll be real.

"Look, Ali. You're a girl who *chose* to have sex, or whatever. Who gives a fuck who you fuck? Anyway, when you get to college, forget it. Everyone has sex with everyone."

I shudder, thinking of Sean's hands all over me. The blood on his jacket.

"I've practically slept with half the guys in my dorm," Cherie says.

"Wait, what?"

"I'm just kidding. But seriously. If I wanted to, whose business is that? Anyway, if you're fine with it, then that's between the two of you," she says. "Are you fine with it?"

Am I fine with it?

Cherie was Miss Cheerleader–Key Club–Peer Leadership– School Spirit Girl all through high school. Something changed last year when she was a senior. She was done with cheer. Done with the C-wing bathroom, which is basically Invite Only. She joined the Feminist Club, started preaching to us about Tarana Burke, Liz Phair, and Kathleen Hanna. Now she's a women's studies major. Cherie really went after the Core Four when she was a senior. Rumor is that Cherie told Blythe group names are a sign of insecurity.

When Sammi and I asked her about it, she went silent, which was weird at the time because Cherie told us everything. "I don't want to talk about those girls," she'd say, until finally she told us this: "There's a lot that those girls have done to get accepted in this school. Stuff that no one should have to do."

I like to make fun of Cherie—as in "Oh, Jesus, no bong hits until we recite some feminist manifesto or learn the lyrics to Bikini Kill's 'Rebel Girl,'" but I know she's right.

My vagina and my body are mine.

Am I fine with it?

I'm not at all fine with it.

I *chose* to do this with Sean Nessel.

Well, not really.

Well, not at all.

At dinner with Sammi's family. Mom. Dad. Sammi. Cherie. Pretend like everything is fine. Please pass the red pepper flakes. Yes, thank you, it was delicious. Sorry I didn't eat all of mine. I guess I wasn't that hungry. How am I? I'm great. I'm great. I'm fine.

Back on my street, just as I turn the corner, my bike light shining on the leaves, I see my dad in the doorway talking to Raj.

Raj is standing there all sweaty as I get closer. No glasses on. His face is flushed. And though I love his glasses, you can really see those soulful green eyes without them.

There have been times when I've considered Raj. Considered kissing him. Considered him as a possible boyfriend. Weighed it over in my mind. How my body sometimes lights up around him. And then sometimes nothing. We tried it once. It was at a party. He was leaning against a wall. Just easy.

"I think we should kiss," I said, real business-like. Big smile. He reached forward and took my hair in his hands, and I stepped forward into him. We kissed, and my heart stopped. I bit my lip. Covered my mouth. My hands shook. I looked up at him, his hair drooping in his face, those eyes.

"Nothing," I said, stepping back. "Like kissing a wall."

"Same," he said. Those eyes, not off me once.

And we never talked about it again. I promised Sammi it was nothing. Just a drunken experiment.

Raj knows how I feel about Sean Nessel, anyway.

Felt. Fuck. *Felt.*

My dad smells like pot and patchouli. He must be so stressed out about this whole thing with me and Sean Nessel that he had to light a late-afternoon joint. He can't even wait until I go to bed, which is when he usually gets high. This isn't something we discuss. This is just something I am *aware* of. What would he say? "I smoke weed." So I've figured out his *I'm going to bed early* is code for *I'm getting high. Give your old man some space.*

Raj tells me he's been running in the neighborhood and he just thought he'd stop by.

My father pulls me into the hallway, and Raj waits outside. He hands me a white paper bag. "Aunt Marce dropped this off," he says, his eyes so serious.

I open the bag and look inside. It's a small mint-green box that says PLAN B. I look up at him, horrified. "Dad, oh my God."

"Don't *oh my God* me, Ali. You need to take this tonight."

Plan B is the pill you take when you don't want to be pregnant. Pregnant. The word makes me sick. I think of Sean Nessel. What he looked like. His face. His hair. I pinch the inside of my wrist until I can feel pain shooting down my hand.

My father sighs deeply. I can see how upset he is. And stoned. He keeps licking his lips.

"She said not to take it on an empty stomach," he says. "Maybe have it with milk and cookies before bed. I don't know." And he shuffles off.

There's a note on the box inside.

Ali, don't worry about this being any more than a light period. You might get a little spotting. Some cramps. Take some Advil. You'll be fine, I promise.

I love you,

Aunt Marce

I shove the bag in the bathroom, my eyes tearing up.

Raj and I wipe off the leafy lounge chairs out back. They're moldy from the fall—no one's cleaned them off in a while. I'm wearing black sweats and a black Pixies T-shirt, so I don't care about getting all smudged. Besides, I feel so dirty still anyway. Sitting in sludge is somehow fitting.

"You cut your bangs," Raj says.

I shrug. Place my hand over my forehead.

"Just wanted to see how you were."

"I'm fine," I say defensively.

I don't like that he's saying this to me. I don't want him to remind me that he knows something. Or that something happened. I don't want anything to have happened.

"Okay." He looks away.

"Why are you even asking me?"

"'Cause I saw you run out of there last night all freaked out. I couldn't catch up to you. Too many people. And then you didn't text me back. And Sammi wouldn't say anything today when I talked to her."

"I didn't notice that you texted me."

I didn't notice because I had my phone off. Because I chose to ignore everyone.

"Anyway, I saw Nessel this morning at soccer practice," Raj says.

"Yeah?"

"He said that I should check on you."

"Oh? What a *nice guy*." I crunch my knees to my chest. Hang my head over them like a pretzel.

"Did he say anything else?"

"That you were shaken up."

"Did he say *why* I was shaken up?"

I hear Sean Nessel saying it, so innocent. *Check on her, dude. She was shaken up, man.* And then a surge of rage comes over me, and I turn into a human volcano of spitfire, shaking and sputtering. So I say it because I'm fuming and I can't hold it in.

"We did it, all right? We did it and it was awful. Like the worst night of my life. Like the worst, worst thing ever. So bad that I don't even want to talk about it because I can't believe that it's me talking to you about something that I feel so fucking embarrassed about."

I smash my feet in the grass. The damp grass pokes through my flip-flops. It's the first time since last night that I can feel anything besides my sore thighs and crotch. I don't want Raj to see me like this. But he's here. In my yard. And he's listening.

I cover my face with my hair like that Addams Family character Cousin It. If I could just walk around like this for a few days. I fantasize about finding an escape route through my hair.

I don't want Raj to worry about me. I know he doesn't know what to say to me. He knows I'm a virgin. That I was a virgin. We're close enough for him to know that. If there was a way to bury it. To cover my body with leaves so no one could see me or hear me or find me. Every part of me is telling myself not to speak about last night and to just shove it down into a dark place in my soul so that it just goes away.

Raj curls forward and plops his feet down, leans over so that our knees touch.

But I don't want to be touched. So I move my knees away.

"What are you thinking about?" Raj says.

I stare at my rusty swing set that is still taking up space in the yard.

"I'm thinking about how my dad needs to get rid of that old thing because the only person who uses it is the little kid next door."

9

BLYTHE

Monday morning. It's not difficult to find her.

In a matter of asking three juniors, I learn that Ali Greenleaf has fourth period class right down the hall from me. I've got my leather tote bag packed—I haven't worn a backpack since freshman year—so when the bell rings, I zip right for the door and zoom down the hall, waiting in front of her classroom like I've been there all my life. Her face looks drawn and tired. She has greenish bags under her eyes. And something else. These too-short bangs that are different from that loose-curl-over-the-eye look I saw her with the other night.

She's fumbling with her books as she walks out. I tickle the back of her arm to get her attention and she turns around. She's wearing faded jeans, Converse sneakers, and a black T-shirt. I see why Sean thought she was cute. She's a little rebel. Nothing like me.

ALI

Blythe Jensen is standing in front of me. Smiling. Blythe's best friends with Sean Nessel. So if she's talking to me, then it means it has something to do with him. And it has something to do with what happened. I take a step back. My heart stops, almost.

BLYTHE

"Ali, right? You're friends with Cherie's little sister."

She stops and nods at me. Says nothing, her eyes vacant. I wonder if she remembers me from the party.

"Hel-lo?" I laugh. She's still staring. Like I'm a ghost. "Do you smoke?"

"Smoke . . . weed?"

"You're funny—uh, no, do you smoke cigarettes?"

She looks at me. Watching me. Her eyes like green sapphires. She takes a deep pause.

"As long as they're unfiltered."

"Is this a joke?"

"No, I'm just tough like that. I break the filters off before I smoke," she says, almost slurring, and stares at me blankly. Then smirks. "Of course I don't smoke unfiltered. What am I, a maniac?"

I laugh, and I didn't expect to laugh. Maybe I've underestimated her. I ask her if she wants to come with me somewhere that we can talk. She says sure.

Ali trails me as we walk over to the C-wing. "You don't have to walk five feet behind me. You're not a servant," I say. So she scoots next to me, just staring. Which is fine for now.

It can't stay that way—it's too annoying. Besides, the other girls won't like it. They'll see it as a weakness.

I think about texting Cate and Suki so that I can give them a heads-up about Ali, but surprising them will be a better tactic. Anyway, I need to keep those bitches on their toes. I can bring anyone into the C-wing bathroom I want.

ALI

Have you ever walked next to a girl like Blythe Jensen? Her hair is a commercial. It's blond and has a wave and somehow no frizz. It swings from side to side. Her skin is so smooth that she has no bumps. It's glowy and flawless. I rub my own scaly elbows and make a note to myself: use more moisturizer.

I'm going to have a minor breakdown. She's bringing me into the C-wing bathroom. The C-wing is designated as a senior bathroom. This is not a school designation. This is just a known fact. If you're not a senior and you have a class in C-wing, you do not use that bathroom or else you might as well transfer to another school. A select group of senior girls smoke cigarettes in there. (Everyone's gone back to cigarettes. Because if vaping is going to kill you, you might as well just smoke the old-fashioned way.)

There's some code. You have to knock a few times. But I've never even tried to get in. I know this sounds implausible— hello, this is a school—but we have a big school. Three wings! Three floors in each wing. Two bathrooms on each floor. Three different vice principals even. No one gets busted for smoking up in C-wing. Teachers aren't interested in going up there, to the third floor, all the way down the hall. Practically nowhere. They've gotten away with it for years. And I've learned to just fear it. To stay away.

BLYTHE

Even though no one has caught us smoking in the C-wing bathroom, we're all still a little on edge about someone busting in. You just need to say, "It's cool," or rap on the wall a few times before you walk in, but I never see anyone new here. People are scared. It's fine with me. The fewer people who come, the less attention it gets. It should be exclusive. It should be hard to find.

I turn to Ali outside the bathroom door and place my index finger on my lips. I whisper: "Don't say a word."

I kick open the bathroom door, and Suki, Cate, and Donnie all gasp. Suki chokes, coughing on her inhale. They shove their cigarettes behind their backs, as if that would help their asses if they had gotten caught.

ALI

It's the Core Four. Suki Fields. Cate Sandoval. Donnie Alperstein. Blythe Jensen, their fourth.

I take a quick look around. Cate has these big gold hoop earrings with her name spelled through the middle: CATE.

Suki is wearing a floral skirt down to her calves. A tiny T-shirt that says SO TIRED.

Donnie Alperstein in denim shorts. Button-up shirt to the collar. Black Converse high-tops. She has smoky blue tips in her curly hair, and I flash back to seeing her at Sophie Miller's party, laughing in a crowd of people.

The party. That night.

Sean Nessel on top of me.

Shake it off. Close your eyes and make it go away. Breathe, Ali. Breathe.

The girls collectively hold their breaths and hide their smokes behind their backs. When they see it's just Blythe, they exhale, and a massive cloud of smoke hits my face. *Don't cough*, I tell myself. *Just breathe.*

BLYTHE

"What's up, bitches?" I have a big smile on my face.

"What the fuck, B?" Suki says.

"Thanks for giving me a heart attack at seventeen, Jensen," Donnie says.

I introduce the girls to Ali; though I might as well say, *I've got the girl who fucked Sean Nessel.*

Does Ali know that's her story? That she's the girl who fucked Sean Nessel this weekend?

I pass Ali a cigarette and let the girls give it to her a little. Suki eyes Ali, then turns away, uninterested.

"So. Why did you bring her here?" Suki says. "Is she going to do a tell-all with us?"

"Yeah, Blythe is, like, going to interview her about Sean," Donnie says, laughing.

"Give us the lowdown," Cate says, laughing. "'Cause I bet she got real low."

"Ever heard of don't kiss and tell, you sluts?" I say. "She's not going to tell you shit about her relationship with Nessel. And he wouldn't expect her to."

I frame it like that. Relationship. Ali doesn't even know what I'm doing, what I'm giving to her by framing it like that. She doesn't know what these girls could do to her. What I could do to her. I'm donating status to this girl Ali Greenleaf—she better take it.

A L I

Donnie hikes herself up on the bathroom sink. Swinging her legs and blowing smoke rings. She calls Blythe by her last name, Jensen—almost like she's taunting her. "New pair of boots, you shoe-whore, Jensen." Or "Oh, Jensen, you're so cute when you're being head slut-shamer in charge." But Blythe smiles with every one of Donnie's digs. She seems to like it.

I stare at Donnie because she's so pretty—I've never been this close to her. I always thought Blythe was in charge of this group, but now I wonder if it's different. There seems to be a divide. Blythe and Donnie, top tier. Suki and Cate, underlings.

"Like something you see, Greenleaf?" Donnie says, taking me by surprise and flicking her ashes at me.

I just kind of blink.

Cate starts at writing on the bathroom wall. *THE CORE FOUR.* "The asshole janitor scrubbed my last design."

"That asshole janitor is my father," I say.

I don't know what makes me say it. It just flies out of my mouth, and I automatically want to apologize for it, say something like, "I'm just kidding," but instead I smile and say nothing.

Then all of them, the Core Four, start laughing, even Cate. And then it's a whirlwind of laughter. They think I'm funny.

I finally breathe.

BLYTHE

"So," I say, turning my body to Ali. My knee touches her knee. She doesn't pull it away, and I whisper, "My boyfriend, Devon, and Sean are best friends." I click my mouth, making smoke rings. "Do you know Devon Strong?"

"I know who he is."

"Anyway, Sean really, really respects you. He's waiting to hear back about early acceptance from Duke and then there's the State Champs and then he's going to build huts for needy

Costa Ricans over Presidents' Day weekend, which means he needs to be in great shape, because ten huts in three days, he's kind of inhuman, right?"

Except we both know he is human. And humans cry. And humans make mistakes. Especially male humans.

"He doesn't usually drink that much, Ali. That's not his style."

I don't even know why I'm saying this. I know it's not true. Everyone knows it's not true.

But Ali glares at me. Her eyes don't exactly tear up, but they get squinty. As if she's insanely angry. Because I've said something so awful. I've insulted her. She gasps. She tosses her cigarette toward the toilet, and it flies by Suki like a rocket.

"Nothing happened," Ali says.

Except something did happen. And we both know it. And Sean knows it. And Dev knows it. And too many people know it to pretend like it didn't happen. My fear is that a month from now, when she's ready to talk, there'll be accusations. Crying fits. Post-traumatic stress, or whatever. Anyway, I promised Sean.

I can't stop thinking about him crying at my car. And I know I should think of the way Ali looked traumatized as she ran out of Sophie Miller's house the other night. *Find empathy in my heart.* But my loyalty is with Sean. It just is.

"Look, I've had experiences too," I say. "Experiences that I'm not so happy about. Do you know what I mean?"

But she's blank.

"I don't know what you're talking about," she says, and looks down at the floor.

"Uh, Ali, you ran out of the party like a crazy banshee—I mean, *everyone saw you.* But Sean's a good guy. He doesn't want to, you know—he doesn't want *you* to be all freaked out."

ALI

Everyone saw you. That's what she said.

Everyone saw you. I don't want to be known as the girl that everyone saw. I just want to be known as the cute girl. Or the hot girl. Or the cool girl. Or the whatever girl. Not the girl everyone saw with blood smeared on her jeans.

What does Blythe mean when she says, "I've had experiences"? What does that even mean? Was what happened to me an *experience*? Is that how they're defining it?

I feel my legs tingle and my stomach cave. I hold my hand against the cool bathroom wall, and it's the only thing that's keeping me from completely passing out right here.

"You okay?" Blythe says.

Oh, yeah. I'm so okay.

Not.

And then the bell rings.

10

ALI

I race down the hallway to get to my physics class and my teacher, Mr. Chui, gives me a late notice, my third this month. I slip onto my stool next to Sammi.

Terrance Carter from the school newspaper sits on the other side of me.

"You smell like smoke," he says.

"Wow, you must be a real investigative journalist," I say, sneering. "You should get a hat that says *scoop* or something."

He turns away. Terrance and I go way back. We were in an advanced reading class together in third grade. Now he walks around in this trench coat like he owns the school because he's the newspaper editor. My entire relationship to the school newspaper is based on how they cover Sean Nessel. If Sean Nessel was in the paper, I'd bring it home. I'd cut it out. I'd stick it in the collage book.

Sammi opens up her notebook and starts scribbling to me.

Where the hell were you?

C-wing bathroom

How??

Blythe Jensen.

"What the fuck?" she whispers.

I shrug because I don't know, which is really the truth. I rub my stomach and groan.

"Is it hot in here?" I say to Sammi and throw my hair up in a bun, the back of my neck sweaty.

She goes back to the notepad.

I'm worried about you.

I know. We'll talk after class. PROMISE.

Mr. Chui draws a rocket on the board. He says the rocket is going to launch a projectile with a strong velocity.

My body gets real hot. Like clammy-sweaty hot, and I can't stop it, and then I launch my own projectile . . .

I puke.

I convince the nurse that I'm fine. Just a nervous stomach. I slap my cheeks. Look. I'm perfect.

"I have to call your father anyway. And if you feel at all nauseous again, you need to come right back here."

"Fine," I say. Anything to avoid going home. I don't want my father eyeing me all afternoon.

Lunch room. Sammi doesn't say a word to me in the lunch line. She waits until we get to a small table in the back. Just me and her. She gets in my face and does that yell-whisper. "What the fuck is going on? You smelled like smoke in class. C-wing? Then you puke?"

"Shhhhh."

"Ali, what really happened with you and him?"

"This isn't something I want to even admit to myself."

She practically chokes on her tater tot. "What does that even mean?"

Sammi has been my best friend since second grade and telling her is like telling myself. That's how close we are. That's why I don't want to say it out loud. I pull her face close and put my lips to her ear.

"Why are you breathing in my ear?"

"Shhh. Just listen." I hear the echo of my breath against her earlobe. Back and forth. Breathe in. Breathe out. "Remember I told you about what happened with Sean Nessel?"

She nods. Her face frozen. Eyes bugging out of her skull.

"He forced me."

She pulls her face away. Her eyes squint in that way they used to around that time my mother left and I would make up stories about where she was. *My mother is exploring the moon, actually. My mother decided to be a rock climber.* Anything sounded better than *My mother went to rehab because she has the alcoholic disease and also she's moving to this weird place in New Mexico.*

He put his hand over my mouth, I want to tell her. But I can't say it out loud. I can't say any of it to her. If I say it to her, it'll never stop. That voice in my head will keep going. I'll relive that night on repeat. And I want to get it out of my mind.

So I pull my T-shirt down a little on the one side. Since we're in the cafeteria, I hold back my tears; they're choking me.

I hear her gasp. I know she sees it, the bruise above my collarbone, close to my shoulder.

I quickly cover it up. No one's going to see that again. Sammi's circling her eyes with her hands. Rubbing them.

She whispers, "Is that why you ran out of there?"

I nod.

"And you just left this information out when you were at my house last night?"

Her eyes tear up. Her face reddens. She covers her face with her hands. Tears stream over her knuckles.

"We are not telling anyone," I say, breathless. "Not anyone."

"Cherie? Can't I at least tell her?"

"Oh my God, Sammi, especially not her. She'll make me go to a protest with a uterus strapped around my head."

"But you have a bruise on your shoulder. He *forced* you. I mean. This isn't right, Ali."

"I was drinking those tiny bottles of vodka. My stupid collage books?" Saying it out loud takes my breath away. I grit my teeth. "He was my target. Everyone saw me."

"But, Ali—"

"You saw me, Sammi. You said it yourself. You saw me drinking with him. Everyone saw me drinking with him."

"So what? We've learned about this a million—a zillion—times. It doesn't mean it's consent just because you were drinking."

"But don't you see, that's *everything*. Because—I wanted to do it." I think about my back scratching against his soccer jacket. His hand over my mouth. I rub my eyes. I wonder how long I'm going to have to do this just to get rid of those images. Then if I have to tell people? And if they don't believe me? It's one thing for the stupid health teacher to mindlessly talk about consent because it's in the curriculum, because that's what's expected of her. She wants to preach consent and #MeToo and #GirlsToo. But I've seen too many news stories, too many articles, I know that in real-life situations, girls don't get the chance to defend themselves. Especially not when it comes to the captain of the soccer team.

I try to explain this to Sammi. That my whole life is on the line here, that she can't tell anyone because if she tells even one person, my whole life is going to explode. That Sean Nessel will ruin my life. But she keeps pressing. She won't stop. So I just shake my head, close my eyes, pretend I don't exist. Like this is happening to someone else.

"And then?"

But I say nothing.

"And then what happens? He just gets away with it?"

I shake my head. Nothing comes out. I'm nothing. I'm not even here.

"If you said no. If you have a bruise on your shoulder. Ali," she says, looking around, covering me up, holding my hands, pulling me closer, her voice so low and quiet. "You have to tell someone."

"Oh, like who?"

"Someone other than Blythe Jensen."

I forgot that I was just in very close quarters with Blythe Jensen and that Sammi is not happy about that either.

"Blythe doesn't know anything about it." She looks at me like I'm crazy. "I know she brought me to C-wing, but she doesn't know about that. I didn't say anything to her about it."

"Come on, Ali. He must have told her to be friends with you. So that you wouldn't say anything." She's trying to be protective, but it feels really condescending, so I sit back in my chair and pull my hoodie out of my backpack. I suddenly have the chills. Maybe it's Plan B side effects. Maybe it is a stomach bug. But of course it's not. It's me. It's just me.

"Obviously I know why Blythe brought me to C-wing. I'm not stupid."

And of course she's right. It was more than that. I'm not going to pretend—at least not to myself. I know it's transparent. I know Blythe picked me to go because it has to do with Sean. Blythe has three entities she's loyal to: the Core Four, Devon Strong, and Sean Nessel. She told me while walking out of C-wing that she, Dev—that's what she called him, "Dev"—and Sean were like *this*. She curled three fingers so they entwined.

But I liked it. I liked going into C-wing with Blythe. I liked being around her. Her command of those girls in that stupid bathroom, it made me want to follow her. The way she throws her hair to the side, like no one can touch her.

I'd like to feel that way right now. A glass wall. Like no one can touch me without getting cut.

I can't explain this to Sammi. She's got this tornado of anger behind her eyes that I see is building in the way she stirs the ketchup on her napkin with her straw.

* * *

Later, we're walking down the hallway. Both late for class. Saying nothing. She doesn't want to let me go, she says. Sammi is afraid for me, she says.

"You can't pretend like this never happened, Ali."

"I'm thinking that pretending will work really well, actually."

"It'll work until you get severe panic attacks and can't leave the house and then have a nervous breakdown and they have to put you in a psych ward and you'll be babbling about bananas and lobotomies. That sounds like a great way to live."

She grabs my hand. Her unfiled nails scratching against my fingers.

"You have to promise not to make me talk about this—"

"Ever again? I mean—"

"You can't push me."

My face gets hot again. I might puke. I see her eyes busy and scared.

A hall monitor walks into the hallway. "GIRLS," she says. "GET TO CLASS." Hissing.

"She just threw up, so I'm walking her to class," Sammi says.

"Oh, then where's the note from the nurse?"

There's no note from the nurse. The monitor knows this.

Sammi turns to me. She's scared. Biting her rosy lips. She begs me to let her take a picture of my bruised shoulder later at her house, later tonight. Just for insurance. I say yes. Anything to make her happy. Anything to get her to stop asking me questions. She holds my hand, takes it tight, cupping it. Then

she sings to me. Our song that we hate so much that it's become
our theme song. Journey. "Open Arms."

"'So now I come . . . to you . . . with open arms . . .'"

"'Nothing to hide . . . believe what I say . . .'"

I'm trying so hard to be us. I'm trying so hard to be me.

I pull away first, but we both expected that.

11

BLYTHE

After school. Sean meets me at the gym before his practice.

"So? What did she say?"

I have so many responses to this question. One: Why do you care what she says?

We're talking about a girl whose name I didn't even know until three days ago and now I'm being asked to bring her into my most secret cave, C-wing, which is basically this school's equivalent of a lioness's den. There's a part of me that wants to tell him to fuck off.

What did she say? She was funny. She was smart. She doesn't deserve this. That's what.

But this is Sean Nessel I'm talking about. Sean has had his flaws and his mistakes, like that time with Suki, and yes, all the other times with all the other girls. Isn't it also true that no one is perfect? That's not me trying to make excuses for him. That's just me having empathy. Right? Isn't everyone entitled to forgiveness? Look at how much he cares about Ali's feelings. Isn't that Sean trying to change?

"She didn't say much. She's kind of reserved. She snapped at me actually when I asked her."

"Well, that's probably good, then, right?"

"Just because she's saying nothing happened now doesn't mean she's not going to say something later."

"Well, can't you just talk to her?"

"Sean, it's not that easy. I mean. I am talking to her. It's just going to take some time."

"This is the only thing I have," he says. He runs his hands through his hair, worried, but it comes off as super cool, like posed. And for a second, I think, how am I going to help him? How can I be in charge of something like this, something so perverse and weird? How do I make it so it doesn't reek?

And then Sean stares at me, his eyes lowered. His eyelashes, so long and thick.

"I can't stop thinking about it, B. I can't stop thinking about how bad this could turn out."

He coughs, a nervous cough, and takes a step in. So close to me.

"I need you so much right now, to help me through this. I don't even want to run into her in the hallway because I think she'll, like, spit on me or something. And I didn't even do anything. It was an accident. The whole thing just got out of control."

I look around and see people staring at us. Usually it's not just me and Sean talking like this, so close, face-to-face. Me, Dev, and Sean? Yes. Me and Sean? No.

I pull him around the corner so fewer people can see us.

"Shhh. Listen. We have a plan. We'll stick to the plan. Everything's going to be okay."

He nods, his face blank. I put my hand on his, gently, his hand, calloused and rough, scaly almost, and so I run my fingers over his knuckles.

In the gym, I can hear the volleyball team practicing. Girls in tiny shorts. Spiking balls over the net one after the other. Click-swoosh. Spike. Click-swoosh. Spike. Their sneakers squeal against the gym floor.

He places his hands on my shoulders and backs me up against the wall.

"What are you doing, Sean?"

He's flustered. He shushes me. "Sometimes . . . when I'm with you . . . I . . ."

My face is hot. I can barely look at him.

"What?" I whisper this. "What?" Because I'm scared of what he's going to say to me. So breathless, so on the edge.

"I need someone to set me straight. I feel like you can help me, B."

I exhale like I've never heard better news. What could he have said otherwise? That he loved me? *Sometimes when I'm with you* . . . his soft voice, pulsing inside me. Anything could have come after that, couldn't it? A declaration. Even a kiss.

And I don't know what I would have done. I don't know if I would have wanted to turn him away.

12

ALI

"I want you to ask me any questions you can think of before we get there," my aunt Marce says.

It's Tuesday morning. We're going to an emergency visit at my aunt Marce's gynecologist in Jersey City. Marce told her I had unprotected sex, so I need an STI test. It's my first time seeing a gynecologist and I know I should have so many other thoughts right now, but I seem to be fixated on all the women who have been in her office. All the mothers and the babies. All the vaginas.

"Are adult vaginas the same as teenage vaginas?"

Marce smirks. Gives me a quick look.

"Less pubic hair," she says. "Pubic hair is like a gift that keeps on giving as you get older. It turns gray too."

"No. It does not."

"I am here to tell you, my darling, that it does. Sprouts of gray."

I plunge right into an image from when I was little. Of my mother's massive pubes. She was the kind of parent who walked around nude a lot. That was just her thing.

I called her pubes a gorilla for years, which she always laughed at. They would pop up in the bathtub when she'd soak there for what seemed like hours. And then I'd sit on the floor painting my little kid nails, nail polish all over my fingers, waiting for her to come out, and her gorilla vagina with all its dark curly pubes would hang down, dripping water all over the floor. Her vagina needed a separate towel.

As I've gotten older, I've told her to trim it up, and she accused me of being a bikini-line fascist. "Women are supposed to have hair down there, Ali," she said.

We're at a stretch of road near the New Jersey Turnpike that runs along the plume-filled wetlands, and Aunt Marce pulls over. The plumes are these giant feathery tusks. In the distance, a steel bridge crosses over a railroad track. Trucks whiz over the bridge at full speed. Train tracks run side by side with the water. I don't understand this part of New Jersey at all.

"Ali, I love you and want you to listen to me," she says.

"Just say it."

"Say what?"

"That I'm a whore. Or that I'm a slut. Or that I'm stupid."

"I wasn't going to say anything like that, Ali. I would never say anything like that to you."

"Then why would you start a sentence with a 'but' clarification. 'I love you, but . . .'"

"For the record, I said 'I love you and want you to listen to me.' There wasn't one single 'but.'" She shifts her hands on the steering wheel. "What happened the other night? I'm just trying to figure out what happened."

"What do you mean?"

"Why did you go up to the bedroom with him?"

"I can't believe you're saying this to me. Are you blaming me now?"

"No—" Her voice is getting higher, defensive. "I just want to figure out what's going on."

"Then you would know why I went up there!" I lower the car window. The dry wind moves through my hair. "I wanted to have sex." I replay the whole thing over in my head. Going there with the intent to see Sean Nessel. Taking those drinks. Walking up those steps. Part of me wants to tell her.

"Honey, Sean Nessel—and let's forget the part that happened in the bedroom—he was someone who was unattainable. Someone you kind of fantasized about."

"I didn't see it that way. In my mind, I knew him very well."

Except I didn't at all.

"But there's more than that. For your first time, you want to have sex with someone who you love and care about. Not just a onetime thing at a party. When you've been drinking."

"Who says it was my first time?"

"Ali."

"Okay, fine. Fine."

I slump deeper into my seat. Stare out at a mall in the distance. Something giant. More wetlands removed for it. More birds gone.

"Maybe there's an emptiness inside. Maybe there's something that you're trying to fill up that empty space with."

She's talking about my mother, I know. She wants me to do the messy cry. But I won't do it. I can't do it right now.

"Sometimes when we have an emptiness that's so great, we

try to stuff it up and fill it up. And I think that's what you did by having sex with that boy Sean."

I'm dying to say: yeah, I *filled* it up—with Sean Nessel's dick.

God, I'm disgusting. I'm just disgusting.

"I can't do this with you right now," I say. I can't do this because she doesn't know the full story. She doesn't know what he did. How he held me down.

I start to tear up and lean my head over my knees. Aunt Marce rubs my back. "I know it hurts when you like someone so much. I know how much it hurts."

She doesn't know though. She doesn't know all of it, and that's not her fault. It's mine.

Dr. Diaz tells my aunt that she doesn't have to come in and that there's a medical assistant. Is that okay with me? I nod. I don't want Aunt Marce anywhere near this exam.

I sit on the table, trying to cover myself with the paper towel gown. My legs crackle over the waxy covering. Too much noise. I'm making too much noise.

Dr. Diaz knocks on the door and comes back in with the medical assistant who gives me this weepy smile. I wonder how many vaginas she's seen today. It's only morning. So one other vagina? Maybe two?

"Have you had a talk with anyone about condom use, Ali?" Dr. Diaz asks.

"Yes, I know I'm supposed to use them."

"But what happened this time? Heat of the moment?"

I squirm. "You could say that."

She asks about the Plan B. How am I feeling? Fine. Everything's fine. She's going to show me the speculum now, is that okay? Sure, I nod. The word *speculum* sounds like an electronica band. When she holds it in front of me, I realize it's a metal clamp. A carpenter's tool.

"That's going *in there*?"

She tells me there'll be a little pressure. That she'll use lube to make sure it just slides right in. How she uses a heat lamp. She says it'll feel like light pressure.

"Is this code for *it's going to hurt*?"

Not hurt. There's no hurt. Some people don't even feel it, she swears. I cross my legs and wrap the gown around my knees. The panic in my stomach churns more, and I look over at the door.

"Look, Ali, if it makes you uncomfortable, we can do this exam over a number of visits. And if at any point you don't feel comfortable, we can stop."

"What do you mean 'stop'?"

"I mean we can just stop right in the middle of the exam. I'll take out the speculum immediately, and we can either start again or reschedule."

This is hard to believe.

"And you'll just stop?"

"I'll stop right away," she says. "That's my promise to you. One that I will never break." She looks at me with her dark brown eyes. She's probably always had sincere, trusting eyes. Maybe it's why she went into medicine, because people wanted her to take care of them.

"Do other girls freak out like this?"

"Well, it depends on the girl. Everyone's got a different feeling," she says. "For the record, I don't think you're freaking out. I think you're a little nervous. You're asking questions. And I love questions."

But she's lying. I'm totally freaking out and making a spectacle. I think of other girls and wonder if they sat perfectly still for their first gynecologist's visit. If their visits were all easy with their moms right next to them.

I want to leave, but I feel like I'm stuck here forever in the prison of lube, heat lamps, speculums, and vaginas.

I cross my arms over the gown. I wish I were wearing my T-shirt.

I wish I were wearing my pajama bottoms with the kittens on them.

I wish I had a pair of zip-up pajamas like I saw at the store last week. The kind with the footies. The kind that snaps at the top so that no one can get in them.

I glance down at my fingernails. They've taken a beating over the past few days.

Dr. Diaz takes a long stare at me with her big, brown, trusting eyes and then rolls her little stool over to the table. It whirs in the moist air of the office.

"How about this? How about we don't do the exam at all today? I can just do an STI swab. That's all." She shows me a long Q-tip with a wooden stick. It looks like the kind they swab your throat with at the doctor's office. "No speculum whatsoever. Really, I want you to feel comfortable," she says. "We want to be in control of our bodies, right? So you'll come back when it feels right to you."

Control is not a word that I can associate with right now. Right now I feel more out of control than I've ever felt in my life. Why is this? Because of Saturday night? Because of Sean Nessel? Her words bounce in my mind—they're like a weird language I don't understand. *Control. Stop. Promise. Speculum.*

I convince her that I just have a serious case of nerves. I'm good at convincing people I'm fine. This is something I've been doing since I was twelve.

I imagine just telling her. Right now, just like that.

I want to tell her about that night. How I lost my virginity to the boy I love.

Excuse me. Loved.

Obsessed over.

Stalked.

A boy whose face I decorated with flowers and hearts. The kind of boy I would have jumped off a rusty bridge with. Even if he left me in a pond floating with tires. Which he sort of did in a metaphorical way, didn't he?

I shake my head. If I talk, I'll cry. I'll cry so hard I might not be able to end it.

My eyes water. I wind my elbow around my face. I suck in my cries, and my throat burns from it. I can't hold in the tears though. It's physically impossible. When tears are ready to explode, you just have to get out of the way. I heave into my elbow and it comes out like hiccups.

"Ali, what's going on?" Her voice is low now, concerned. I can't even see her because I'm hiding in the crook of my arm.

"I don't know why I'm crying." And that's the truth. I don't know. This shouldn't be such a big deal. Maybe a weird deal. But not a traumatic deal.

"Really, everything's fine," I say. "I'm just shaken up and dying from heartbreak like Ophelia, that's all." I smile. Everything's fine. Everything's fine. If I keep saying it, it'll eventually be true, won't it?

She asks me to lie back on the table because she's going to do the swab and that's it and I do, but I tighten my knees together and pull the paper gown over my thighs. She's wearing little glasses now and glides her chair over to my feet. She places my feet in the stirrups and tells me she's going to open my legs. I feel the silliest and weirdest I've felt in a long time.

Dr. Diaz's hands separate my legs. Gently. She's very gentle. She tells me when she's going to touch me. I stare up at the turquoise parrot mobile that spins in a perfect circle above my head.

I close my eyes and get dizzy with all these weird images of people bending over and lifting their legs like they do in the *Kama Sutra* and Sean Nessel unzipping his jeans.

It's possible that I'm a fake. That I duped Sean Nessel into thinking I was experienced. That I was complicit in what happened to me. That I was ready to drink vodka and go upstairs. That I was ready to take my clothes off. Maybe it's my fault.

"Okay, all done," she says, and closes my knees together, then hands two thin tubes to the medical assistant, who walks out of the room with them. Dr. Diaz covers my thighs with the paper gown and helps lift me so I'm sitting up.

"Sometimes you think you can love someone, but then they show their true selves," she says. And I nod, her voice going in and out, *mwa-mwa-mwa*, like the absent grown-ups in Charlie Brown. "You're entitled to the same confidentiality protections as an adult. Anything you tell me stays in this room, okay?"

I nod because I can't speak, and she smiles, that warm smile, tells me to get dressed, then closes the door behind her.

I jump off the table, kicking one of the stirrups aside in the process. The metal poles clang against each other as they ricochet back and forth. I snatch my jeans off the chair. I don't even put on underwear. I just shimmy my jeans on, hiking one foot into each leg and jumping a few times.

Zip up.

Button up.

Closed shut.

In the car ride home, I'm numb.

I have only a few words. Something happened to me. I want to say it to my aunt Marce, who's telling me that it's okay that I want to reschedule. That there are plenty of girls like me who get really scared the first time they go to a gynecologist. That it's perfectly normal. That we'll try again in a few weeks.

She reminds me that I can tell her anything.

That I'll never be in trouble for telling the truth. That Dr. Diaz recommends counseling. That maybe there are other things going on.

Something happened to me?

Something happened to me.

13

BLYTHE

Come over, I text Dev. We go for a run. Nighttime. It all feels safe with him. Not crazy. At the same pace. Him turning to me. His smile. His warm smile. We stop at the old cemetery, both of us out of breath.

"Sean's freaking out," I say. It just sputters out of my mouth.

"Come here," Dev says.

"I'm all sweaty."

"Even better."

"Dev, gross."

He whines, making fun of me. "Dev, grossss."

His neck tastes like salt and sweat. His body is so warm. I lean against the black iron cemetery gate and he presses into me.

"Nessel gets himself into these messes and you're such a good listener. You're so good at talking him down. And you're so nice to all these girls. But you don't have to be his caretaker."

Over the summer, there was a freshman. Sean swore they didn't have sex, but Dev asked me to check up on her. She looked confused afterward, disoriented, like she wasn't supposed to be there. And what did I say to her? I asked her if she was okay. I told her she could call me. I pressed my hand against hers. Gave her empathetic eyes. She never did, not that I expected her to.

We walk back to my house. My mother's in her room watching TV. My father's home, in the kitchen drinking whiskey and reading. He waves and goes back to his book.

Dev is behind me on the stairs, rubbing my hips as we walk up to my bedroom. Sweat and slippery lips. I lock the door. I lead him onto me. Dev's strong fingers dig into me. Usually I have to tell him to pull back, to calm down. But this time I want it harder. My body becomes this crushing wave. Everything lights up.

My eyes are closed the whole time as I think of Sean. Sean. Sean. I wish I could get him out of my mind. Does he do this with all these girls because of some unbridled love for me? This is ridiculous. I'm being ridiculous. But his face. I can't stop imagining his face. I want to wrap my arms around him and make everything go away.

Dev's running his fingers through my hair.

"All these strands. Just coming right from your head. And your lips. Where do they come from?"

"Science."

He scoots into me, his shirt off, and I run my hand across his collarbones. His hair drooping over his eyes. It reminds me of the first time we kissed, just a few days after that party down the shore. At Cate's house. He and I on Cate's bed. Just talking and kissing. Just like that. He didn't want anything.

He didn't try anything else. I told him about the Initiation that night. "You know about it, don't you?" I said.

He nodded.

"Do you judge me because I did it?"

"Judge you? Of course not," he said. Then his face scrunched up. "Lucky those guys aren't still in this school. No, man, I hate that shit. I promise you that I'll never do that Initiation. I'll never be one of those guys. I don't care how many guys are doing it—I won't be part of it."

"What if the girls want to do it? How about then? To get it over with. To hold the power, like Amanda Shire told us." I don't know why I said this. Maybe I was testing him. Maybe I wanted to know if he'd see me that way. The way those guys did that day. Looking down on me that way.

After the Initiation, I felt like people were staring at me. Not just because we were considered royalty all of a sudden. But because it felt like the whole school knew what I did. Like they knew what I was asked to do to those guys.

I was floating around so confused and angry when I was a freshman and sophomore. Hooking up with older guys. Bashing freshman girls. Being with Dev did something to me. It stunted some of my shame. Not all of it, but a lot.

Any of the feelings I've been having for Sean lately—I've got to erase them. I'm embarrassed for even thinking about him. I've got to crush them, even if it's just for Dev.

Sean and I are in my bedroom. There's a white glow between us. A warm light. Like spring. Like the way the sun shines on you in a hot meadow. But then it starts to feel dangerous, and I can't breathe. Sean is sitting on top of me, and I'm saying, *Sean, Sean, I can't breathe. I can't get up.* Someone grabs my hair from behind and people are laughing. Sean is laughing. *Why are you laughing?* I scream. I look over and see Donnie on her knees crying.

I open my eyes.

I'm in my room.

The clock says three A.M. I hear my mother sniffling in the hallway. I jump out of bed and run to her.

Her face is a mess. White and puffy. Like she's been sitting there for a long time.

"Where's Daddy?" I say.

"He took a sleeping pill. I shook him and shook him, and he can't get up. He was drinking earlier. He shouldn't have done both."

"Well, Jesus, Mom, is he breathing?"

"Of course he's breathing, Blythe. I would have called 911."

"What about you, Mom? Did you take your medication?"

"I took it, but it's not working." She's rubbing her hands through her hair, but then they just land on the crown of her head like they're stuck and she can't move them. "My body chemistry is changing again, Blythe. None of the meds are working anymore. Everything is just falling apart all over again."

I sit down next to her, even though I don't want to. I don't want to touch her. I don't want to kiss her. But she's crying and she can't stop. I can't do anything but help her. I can't do anything but tell her it's okay. I feel like this is my new saying lately. This is what I've been telling everyone. My mom. Ali Greenleaf. Sean. Everyone.

Who is going to tell me?

Before the medication, my mother was so unpredictable. When I was younger, she was exciting in a way even though it was a roller coaster being around her. I thought it was cool when she woke me up at one A.M. to go on a night walk when we had a place in Upstate New York because that's the only time you can see the stars, in the middle of the night when all the lights are really, truly off. It didn't matter that I was in my pajamas, or not in any shoes at all. Or that the ground was cold, or that I was stepping on rocks. Keep going, Blythe. Keep going. Keep pressing on.

Then there was the time she brought me to this big adventure park down in South Jersey when I was eleven years old and left me there.

"It's time to teach you about materialism. See all these people here with their short shorts and their cotton candy and their SpongeBob rides? They're all falling into something called consumerism. The only way for you to not be anywhere near that is to immerse yourself in it without me. I want you to be scared of it, Blythe. I want you to be fearful of it because no one should live like this."

I walked around for a while buying myself popcorn and juice and then, after going on something called the Dare Devil Dive four times in a row, I finally puked right next to a young mom and her daughter.

"Who are you here with?" she said, wiping my mouth. That's when I said, "My mother left me here." So she called the police and then my father came.

It was breathtaking how concerned people were. You can't just leave your daughter at a park, apparently. My father and my grandmother excused it up to the hilt, but the police don't deal with incidents that way. They pressed charges against her. That was the first time my mother was hospitalized. Bipolar.

My father started taking me to my shrink then. The same person I'm seeing now.

"It's okay that you feel bad that your mother is in the hospital, Blythe. But no matter what you think, it's not your fault," my therapist told me at the time.

I never thought it was my fault, by the way. They say this to kids a lot. *It's not your fault.*

"I don't think it's my fault at all," I told her.

"Oh? Okay. Good."

"I was glad not to be around her," I said. I think I was hoping for a reaction, but she only gave me a twitch. "I had those few hours there by myself at the park, alone without her acting nuts or starting a fight with someone because she thought they ripped her off. Do you know how many fights she starts with everyone? Do you know how embarrassing it is to be around her?"

That's when I started screaming and crying. That's when I raked all my dolls across the sand tray. That's when I kicked over the pottery lamp in her office. It broke into triangular pieces all over her black-and-white chevron rug.

My father came running in from the waiting room. "I heard a commotion," he said. "I heard things breaking." His face looked freaked. He had a lot of looks like that during those days.

My therapist was on the floor cleaning up the pieces of her lamp, saying, "It's all right. Honestly, it's all right."

"Oh, now you're coming in," I yelled. "Now you decide it's time to step in? Father of the year, aren't you?"

"Blythe, it's not like that, honey. None of this has been easy on any of us."

"I wish I could just leave. I wish I could just leave all of you," I said. I threw myself onto the couch and cried and cried.

I heard my therapist coaching my father.

"Tell her that you're going to do your best to protect her."

So he walked over to me. I could hear his feet creak across the room, his footsteps so quiet and calculated. He was so concerned. Not sure if it was about me, or about how to handle this situation. This tween girl falling apart at the seams.

I sat up. Wiped the tears from my face. My cheeks burning.

"Don't worry, Daddy. I'll be fine," I said.

I let him off the hook again. And that was probably the end of my childhood right there.

"Blythe, you don't have to say it's fine."

And they talked and talked. But I faded out into nothing. I felt all my memories of my mother slipping past me in a fuzz, like the kind you pick off your pillow. You have to deal with bad things in life like that sometimes. Like lint. And so that's how I learned to deal with a lot of painful things. Like lint.

14

ALI

I've been going to the C-wing bathroom with Blythe Jensen for about a week now, which is causing problems between me and Sammi.

Sammi wants to know if I'm going back to the gynecologist. Sammi wants to know if I got the STI test back. (I did. It was negative.) Sammi wants to know if I'm sleeping. If I'm eating. If I want to get disco fries at the diner. If I've talked to someone about the thing that happened, because we can't name the thing that happened. I won't let her. I won't let her tell Raj. I won't let her tell anyone. And I don't want to answer any of Sammi's questions because I don't want to think about that night. I don't want to think about anything at all.

I walk out of my third period class, and Blythe's standing there waiting for me like she said she would be. The hallway is chaotic between periods and so many kids and schlumpy teachers bump into each other, and there's Blythe, this lone spirit, standing right under the MUSTANG PRIDE signs, watching me. Her greenish-blue eyes shimmer as I step closer. I blush. I've never had this kind of attention from another girl before. Not like this. Not like Blythe.

She nudges me with her elbow. Wraps her hand around mine.

"Stand against the locker," she says.

"Huh?"

"You heard me. Stand against the locker—I want to show you your posture. You're a sloucher, Greenleaf."

Blythe is Eliza Doolittle–ing me. She's going to turn me into her little smooth-armed robot. Her little fashion princess. She's going to dress me up like a doll next and curl my hair. I back up against the metal locker, trying to get my body straight. Blythe pushes my shoulders back.

"Relax," she says. "Drop your shoulders."

I do what she says. But I slept funny last night. Every night since the party. I stretch my neck to the left. Then to the right.

"Ugh! What are you doing?"

"I'm loosening up my neck."

"You're going to give yourself fucking whiplash, Greenleaf."

"I don't think you get whiplash from standing."

She softens her face, her perfect teeth white and gleaming like she has the answers to everything, and maybe she does. "We'll work on it. Getting your shoulders down," she says, and then zeroes in on my triceps. Blythe has a hot-pink reverse French manicure. Her nails are clear and the half-moons are neon. She runs her nails down my arm. It tingles. "Then we'll work on the pimples on the back of your arms."

My skin is bumpy. A little freckly, but I don't have pimples. I don't think I have pimples. At least I never thought I had pimples until this moment.

"Touch my triceps." Blythe hooks her elbow toward me and makes a muscle. I laugh, a nervous laugh because it sounds so strange, like she's showing off. "I'm not going to bite, Greenleaf."

So I touch her skin. And it's so smooth. So shiny. So much softer than mine. I'm in a trance from her arms. And I stare back at mine. How did my arms get so ragged? How did mine become so neglected?

"See how smooth I am, Ali? See how shiny my skin is?"

I touch her because she asks me to, and I want to, just to be closer to her because Blythe's skin glows like every other part of her. None of it seems real, except it all is.

"How do you get your elbows so pale? And how do you get all those bumps off?"

"You have to exfoliate. You gotta dry loofa that shit out. Then alcohol. Then almond oil."

"Wait, doesn't alcohol burn?"

"Of course it burns. What are you, a pussy?"

"Hell no."

"Do you ever go to yoga, Greenleaf?"

"Not really."

"You should take a class with me one night. It's really good for your posture, and your mind too."

"I know what yoga is, Blythe. I don't live under a rock."

Blythe's face gets crumply and weird. She's not used to someone being irritated with her, or snarky. They're all yes girls. And I'm supposed to be a yes girl too. A fangirl. She doesn't know that I've watched her for years. I'm not alone. Who hasn't watched Blythe Jensen? How do you not stare?

"The only time I stopped doing yoga was when I hurt my

ankle. And I had to walk around on a cane for a little while—"

"I remember that," I say, but it's too quick. I shouldn't remember that. I shouldn't have been so quick to admit that I noticed her cane. An old brown carved cane. She walked around with it for at least a month.

"You *remember* that?"

"I mean, it was a pretty unusual cane." Trying to shrug it off.

"My dad got me that cane in Africa."

"He travels a lot? Your dad?"

"Yeah—he's away a lot. I'm, like, the house babysitter," she snorts.

"Oh, do you have a younger sister or brother?"

She looks away. I want to ask her where she's looking, but maybe I already know. It's the anywhere-but-here look.

"My mother is sick. She has an illness. I shouldn't say babysitter. I'm just needed around my house."

"What kind of illness?"

"She's fucking crazy," Blythe says. "No. I shouldn't say that either. That's mean. She's bipolar." She slows her walk down to a stroll. Everyone else is speeding up, but we're slowing down. She's told me something now that she can't take back. I'm supposed to give up something private and secretive about myself in return.

"Well, my mother's fucking crazy too," I say.

"Everyone's mother is crazy," she says. "But unless you have a crazy mother, a real honest-to-goodness, clinically crazy parent, you just don't understand what that's like."

And so now we're at a standstill, kind of. And I wish I had a joke. Anything to break that silence.

"You want to have a crazy-off with me? Is that what you're trying to tell me?" I say and smile. I drop my hands down like I'm about to fight her. Rock my body back and forth. Hop up and down. "Let's have a crazy-mom-off. Let's do it."

She stops. So I stop too. And everyone walking behind us trips over themselves because when Blythe stops walking, everyone stops walking.

"Greenleaf."

"I'm serious."

She takes me by the arm and drags me into her, close to her hip. I'm in a little cocoon with her.

"Did you just say *crazy-mom-off* to me?"

"Yeah, man. Let's go. I promise you. My mom can out-crazy your mom."

"How did you get like this?"

"Years of self-preservation." Which is true. You can either get really depressed about your life or you can shove that depression so deep inside you and hide it with snarkiness. I'm not saying the second option is healthy. I'm sure I'll die of an ulcer at age forty-six. It's just what I've done.

"So you want to play?" I say.

Blythe nods. Takes a deep breath. This is weird for her, I can see. She's not used to talking about private stuff. About stuff that you're supposed to be ashamed of.

"I'll go first," I say. "My mother decided when I was twelve that she didn't want to be a mother anymore and moved to

Truth or Consequences, New Mexico, to drop out of life." I draw myself closer to Blythe and slow the pace down even more. People are just bypassing us now, scrambling to their classes. I lower my voice. "My father caught her in bed with another man. In our house. Let's see . . . she used to be a drunk. She's on three years of sobriety now."

"So now that she's stopped drinking, does she just get high all day?"

"I don't know, probably. When I go there, I sleep on the couch. She lives in a peach-colored house in the desert."

"Do you still talk to her?"

"Talk to her? Yes, of course. I mean, she's my mom."

"That doesn't mean anything," she says, her voice breaking. "I live with my mom, and I barely talk to her. I try as much as I can to stay away from her."

I shouldn't have started this game with Blythe. My mother is crazy, but in the not-so-harmful way. It used to be bad. When I was younger, it was bad. But it's not destructive anymore.

She stares at me hard, then loops her arm around mine tight, locks it in, so I can't let go. She leans in as we walk, her breath in my ear.

"My mother used to be one of Oscar de la Renta's designers in her early twenties. She worked for Louis Vuitton for years. And when she's not in a robe, everything she wears is tailored or silk. It was good to be manic and have these grandiose episodes when she was creative and when she didn't have me," she says, bitter. "My mom got arrested when I was eleven for leaving me in a theme park by myself on purpose and then got institutionalized by the state. Now she's at home under lock and key and medication, of course, when she decides to take it. She goes up and down. Mostly, I've gotten stuck driving her to doctor's appointments because most of her meds have a sedative side effect and because my father is always traveling."

She stares at me matter-of-factly, her eyes wide open.

"DAMN."

"Top that, bitch."

"I think you won," I say.

"I think my mother out-crazies your mother by a long shot."

I'm attached to her, a loop on her belt. We stare at each other so serious and then—I can't help it. Nerves. The exhilaration of saying it out loud. *My mother's crazy.* And like a flash, we're hysterical. Laughing so hard that we're going to pee. We keep walking. Part of me wants to hug her, because to get left in an amusement park? That sounds awful. My mother left me too—but not in an amusement park. I can't imagine being left like that.

Blythe and I can shove the painful shit down. And laugh ourselves to tears until we explode. Look at us. So happy on the outside, neglected on the inside by the women in our lives. That's what we have in common.

I tell her I'll meet her after fifth period near the cafeteria, and I run off to class. I turn around in the hallway to see where she is, and she's already gone.

15

BLYTHE

Morning. I look around the kitchen. My mom in her robe. Shuffling around in slippers. Dinner from last night still on the table. Cartons of takeout Mexican food.

"Where is Dad?"

"He left super early this morning."

"Is Rosita coming?"

"No, Rosita is not coming— Do you understand what a spoiled brat you sound like?"

"I'm not asking if Rosita is coming because I want her to clean up."

I want to know if Rosita is coming because I want to leave the house, and I can't leave my mother unless someone else is here. I promised my father. She got kicked out of group therapy the other day. She doesn't like her meds. They're making her paranoid. She accused someone of stealing her phone, when really, she just left it at home. She got in the woman's face. Threatened her. I prefer her when she's drugged on Klonopin.

Her eyes travel off, looking at the mess around the kitchen, maybe, or just looking at the mess of her life.

"Rosita will be here soon. In twenty minutes. She's running late."

I can leave her for twenty minutes. What damage can she do in twenty minutes? I know. I'll clean until Donnie gets here. I toss the plates into the sink. There's an empty popcorn bag. There are tissues near the garbage that haven't been thrown out. I'll just get things started, that's all. All my nervous energy around my mother, festering inside me. My therapist would say, *Give yourself healthy advice. Channel that discomfort.* So I'll channel it into the dishes. Here I am, a good daughter, washing the dishes.

"Blythe, don't start throwing dishes around."

"I'm just clearing the countertops—"

"I'll do all this. Stop—" she says, and reaches for the dish in my hand. Neither of us holds on to it. The plate breaks in pieces. White porcelain shards scatter across the wood floor.

It all gets so harried and crazy with her so fast. I only want it to slow down. So I stop. I breathe like my therapist told me to. I step over the shards.

"Mom, I have to go to school."

"It's fine. Go. I'll clean this up."

I grab my backpack and don't look at her, even though I'm on the verge of punching something or throwing a chair.

"I know you want to blame everything on me, Blythe. But I want someone to blame too. You don't understand that though, do you?"

I want to say things to her about her taking away my childhood and how since I was six I realized there was "something wrong with Mommy" and sometimes "Mommy isn't rational," and how it's "not my fault that Mommy is sick."

But I say nothing. My mother scares me in a way. I don't want to be too vulnerable in front of her because I don't think she can handle it. And if I break down and cry, tell her how I really feel, let it all pour out, she'll fall apart. She'll beg me to understand her side. To talk to me endlessly about her mother and her father. About her sister who died ten years ago. I don't always want to understand her side. I just want to be a person who doesn't have to take care of, or worry about, her mother— but I don't get that option.

I want to call Ali. Isn't that strange? That pull I have toward her? Suddenly, there's some connection between us. Because this is something Ali would understand—especially about mothers—that no one else would. Even Donnie, who I turn to for everything. Her mother and father, they're still together. Her mother is a scientist! Dr. Alperstein, the famous scientist.

And just like that, Donnie, Cate, and Suki are at my house. I lock the door behind me and text Rosita: *Let me know when you get to the house.*

I'm outside so fast. There's Donnie with a cigarette, her hand hanging out the car window, her silver cuff around her wrist sparkling in the sun. I cram in the back seat next to Suki. Cate's got shotgun, and usually I'd fight her for it, make her get in the back. Today I don't care. Can't get out of here, away from my mother, fast enough.

Donnie hands me the cigarette. Deep inhale. Smoke in my lungs. Exhale smoke rings. "Where's your little friend?" Donnie says. "I thought you'd be walking to school with her. Maybe holding her backpack."

"You sound jealous."

"I, for one, don't care who you're friends with, but I also

am kind of curious," Suki says. "Is this an actual friendship? I thought this had something to do with Sean."

"It does have to do with Sean. At least it started that way. But I like Ali."

Cate turns around from the front seat, shoots a look at Suki, and they laugh.

"What's so funny?"

They laugh more. There's nothing funny. It's a game they want to play. They're scared that they're going to slip from my fingers and they'll have nothing for me to hold on to. Maybe that I'll trade them in for Ali.

"Playing with fire, gonna get burned," Suki sings, making up her own song.

"Ali? She's innocent. What could she do to me?"

"Not her," Suki says. "Sean."

"He's a baby," I say. "You didn't see him crying that night. You guys don't understand how I pick up the pieces for him. How that's part of our friendship now. He doesn't come to you like he comes to me."

Especially lately. That was a job Dev and I both handled. But now, it seems to be just me. The other day in the hallway. *I need someone to set me straight.* And then, *Sometimes when I'm with you.* I haven't told anyone about that. Kept it hidden, all the way down.

"Crying about what, B? That he broke some other girl's heart? That's his MO," Cate says.

"Oh, and what guy's not a player?" I say.

"Dev's not a player."

"Maybe that's why Sean hangs out with Dev and looks up to Dev. Because he wants to be more like him."

But I have no idea if that's true at all. It feels like it could be.

"You guys have never seen him cry like I have. You've never seen him spilling his guts like I have."

"About what? His hair?" Suki says.

"His SAT scores?" Donnie says. "*He has a soft side. You guys don't understand.*" Donnie, mocking me.

"That soft side is his pretty face," Suki says.

I slump down into the back seat, my knees up against the passenger side. I close my eyes. I can see his face right in front of me. The way he looked that night. *I would never hurt anyone.*

He wouldn't, would he? Not purposefully. Right?

16

ALI

It's been two weeks since I first met Sheila the She Woman. Two weeks since that night.

My dad wants me to meet her again. The right way.

"You mean, not with her ass sticking out?"

I try not to laugh. I love teasing my father. It means everything to me.

"Alistair."

"Dad."

"You seriously have got to get a handle on that mouth of yours."

So Sheila is coming over for dinner. My father is cooking. This means he bought a rotisserie chicken and is microwaving frozen broccoli. If he really wants to charm her, he'll open a can of beans and chop up some cilantro.

Sheila comes in with flowers for me. A dozen orange roses, which is sweet actually.

"They're from an organic farm in West Jersey," she says.

"I thought roses came from a florist," I say, deadpanning.

"Jesus, Ali. Give it a rest!" my father yells from the kitchen.

"Your father told me about your great sense of humor," she says. She's smiling. She's not so offended.

✹ ✹ ✹

At dinner Sheila wants to know about my interests.

"Boys."

This used to be a funny joke in my family before Sean Nessel. Before my father thought I was a slut. Before I had to go to a gynecologist. Before my aunt delivered Plan B to me. It slipped out of my mouth too fast. My father stares at me like he's going to slap me from across the table.

"New answer," he says, gritting his teeth.

I sit up in my seat. Serious now. "I write a little. I also make collages. I guess I do a lot of things."

She tells me that she writes too. That she used to be a journalist. Now she just teaches more than she actually writes.

"What made you become a journalist?" I say.

She perks up. Surprised that she caught my interest.

"I saw a movie on Woodward and Bernstein. Ever hear of them?"

I shake my head.

"They're the journalists who uncovered Watergate. The reporters who found out that President Nixon had hired his men to break into the Democratic National Committee offices that were in the Watergate building to steal information. That he lied to the country and then resigned. They ended up uncovering layers of Washington secrets about the president that no one was willing to talk about."

"It was a defining moment in history," my dad says.

Of course I know about Watergate, but I don't feel like explaining myself. Too much effort. So I nod. Watching her.

Wondering what her articles were about. Why she started teaching.

"The only journalists I like are comedians," I say. "At least they make you laugh while talking about how depressing everything is."

"Apathy, apathy, apathy," my dad says.

"Hey! Apathy! That's on my PSAT."

He shakes his head.

"Do you have a school paper or something? Do school newspapers even exist anymore?" she says.

"Actually they do have a school paper. Didn't it win an award last year?" my dad asks.

"Yeah, we have a great school newspaper. And I know all about it because the boy that I used to be in love with was in it all the time. I used to cut his face out of it."

More deadpan. My dad looks down at his plate.

"Are you interested in journalism, Ali?" she says. She's not letting this go. She's insisting on a serious conversation.

"I don't really know what I'm interested in right now." That's the pathetic truth.

"Okay," she says, uncomfortable. "Well, if you're at all interested, maybe you could look at some places online. There are a lot of female journalists out there writing great stuff about college campus rape, eating disorders, abortion rights . . ."

I think of the first thing she said: college campus rape. Rape. My mind buzzes and buzzes as I stuff food into my mouth, nodding, *Yes, sure, send me something,* I think I say, my mouth filled with food because there's not enough food, not enough of anything to fill me up and make this feeling like I'm disintegrating go away.

Later that night, I'm watching what seems like an endless stream of YouTube videos on babies who can't see. A doctor places glasses over their little, confused faces and then their world becomes clear. Imagine your world so fuzzy. That you can't see. That you don't know anything is different about that fuzzy green thing hanging from the tree. Then it becomes shockingly clear: that fuzzy green thing is a leaf.

Blythe texts me: *What are u doing?*

Watching babies with bad eyesight see for the first time on YouTube

ALI

YES

Can I come over?

I look around my room. Some of my room seems so babyish. I bet Blythe's room is glamorous. She's got like silver wallpaper or something. A canopy bed with long white silk drapes hanging from each end. Some chic white chair in the corner with black fur pillows.

My room on the other hand. My desk is painted turquoise because my dad and I painted it together. My mirror is from the 1970s; it's got tiny little daisies painted in clusters except for the center. My mother picked it up at a garage sale years ago. "When you look at yourself in the mirror," she said, "you'll always be surrounded by flowers." There's a Nirvana sticker in the corner that came with it, otherwise it would have been worth something. God. Do we have to be so fucking quaint?

Mother driving me crazy.

Sure, come over.

Blythe will be here in ten minutes. That's not nearly enough time to clean up. I assess my room. What's the most messy thing? My bed. My bed has to be made first. But oh my God, why do I have Dora sheets? What am I—two? Everything else was in the laundry, I'll tell her. It's the truth! I found them at the back of the closet. Everything *was* dirty! But Dora sheets? How has it come to this?

"Dad! Where are those white sheets that you got me from Target?"

He's downstairs, yelling something I don't understand. I'm at the top of the steps.

"The white sheets from Target! Where are they? The new ones!"

"Still in the bag. Next to the washing machine."

"Ugh, they're not clean?"

"If you had cleaned them, Ali—"

"Does everything have to be such a chore?"

I run down the stairs, and he's calling after me.

"It's only a chore if you make it a chore."

I unwrap the sheets and a duvet cover. Everything has to be white. That's what it means to have a normal bed that's not a loser bed. That's not a baby bed. Everything white.

I kick the bags to the side and race back up the stairs.

He follows me, stairs creaking behind me. "Why are you doing this now?"

"Blythe is coming over now."

"Wait . . . now?"

"Don't start with me, Dad. My room is a mess—"

"What are you doing with those?" He points to my Dora sheets on the floor.

"I'm throwing them out. That's what I'm doing." I'm standing on my bed trying to shove my pink comforter into the white duvet cover.

"I want to save those, Ali."

"What? Why? Even if I have a kid one day, which I won't, I wouldn't let her watch Dora because her head is too big for her body and she doesn't even look like a real person."

"When did you decide you're not having kids? I'm so lost—"

"Dad, seriously. Be cool when Blythe comes over. She's upset about her mom. And I don't want her freaking out. This is a new friend."

All of a sudden my bed is white and sparkly. And I'm so proud of myself. I throw all my shoes and clothes into my hamper—shove it in the closet. Everything. Boxes. Books. Everything goes in the closet. I stack two bowls with pretzel crumbs and three empty water glasses together and hand them to my father, pressing them against his chest.

"Please take these down for me."

"What's wrong with her mother?"

"Bipolar."

"Oh."

His face looks worried. I see the crease between his eyebrows.

"Everyone has problems, Dad."

The doorbell rings. It's Blythe.

"Dad?"

He looks around my room. "It looks great. Don't worry. I'll be cool."

I stand at the middle of the steps watching my dad let Blythe in. I think even he's surprised how together and pretty she is. Her hair tonight is all swung to the side, wavy. Shiny. She's wearing a strategically washed-out sweatshirt and tight black jeans with holes in the knees. She gives my father the whole *it's so nice to meet you* shtick. I wave my hands toward her, grab her hand, and lead her up the stairs.

"Aww, your room is cute," Blythe says.

"Can you stop calling everything I do cute?"

"You *are* cute, Ali. Can I have a tour? Show me everything. I want to see everything."

I look at her strangely, because I don't know exactly what that means, but I laugh and show her all of the main points of my life. The third place ribbon I won the year I was on the swim team. The old dollhouse I had with the super put-together nuclear family.

"What do you keep under there?" She's staring at the black boxes under my bed. They're filled with my stupid pictures of Sean Nessel. I never finished ripping up all the scrapbook pictures.

"Nothing is under the bed."

"There's always something under the bed. No one has nothing under their bed. And you have black boxes."

Blythe bends down on the floor and eyes the boxes. She looks up at me with puppy dog eyes and smiles sideways. "Ali. There are secrets packed away in these boxes, aren't there?"

"Honestly, it's nothing."

"Oh my God, I have to see now."

She pulls at one of the boxes, laughing. She thinks it's something embarrassing from my childhood, and because Blythe Jensen isn't used to hearing no from anyone, she won't take no from me. I'm telling her to stop. She's not listening.

"You said you had to talk about your mother!" I say now, my voice shaking. I shove her back with my foot and then try to block her with my thigh down to the ground. I'm all contorted in front of her, between her and the black boxes filled with photos of Sean Nessel.

She crawls away, coughing because I guess I got her in the belly.

"Seriously, Ali, what the fuck?"

"What the fuck *with you*? I told you not to look at those boxes and you—you just can't stop."

"I didn't know it was so serious. I thought you were doing your Ali snarky thing."

"It's pictures of Sean Nessel if you really want to know. I was in love with him. Stupid me. So in love with him. I used to clip pictures of him. I used to clip out everything he did."

Does hiding it matter anymore? It just makes me look crazier than I already am. What am I trying to protect anyway? Myself? I've already lost it all. I drag one of the boxes out and dump it in front of her. All the cutout hearts and cutout tiny stars and the black paper and the glitter and the markers and the newspaper clips and the printouts. The feathers and gold ribbon that I used to line the book.

"Here it is. Here it all is. My life before that horrible night. This was everything. Everything that I dreamed of is here right in this box and now it's just nothing." I start ripping up collages and pictures. Just tossing them to the side.

I see that I've freaked out Blythe now. I'm crying and she's just sitting there on her knees, not realizing what she got into with me and this black box thing. She's going to leave. She'll leave and we'll never talk again.

But she takes a deep breath instead and stares at me. She's not laughing anymore.

BLYTHE

I want to tell her everything. I want to tell her how Sean cried to me. That I understand her having a whole box filled with photos with idiotic hearts glued to the edges. I want to admit that I have this weird loyalty toward him that I don't entirely understand. That my friends don't entirely understand. My boyfriend's best friend. That I've become his confidant. I recognize the collage books and I know what it feels like to be obsessed with someone. I get it. Some of Ali, in a way, reminds me of Dev. So honest and good. Her face, the way she's so scrunched up and confused. It reminds me of how Dev gets frustrated about the injustices of the world. It makes me want to tell her things.

She's crying and I feel bad. It's a soft cry. Her father is downstairs, and I know she doesn't want him to hear.

"Have you ever heard of something called the Initiation?"

"A little. I always thought it was a rumor."

"Not a rumor. It's a thing that happens when you're in the ninth grade. And you have to be really hot."

She laughs, snorting out her tears. "Oh, I guess I wasn't really hot."

"Not hot. You have to be . . . you have to be developed. You have to seem older. You have to seem like you're down for anything."

Ali sits back, wraps her arms around her knees.

"I was asked to be in the Initiation. You get asked by senior girls. And I stood in a room with a bunch of senior boys. Me and Donnie. We . . . we sat on the floor. Got on our knees. And we . . . you know."

But Ali is staring at me. She's not filling in the blanks.

"Know what? What do I know? What did you do?"

"You really never heard this, Ali?"

"I heard that girls get chosen and people hook up."

"It's more than that. It's like we walk into this room. And all the guys are sitting there on chairs. They're all smiling, but they're not supposed to. My initiation leader, Amanda Shire, is yelling at them. Like a dominatrix or something. 'Get that smile off your face. I'm going to smack it off your face, you pervs.'"

And it's true, everything I'm telling her. I remember thinking to myself when I walked in there, all of us in a straight line, that maybe this won't be so bad because Amanda Shire has the whole thing under control. Maybe it's even a joke, I thought. Maybe it won't happen at all.

"And then she reads out all these rules. She starts saying, 'No touching. Keep your hands in your lap. No touching heads. No touching hair. No moaning. Keep your mouths shut. We don't want to hear a word. Not a fucking word.'"

"And you . . . just stayed there?"

"What was I going to do, run? I thought it was an empowerment thing. I thought we were in charge of it. Amanda Shire. Calling me lil sis. Telling me that this would put me in control of my body. There were a lot of girls getting attacked by guys in school. A lot of cover-ups. And so this was her antidote. She said it would put us in charge of the act. Get it out in the open so that we were no longer conquests.

"But I knew that was a lie. That was a lie right when I stepped in front of Kramer, this senior. He smirked. Jittery. His nails bitten down to the edge like some attention deficit hyperactive maniac.

"'Stop smiling, Kramer,' Amanda Shire was saying. 'I'm going to tell her to cut it off.' This made them all laugh more. They loved it. They loved the challenge of it.

"She was like a drill sergeant. 'Get on your knees, girls.

Guys, unzip your shorts. Do not pull down your pants. If you pull down your pants, you're out of here.' I sat on my knees and looked over at Donnie, who sat on her knees, staring at me like *what are we doing here*. Her face blank when the guy in front of her pulled it out. Jason something. I can't even remember his last name. Isn't it weird how we blank out those details?

"It was the first time I saw a penis in the daytime. Hard and long, like it didn't belong here. Like they were grotesque animals with masks covering them, skin stretching and veins. All the most vile parts of the human body. I closed my eyes tight.

"'Girls, you're going to sit up and put your mouth over it. These perverts aren't going to come in your mouth. I'm not going to let them. You're going to do a few sucks, and I promise a few sucks will get these hormonal assholes off. Close your eyes, you fucking perverts. Close your eyes because you're about to get the best thing you have had in your life. Virgin mouths. Young mouths.'"

Ali just stares at me. "This is crazy, Blythe. You never told anyone this?"

"I know girls came before me and they came after me. And now I'm the one who is supposed to run the Initiation. It was passed down to me by a senior last year. To me. *Me*. 'Good luck,' was all she said. Imagine the hypocrisy of it. Screaming at eighteen-year-old boys, 'Don't touch them! Don't touch them!' As our mouths are wrapped around their penises. In broad daylight!"

I don't even know how to process the whole thing. I don't. I never have.

But now I've told this to Ali. This secret that I've never talked about with anyone. I've only told Dev the surface details. Not everything. I never talked about how when we left, guys were shaking hands and laughing. Pointing at us as if we were cattle. Two of the girls were crying. I never told anyone that. How Amanda Shire screamed at them for crying— *This will make you stronger. You're not weak. Stop acting like weak bitches! You want to get raped? You want them to think they can have you? You just had them. You have the power.*

"Donnie and I walked home that night spitting on the ground. Trying to wipe all traces of them. Kramer drove up next to us. Another guy was in the passenger seat. 'You girls shouldn't walk home alone. Let me give you a ride home.' We were so scared they were going to kidnap us or something, I don't know what we thought. Crazy thoughts. I snatched her hand and ran the opposite way, tearing through someone's backyard. 'This was supposed to make us more empowered?' Donnie kept saying after that night."

"What was it like the next day?"

"It was like Donnie and I became queen of the freshmen. They catered to everything we did. It was crazy. The attention we got," I say. "So I went with it—it was so stupid. What was I supposed to do? *Tell* someone? Cry about it? It would make me seem vulnerable and weak. And if I told someone? Can you imagine the response? 'No one forced you into it, did they?' Those boys looked at us the next day and lifted us up because they felt guilty, and that's why we became queen of the freshmen. I walked around pretending I was happy because that's what they wanted from me. 'See? I'm not damaged. I'm not sad.'"

Ali sits down next to me and our arms touch. I lean my head on her shoulder because, in a way, we are exactly the same person.

We're both holding on to secrets.

And we've held our secrets tight, and we have that together. And we'll hold on to those secrets, maybe forever.

"Sometimes guys make mistakes, Ali. You know this, right? Even in the Initiation. I know there are guys who regretted it. There are guys who wished they didn't do it."

She nods. And I think that I'm getting her to understand.

I reach out for her hand. "Sean's one of those guys," I say to her. "He's not perfect, Ali. But he was crying afterward. Crying to me like a scared child. Doesn't that say something about him? That he had guilt?"

But she doesn't answer. Not a word.

17

ALI

Three weeks into our friendship, and I understand now that there's a difference between Blythe and the rest of the world.

She's the aqua sea. She's the beach filled with shells. The wind that you wait for. Blythe is all the good things. The calm things. The together things. The harmonized music. Everyone else is the clutter.

Blythe and I walk out of C-wing down to the first floor and cut over to B-wing through the freshman tunnel. "You don't have to say hi to everyone you see," Blythe says. The hallway is her runway, and she's a fucking Chanel model strutting with her books tight to her chest and her blond hair blowing back untamed as if there's a perpetual fan on her face. "Flash a peace sign. Or just nod."

We cruise down the first floor of B-wing, and I see Sammi in front of her locker. Her face is in a wild smile, and I almost call out her name, until I think of what Blythe has just said and give her the peace sign instead. It's kind of this jokey thing; I expect Sammi to flash me a peace sign back.

But Sammi slams her locker. She doesn't take it as a joke. "I can make signs too," she says loudly. She gives me the middle finger.

"Lovers' quarrel," Blythe says, smiling. She giggles and walks a bit faster.

Sammi storms down the hall, the opposite way. We can't connect on anything lately, she and I. I almost want to let her go, but the way Blythe looks at me, like I'm a leper for not going after her. What kind of friend am I?

I'm too exhausted by the drama around her, though. I'd have to trail her until she spoke to me, and explain and apologize. I know this sounds awful—it is awful. I don't want to hurt Sammi. The last thing I'd ever want to do is hurt Sammi. But I'm so deep down in my own rabbit hole that it's hard to see anything else.

"A true friend won't take that shit," Blythe says. "If I ever flashed Donnie a peace sign—forget it. She'd cut my fingers off."

I tell Blythe I'll see her later and chase after Sammi. I notice the worst thing—she's got toilet paper on her shoe. I can't let her run away with toilet paper on her shoe.

"Sammi!"

"Fuck off."

"Sammi, you have toilet paper on your shoe."

She looks down, annoyed, rips the toilet paper off her boot, and clenches her jaw.

"That's what you're catching up to me for? To tell me about toilet paper—right after you throw me a peace sign? With Blythe Jensen?"

I look around, tell Sammi to lower her voice.

"Why, is it a secret now? Your friendship with her is, what, something we shouldn't discuss? Maybe it has a password too? Like a diary where you lock it up and only give one person the key?"

I'm too tired to fight her. I'm vanishing. Really. If she only knew how I was disintegrating.

"I'm sorry. That's all I can say right now."

"This isn't what our friendship is about."

"I know."

But this is what happens when you have nothing to say. When everything feels like dust.

"I have to go to class."

"I know . . . Sammi, I'm so sorry about that stupid peace sign."

"You need help, Ali," she says. "I wish you would talk to me."

I nod my head and let her walk away.

Later Sammi texts me.

What is going on with you?

Nothing, I write.

Nothing is the worst answer ever.

I don't write back.

You can't just keep pretending that nothing is going on with you.

Why? It's so much easier that way.

The next day, Sammi texts me when I don't show up for lunch. I'm in Blythe's car. Donnie and Blythe are sitting in the front seat. I'm in the back. In the Blythe bubble, eating hummus and pita chips while they howl along to a song by a crooner with a deep voice filled with pain. It's a song about how if they got hit by a bus or a train, it would be fine, an honor even, if they could just die together.

Sammi texts me through their bellowing.

Where are you?

"Who's texting you, your mother?" Donnie says.

Blythe smacks Donnie.

"What?" Donnie says, clutching her arm. "What did I say?"

"Her mother lives in New Mexico."

"Oh, well, how was I supposed to know that?" Donnie looks over at me, puzzled. "Sorry, Ali."

"It's fine."

"Aren't you going to pick up the damn phone, though? Seriously. You have a stalker. At least change your ring tone."

Sammi's text screams out:

ALISTAIR

Why aren't you answering my texts?

"It's Sammi."

"Shit, you need to straighten things out with her, Ali," Blythe says, her mouth full of chips.

"Isn't she your best friend?" Donnie says.

"Yeah." And I text Sammi back.

Sorry. Just seeing this now.

Bullshit

"You can't blow off your best friend, Ali," Blythe says.

But they're back to scream-singing, their faces so close to

each other, their hands grabbing each other's shirts. The way Sammi and I used to be, that close.

"I'm not blowing her off," I say, but they don't even hear me. I just don't want to talk. I don't want to answer questions. I don't want her to ask me how I am. What's the answer: *I'm fading away, Sammi. I'm disappearing.*

"How many times has she texted you?" Blythe asks.

I look at my phone. Too many times.

"I swear if you ever blew me off like that, B," Donnie says, and shakes her head. "Snap of the neck."

"That's exactly what I said the first time it happened," Blythe says, giving me a playful smack. "Isn't that what I said?"

"Yeah. It's what you said." But I'm far away now. Somewhere else.

Blythe keeps going on about how Donnie would show up to her house with a flamethrower or something. More chips in her mouth. Crunching like she has all the answers. Doesn't she?

"Really, Ali. Why don't you just answer her?"

Because then I'd have to talk. I'd have to explain. And that's the last thing I want to do. Talk about how I feel. Once I say it out loud, it'll be real.

Raj and I are at my locker.

"Why are you giving Sammi the cold shoulder?"

"I'm dumping her for Blythe."

But he squints his eyes in a concerned look.

"I was just making a joke, Raj." I sigh. One of those big

sighs like the weight of the world is on your head and you can't walk straight. He notices it and laughs.

"So cryptic, Greenleaf."

"A person isn't allowed to sigh?"

He sighs loudly, making fun of me, slowly shrinking to the floor.

"That's me?"

"That's you when I try to talk to you. This is an awkward thing between the two of you. Usually Sammi's the Ali expert. But she doesn't know what to say to you anymore."

I know Sammi didn't tell Raj what really happened. Sammi wouldn't tell a soul. I know that.

"She said you were still really messed up about the Nessel thing."

"That's all she said?"

"That you were isolating yourself."

"I'm not isolated."

"Oh, right. You're hanging out with Blythe Jensen. That's not isolating at all."

This is Raj. He's legitimately concerned. I can't just shut him down. "I've been doing this with everyone. It's not just you. It's not just her."

"I'm aware."

"Wouldn't that make you feel better?"

"No. It'll make me feel worse."

"Why? Why would that make you feel worse?"

He looks away, more annoyed than worried, actually. "Because you've just been somewhere else lately. It's not like you. None of this—it feels like I'm talking to someone else."

I want so badly to talk to him about all of it. How Blythe scooped me up and how it just feels good to be wanted by her. To hear her spill secrets she hasn't told anyone else. To know details about this school, hidden things.

I wish I could explain this to him, but I can't get the right words out of my mouth because then I'd have to tell him everything and I don't even know where I'd begin.

"Do you know sometimes how you just feel lost?" I say.

"When my parents got divorced," he says. "And I first started going back and forth to my mom's for three days and then my dad's for three days. That was hell. I hated that. I felt lost. Like I was nowhere. So I made this little fortress around my superheroes. And I told my parents that I was the superhero. And that the fortress was my house. I was just safe inside that little space."

I would like a fortress.

"I get it, Ali. I get how it feels to want to disappear," he says. "I'll talk to Sammi."

I reach out and hug him, which I know surprises him. But I hold him tight because I'm going to cry so hard if I let go. And then I feel his hands across my back hugging me too. My chest up against his. His breath in my ear. I don't want to let go. I want to rest my head in the crook of his neck and be closer to him. There's a buzz all inside me warming my body, and it surprises me. So I pull back to stare at him. That fuzz around his mouth. That hair drooping in his face. Wonder if he's feeling that buzz too.

18

BLYTHE

It's not like people notice when we're standing there together, me and Sean. They don't think, "Oh, those two are in love." There's no conversation when we're huddled together because the three of us—me, Sean, and Dev—are always together. But today it feels like I'm hiding something. It's the way he needs me and how he confides in me about Ali. It feels like I'm keeping something from Dev. And maybe I am.

"So what did Ali say when you were at her house?" Sean says. "You had some enlightening conversation with her."

"She showed me a collage book of you." I feel awful right when it comes out. God. Why did I say that?

"A what?"

"I mean, it's sweet, Sean. It's not something to make fun of."

"What kind of collage book?"

"Pictures of you. You know? Hearts and daisies."

He starts laughing, laughing so hard like it's a joke. Except it's not.

"It's cute, Sean. It's the kind of thing—"

"A stalker does. That's what it is. The kind of thing a stalker does."

"No, it's the kind of thing an immature girl does. An inexperienced girl. Maybe it's kind of normal actually."

"How can you think that's normal, B? She made a book of me? She collected photos of me? Hearts and fucking daisies? And I'm walking around feeling guilty?" he says. "So when I met her at the party she had a plan. She had a plan for us to be together—"

"Well, maybe the plan didn't go the way she wanted, Sean."

"Bullshit. She went up there with me. She took her fucking clothes off, and when I didn't profess my love to her, she flipped out. That's what happened. I didn't call her the next day, is that what it was?"

I tell him to quiet down. He's too animated. Too manic. "Sean, you don't remember in the car after the party. What you said to me? That something happened?"

"Of course I remember. Like maybe I hurt her somehow." He laughs, a grunt. "Except I didn't hurt her, B. Don't you see? She was a virgin. That's why she—"

"I know. I get it."

He's talking about the blood. I don't even want him to say it.

"Could I have been a little more caring? Sure. But I was wasted. It was a big night. And I was freaked out too. But, B. You have to believe me. It was mutual. She was infatuated with me or something, like you said. We both got caught up in it."

I want to slump against the wall. I want to make this go away. How do I make this go away?

"Okay, if she was so infatuated with you, then you owe it to her, really owe it to her, to make sure it ends in a way that isn't so devastating or heartbreaking or whatever."

He takes my hand. "How do I do it, B? Tell me how."

"You're like a whirlwind sometimes, you know that, Sean? You just fly from one emotion to the next."

He leans into my face, his breath so soft and sweet. People just don't understand how complex he is. That's all. They don't get him. Suki. Donnie. Even Dev.

"There are so many things I want to say to you."

My heart is pounding and my breath is so tight. Sean. Sean, who is like a brother to me. Sean, who is my boyfriend's best friend. Sean, who I've known forever. He brushes his cheek against mine. Kisses me there. On my cheek. And I'm shaking.

I'm shaking?

I freeze.

"Sean."

"Thanks for everything, B. Really." His eyes slung low, shoulders down.

"Of course," I say, my body still shivering. "Of course."

Later, at Dev's house. The three of us. Drinking beers outside on Dev's back patio. Dev convinced his mother to give us a few beers now that first quarter exams are over. She lit the fire for us. I snuggle into Dev's body. They're telling jokes back and forth. I can't even hear them. Over the fire, I fixate on Sean, all of it flowing through me. The warm fire. The beer. What it would be like, so close to him that way.

19

ALI

"If you had a list of guys to choose from, how would you list them?" Blythe says.

We're in C-wing. Before the rest of the Core Four is here. Before they can ram their opinions down our throats, Blythe says.

"I'm on a guy hiatus."

"I understand."

"How do you understand? You've been going out with Devon for so long."

"Dev's not perfect," she says, and edges herself between the ledge under the window and the wall. She stares off at the clouds or whatever imperfect thing on the planet that Blythe thinks she needs to add her magical wand to.

Dev. The way she says it. His name rolls off her tongue. Everything she says is so easy.

Blythe's sunny highlights streak down her hair. It's like you can see right through the strands. Transparent. That's the word Sammi used.

"I've never seen Sean feel bad for something like this. And he and I are tight. Super-tight." She does the three crossing fingers thing again. As if I forgot.

I lean into the bathroom wall, the door side. It squeaks,

startling me. I don't know what to say. Everything in my body clams up.

"He wants to make things up to you, Ali. So be open. I know you're pissed—I'd be pissed if Dev and I had sex and then he never called me the next day. But you have to understand—Sean, well, he's a player. There's this surfer from Long Beach Island he's been seeing for years. There's this softball player from Morristown. There's all his matches—the New Jersey State Champs. I mean. There are so many girls. Look at him. He's a god. Do you know what I'm saying? I'd go out with Sean if he wasn't such a player."

Blythe uses the word *god*. Not that I'm religious or anything, but I always saw Blythe and Sean Nessel as equals.

Except she sees him as a god too. Like I do. Did.

"You'd go out with him?"

"Not that I'd go for someone like Sean. He's not exactly boyfriend material."

"I just thought, you and Devon—"

"Well, I'm not oblivious either. You're not the only one who thinks Sean is hot." Her mouth drips with a goofy grin, and she playfully smacks my shoulder with the back of her hand. "He's the untouchable, I guess. He always was."

Blythe and Sean. I never thought about this combination before. That she had any interest in Sean Nessel other than as a friend. But of course she does. We're all drawn to him. Blythe isn't immune.

"Look, is there something going on with you and Rerun?" Blythe says. "Is that what this is about?"

This is Sean's nickname for Raj: Rerun. It came from a television show in the 1970s: *What's Happening!!* The main character is Raj; his friend is Rerun. Sean saw it on YouTube. Now all the soccer guys call him that.

"No, no. Raj is one of my best friends."

"Best friends? Is that like a secret language for fuck-buddies? That's what Suki thinks."

I don't know why this creeps me out, but it does. It really, really bothers me. I'm not anybody's fuck-buddy for *one* reason alone: I don't fuck. Referring to someone as my fuck-buddy implies that I have a sex life and that I'm *choosing* to have a sex life. I didn't choose to have a sex life. I didn't choose to have sex. It was forced on me.

"What did Sean tell you exactly?" I blurt out.

"He feels really bad about that night. He thinks you're a nice girl. I've told you this."

"Wow, I'm so glad I have his approval." I feel my skin wet and clammy. I'm pushing the limits here, and I know this.

BLYTHE

"Whoa, defensive. Why don't you relax with your attitude?"

The girls walk in. Donnie, Cate, Suki. They exhale aggression. They see Ali and snarl almost collectively. They hate her so much.

"Oh, I forgot about our little mascot," Donnie says.

"Maybe there should be an initiation," Cate says. But as

soon as Cate says *initiation*, she backpedals. "I didn't mean that kind of initiation. I meant in, like, a secret girls club initiation like when we were little. Like, you know, when you're kids."

"Ali doesn't have to go through any initiations," I say. "She's passed all the tests she's needed."

20

ALI

The next day in school, Blythe and Sean are huddled in A-wing near the library. She's got her hair hanging down over half her face, and she's whispering in his ear. What is she telling him? My mind switches to paranoia. I'm convinced they're whispering about me.

She doesn't even notice me when I walk by—with her arms animated like a wild tornado—and in Sean Nessel's company, why would she?

She doesn't notice me. But he does. His reaction is plastered and hard, as if he's not looking at anything at all. Like I'm a window.

My scrapbook with all my clips and heart collages and puppy love fantasies crash through my mind. I should have set it on fire.

After school Raj is waiting for me in the parking lot. He's giving me a ride home. Sammi's already in the front seat. I get in the back.

"What are you even doing here, Sammi?" I say, getting in the car. "I thought you hated me."

"Actually, I'm here because I miss you and I think you're slightly misdirected and need emotional help."

"Oh, is that all?" I say. "At least we're on the same page."

"You've been a shitty best friend, Ali."

Raj looks at me in the rearview mirror. He set me up for this confrontation.

"I know. I'm sorry." And I do love her. But my apology comes off as empty and defensive because I can't feel. I'm numb.

We're quiet for a few minutes, the three of us. So I just blurt it out: "Blythe thinks me and Raj are fuck-buddies." I don't know why I tell them this. Now it's out there and I can't take it back.

"Why are you letting Blythe determine anything about us at all?" Raj says.

"When did you start hating on Blythe?"

"When she started hunting you down. I don't like it. It seems fake. She's a fake."

Sammi makes weird grunting noises from the front seat. Her way of agreeing.

"What's the difference?" I say. Drifting off. Isn't everyone fake?

"Because I feel protective of you, all right?" Raj says.

My face beams. I can feel my cheeks heating up. I'm blushing. I didn't expect him to say that. Usually Sammi's the protective one. The one to be scared of. Not Raj.

"What is this, some kind of knight-on-a-white-horse situation and I'm just unaware of it?" Sammi says.

"Relax, Sammi," he says. "I'm not invading your territory."

I know I'm not supposed to want Raj to feel protective of me. I know that I can take care of myself. I know that my father has been teaching me that since, well, since my mom left. I also know that Raj couldn't save me from a burning building, most likely, or save anything, for that matter, but I like it. I like that he said it.

Blythe texts me late. She's like a mermaid. Just showing up to shore when no one expects her.

Drive around with me tonight?

"Who is that from?" my dad says, trying to look at my phone. I cover it with my hand. "Sammi?"

"Not Sammi."

"I haven't seen Sammi around in a while."

"I was just with her today, Dad."

"So nothing is going on with her?"

"No, everything's fine." Which wasn't entirely true. But it was fine enough.

"Ali— It's okay if you got into a fight. That happens with friends," he says. "I had a close friend once. This guy Arthur."

I laugh. "Dad. Stop."

"Really—his name was Arthur."

"His name was not Arthur."

"We called him Arty. Honest to God."

Blythe texts me again.

Answer, bitch. I'm coming to your house in 5 and flicking on my brights twice. Bat signal.

I get up from the table. The chair squeaks on the floor. "I finished all my homework. Blythe is going to pick me up in five minutes. You can tell me about Arty another time."

"It's eight o'clock at night."

"I'll be back in, like, forty-five minutes."

I walk into the front hall and slip on my Converse. I don't even get permission. He just allows it. I hope we're not going to anyone's house. My hair is in a high bun. I'm wearing a ratty sweatshirt. No bra.

"I promise, Dad," I say. "We'll talk when I get back."

I also know that'll never happen.

I get in the car with Blythe, and she zooms down my block. The dry leaves on the street kick up behind her.

"So, Ali. Are you going to the dance?"

This seems to come out of nowhere. Not once have I heard her talking about the dance. The gym, dark and shadowy. Lights flashing. Everyone sweating, jumping up and down. The music blaring. It's the last thing I want to think about right now.

"Is this why we're driving around? For you to ask me about the dance?"

"Did I tell you I'm going dress shopping with my mom?"

"No. I didn't know you spent any time with her."

"She used to be a fashion designer, so it's the one thing we can talk about. Clothes is our *thing*. We shop together. Plus, we don't have to have a real discussion if it's around fashion. Isn't that nice?" she says, irritated. "Such bullshit."

I don't say anything.

"I'm also on the dance committee," she says. "You probably didn't know that either."

"You? I can't imagine you on a committee of anything."

"Basically I get to add 'dance committee chair' as an extracurricular for doing nothing. Except show up. And I have to bring people," she says. "I know it sounds obnoxious, but if people are like, 'Oh, Blythe Jensen is the chair,' then more people go."

"So it's like a paid gig? And you're the out-of-work reality star who shows up at the club?"

"Exactly," she smiles, so much excitement in her eyes. "So you have to go."

"Why do you want me to go?"

"Because you're my new bitch." She smirks.

But there's more to this. I know it. "Just say it—it has to do with Sean Nessel."

"Not everything has to do with him, Ali. Haven't we gotten past that already in our friendship?"

Our friendship.

I forget that I'm here with Blythe, aimlessly driving down neighborhood roads, because we're friends. Because she's choosing to be with me over Donnie, Cate, or Suki. Or Devon. It's also possible they were busy. But no one is busy for Blythe. People make time.

"Cate's mother is going to have a party beforehand. The whole night will be like one big dance party. Think of it like that. What's more innocent than a dance party in a school gym? I kind of love how kitschy it is."

I sink into the seat. Open my window. My hand zips lifelessly through the air.

"Will Sean be there?" she says. "*Yes*. But who cares? Though I will tell you. He wants to make things up to you, Ali. He doesn't want it to be weird between the two of you."

I know this is going to sound sick. And I hate myself for thinking this.

Part of me wants to go, wear something amazing. I want Sean Nessel to think I look hot.

Why do I want that?

I don't want him near me. I just want him to want me. To follow me with his eyes.

That way I can dream of what it feels like to say: *You can't have this.* This is mine.

"Sure, I'll go," I say. The houses on the street sailing past. My eyes glazing over the streetlights.

I'm not going to Cate's house beforehand, I tell her. I'll meet her at the gym. With Raj and Sammi. On my terms.

21

BLYTHE

Today is the day I'm taking my mom dress shopping with me. I watch her in the bathroom as she takes her meds. My parents' bathroom looks like a pharmacy. My mother has boxes of samples of all different kinds of medication from her doctor. For her anxiety. For managing her bipolar. For her asthma. For her blood pressure. For when she can't sleep at night. For when she needs a muscle relaxer for her back.

She can't drive on all these medications, obviously. I'm supposed to understand this and be empathetic, this sacrifice of hers. That she takes her meds because she's committed to our family. To me. But I hate her for it. That slur she gets in the car. I cringe.

"I'm really glad you invited me to go with you, Blythe."

"Are you? I'm surprised to hear this."

"Well, I know you like my input on clothes. I can at least give you that." She pushes her sunglasses above her head. Her hair is beautiful in the sunlight. Her thin arms. Her black camisole with her long wide-legged linen pants. She looks like a movie star. "I want you to talk to me, Blythe. I want you to talk to me like you used to. Remember when you were in fourth grade and you had that whole drama with all those cliquey girls and how we'd talk every night about how you would handle it? You don't tell me about your friends anymore."

Rarely is my mother apologetic. I throw her a bone. "I've made a new friend. Her name is Ali."

"And how did Ali come into the picture? You have such a tight group."

"She came by way of Sean."

"She's a girlfriend of Sean's? I thought he goes from girl to girl."

"He does."

"Oh, I see. So he brought you in to do a cleanup job."

"What? No. I'm just being a good friend."

"Hmm. I suppose you learned that from me. Cleaning up after emotional messes," she says. "So what does your therapist say about all this?"

"About Ali?"

"No, Blythe. About me."

"Every therapist says the same thing, Mom. 'Sit with your feelings, Blythe.' That's what she says."

"My therapist says the same thing."

"Why does everyone always have to *sit* so much with their feelings?"

My mother laughs. It's nice to hear her laugh.

"For one, when you don't sit with your feelings, and you act on them instead, you turn out like me."

It's a red light, and she turns to me and smiles. I see tears in her eyes. She lowers her sunglasses again. I think about what my therapist says, that I can't make it better. I can't make *her* better. That I shouldn't *try* to make it better. When my mom says things like this about herself—vulnerable, honest, self-deprecating things—I should let her say them. And then I should sit with my feelings. All I want to do is tell her it's all right. I want to tell her not to blame herself. Not to shame herself. But I don't.

"Are you sure you want to go to the mall for a dress?" she says.

"Where else should we go?"

"I'm thinking of Bergdorf in the city. Something more highbrow. Something more avant-garde. The mall is for creatures of habit. For the cattle. Girls like Cate Sandoval. Girls who follows the herd."

I look at her, surprised. Eyes back to the road. Her mania still there. The grandiosity not completely squashed.

"Listen, doll, Cate's never been one to think for herself. Her mother used to drive me crazy. Every goddamned top you'd wear, she'd come over to our house about a week later with the same shirt. The same barrette. The same sneakers. It never failed. I don't think I ever told you this, but I finally confronted Lucy Sandoval at the end of the year. I think it was that same weird year. Fourth grade."

"Wait—what?"

"Cate is an *autobot*. You program her like an old-fashioned windup toy. She followed you around like a puppy dog, Blythe. She still does. This isn't a secret about her. And it irritated me to think that people might believe you intentionally dressed like her little twinsie. It bugged me."

"So what did you say to Lucy?"

"I told her that her daughter should focus on originality."

That's why Cate stopped dressing like me once we got to fifth grade. One day I called her in the morning to wear the same shirt as me (I liked that she always had a matching outfit to me back then), and she told me that her mother gave away that shirt—and all the other shirts that were like mine. Such a strange answer. I was too young at the time to put it together, that Lucy Sandoval gave away those clothes not because she didn't want Cate to dress like me, but because my mother instructed her *not* to dress like me.

I pull into the Bloomingdale's parking lot. My mother turns to me and slides her arm around the driver's seat. "Do you want to be one of the followers, or do you want to be a true leader?"

This is a dare that I can't escape. I don't want to go into the city with my mother. This was supposed to be a predictable shopping trip. Not an adventure with unstable Mom. She starts out so empathetic. Now she's goading me. She's waiting for me to say, *Mom, we really shouldn't. It's too much for you.* But there's a light in her eye that hypnotizes me. I like her when she's a little manic. At least she's alive in there.

And then I remember that Sean is in the city today with his grandmother. Everyone can say he's an awful person and uses girls. But really, this is a person who, after soccer practice, spends the afternoon with his *grandmother*. She has a townhouse in Chelsea. Four floors. Six bedrooms. It's like a mansion, but in New York City. She used to be a big art collector in the '80s and '90s. Now she sells paintings every few years and lives off the money. Sean's taken me and Dev there twice, this majestic place with weird sculptures and books and paintings that make no sense. It's only forty-five minutes from my house in New Jersey, but it feels like a world away.

I can text him to meet us. It'll be a little adventure. Me, mom, and Sean. And Sean's grandmother. And maybe a dress.

And so I peel out of the parking lot like her good little Queen Bee.

22

ALI

I don't tell Sammi about how Blythe is pressuring me to go to the dance. I'm not exactly lying, but I'm also not telling her the truth. Let's go to Black Cat Vintage, I tell her. We can buy weird dresses and make fools out of ourselves at the school dance. It'll be fun. She likes that idea.

She files through the racks of velvet dresses because she's looking for something green. She pulls out three that sparkle like the Emerald City. I'm talking bright. As in Oz. The dresses look like they're from the 1970s.

"Tell me the truth. Why do you want to go to this dance?" Sammi says.

"You've been talking about it for years. It's not just me."

"I said that when we were freshmen, Ali. Have totally changed my mind now."

I pick out this black chiffon thing with thick ruffles on the sleeves. I hold it up to my body, modeling.

"I think I want to wear it with red tights."

It's the first time I've noticed myself in the mirror and I'm not disgusted. It's like I'm wearing a costume. A game. I can do this.

"I know this has to do with Blythe Jensen."

"Maybe."

She whips her green dresses against the dress rack.

"God, Ali, how did you become so predictable?"

"You're the one who said it! And she's not the only reason," I say. "I just want to be normal again and do normal shit like other people. Like go to a school dance with my best friend. Or am I going to be punished for that too?"

I can't explain to Sammi that going to the dance, the dance that will be filled with the same people from that awful party, will somehow allow me to get over the humiliation of what happened. That if I show up at this dance where I know he'll be, where all those people will be, I can somehow relive the night. That I can show everyone that I'm not wasted like a freak running out of a party.

"I don't understand what you see in her," she says. "Because underneath it all, she's still best friends with him. The guy who did that to you."

I grab my black dress and head to the fitting room, slamming the door behind me. I don't want to think about what she said. I clamp my hands over my ears and squeeze my eyes shut.

Sammi is standing outside the door apologizing. And I know she's right because everything she says is what I'm already thinking. But it's also what I don't want to admit to myself.

"Come out once you have the dress on," she says, and hollers that she's in a dressing room just a few doors down.

I hate looking at myself in the mirror now. My purple bra, so damaged and affected. It's the bra I was wearing that night and I've been avoiding it for so long. Now I wish I hadn't worn it. I take it off and stuff it under the bench. I wonder if other people like me feel like they need all new clothes.

Sammi's head pops under the bottom of the dressing room door.

"You're like a dreamy witch girl," she says. Her eyes sparkling.

"Get off the floor, you loser."

I open the door and she gets up. She's wearing a teal knee-length dress with a short cape. Her fists on her hips. Looks up at the sky.

"You're fucking Captain Marvel."

She shakes her hair out. She's so pretty. A different pretty than Blythe. A different pretty than Donnie. They're like a perfect pretty—the kind of girls who don't look damaged. The kind of girls who can keep all their secrets on the inside. All their pain.

I pull out my phone. Tell her to pose against the door.

"Don't post this, Ali. I swear—I will hurt you."

"No, it's just that I haven't collaged in a while. And I want to make some different pictures. Pictures of people that I, you know, love. And who, uh . . . love me back."

Sammi stands super close to me. "Can I hand-hug you?"

"Oh my God, Sammi."

"I didn't want to seem cheesy just straight-up hugging you."

"Hand-hug is fine."

She takes my hand and we cup each other's fingers. We

look nothing alike, but sometimes when I stare at her, like now, I feel like she and I are the same person.

"Hand-hug over," she says. "It's time to play dress-up." Like we did when we were younger. Until I gave away all my glittery princess dresses. Told my dad to give them to the babies next door. His face, devastated. It's weird to want to be little again, but I wish I could go backward.

Sammi lifts her cape and tears out of the dressing room, down the aisle of the store.

The woman behind the counter stares at us. She has silver hair slicked back in a small ponytail. Red lips. Cactus and bird tattoos up her arm.

"That cape dress is my favorite. What's it for?" she says.

"School dance."

"Those are some cool dresses for a school dance," she says.

Sammi and I smile at each other. She takes my hand and twists me around. My black chiffon dress, her pink cape.

The woman flips to a song on her phone. "Here. Try this," she says. "The B-52s."

The song starts with one person banging on a high key of a keyboard. A woman sings out in breathless pain, talking to her ex. She begs him: think about how we talked when we were in love, right before you broke my heart.

Then she screams the next lyrics with the kind of heartache that comes from deep within. I've never heard anything like it. Except I have. I've heard it because it sounds like me.

Why don't you dance with me?

I'm not no Limburger.

I don't know what a Limburger is, but I think she's screaming, "No. You can't do this to me. What makes you think you can do this to me?"

23

BLYTHE

My mother scoots me through the first floor of Bergdorf, where the white walls are lined with glass cases filled with colorful purses. The high ceilings, the marble floors, and the enormous crystal chandeliers make it look like someone's Parisian apartment. No. More like their massive walk-in closet *inside* their Parisian apartment.

We take the elevator to where the gowns and dresses are. They're not as much for sale as they're on display. This is a fashion museum, not a store. And there are stores within stores, tiny spaces and hallways filled with velvet couches and rows of gold shoes and masks and paintings. I go to a mirrored spot with a few dresses hanging and get a good glance at myself, because if you're not staring at yourself in this store, then are you even here?

And I pull out a nude dress. Floral embellished with sequins and beads.

"Pick something with confidence. Something that'll stand out. You don't need to blend in, Blythe."

"I have plenty of confidence."

"Really? Because that dress says insecurity."

"Jesus, Mom."

"I'm just being honest," she says.

Before I can escape, a sales rep named Blanche wraps her

arm around my waist, fawning over my hair and my height. "Is this for the Bal Des Debutantes? We have the most gorgeous gowns that don't fit any of these short girls who come in here wishing they were Gisele. Oh my, darling, you are a dream come true. Stunning. Absolutely stunning. I want to cover you in seafoam and strut you down the aisle."

"It's for a school dance."

"A dance? In Manhattan?"

"No. New Jersey."

Her face is stricken. How I've disappointed her. That I'm not a debutante. Just a schoolgirl from New Jersey going to a dance in her gym. *I know*, I want to say, to comfort her. *I feel the same way.*

"I'm just getting ideas," I say.

"Okay, because if money is an issue—"

"Money is not an issue," my mother says, jumping down the woman's throat. Because God forbid we appeared like we had no money. It's all about appearance. No mental illness. No credit cards with $30,000 in charges. No rehabs or institutions. No antipsychotropic drugs. No genetic history. No suicidal grandfather who threw himself off the Golden Gate Bridge when my mother was twelve. Keep it hidden. Keep it down. These are family secrets. This is no one's business.

"I was kind of thinking of something leather," I say.

"Leather? Excuse me. You girls have to start dressing your age and not like a desperate middle-aged postmenopausal mother of four," Blanche says.

She whips a strapless pink lace corset dress off the rack.

Pink so light that it's practically washed out. Practically see-through. High-low bottom. To the floor. Open back.

"Darling. This dress was made for you. Take your hair out of that ponytail and put this on." She pushes me toward the dressing room. Soft lighting. White velvet curtains.

Blanche isn't wrong. The bodice fits me perfectly. I've never worn anything quite like this before. Chiffon peeks out from under the bottom of the dress and wisps against my legs. I shake my hair out. All these girls at the dance will be going to the mall for their dresses. And look at me. A fucking queen.

Oohs and ahhs as I walk out. Blanche shoves her assistant toward me. Another girl from the bag department enters. They guffaw. "You're so lucky. No messy boobies to screw up the profile."

"I'm anorexic just enough for the dress to fit, right?" I say. Blanche doesn't even blink.

"I'm kidding. I'm not anorexic."

But Blanche doesn't care. She just wants me to be the best teenage dream I can be. She shoves a pair of red strappy heels in my hands. Tells me that I will not be wearing any accessories. No necklace. No bracelets. A little rose blush. That's all. I love how Blanche is taking care of me. It's like she knows my mother can't do it, so she's taking charge. I stare in the mirror; it's been so long since I felt this pretty, this soft. Not so harsh. I smile at my mother even. She was right. This is so much better than the mall.

And then I see him.

Well, I see his hair. That unmistakable, shoulder-length blond hair.

Like combing his fingers through silk. Sean. And his art collector grandmother with her white hair and oversize glasses and black caftan.

"Someone get mascara on me quick," I say.

There are so many things I want to say to you.

I can't take my eyes off him. How do you explain something like this? This draw to another person? But why now? Why now am I shaking? Why now that rush? Because of this dress? These red heels? He's seen me in dresses before. Nothing like this, sure. But now it's different. It's the way he *needs* me.

Look at him standing there. With his grandmother! His stylish grandmother. Does anyone have a grandmother who looks like her? And there he is, between the gowns. Scanning the store for me. His eyes everywhere. He's here. He came.

"Ooh, darling, she sees someone." Blanche snaps two fingers at the makeup artist who pulls out black mascara and smears my cheeks with pink blush.

I'm staring at him hard in the mirror. Turn around and notice my reflection, Sean. Turn around, Sean. My heart races. Pounds. Look at me. My pink cheeks popping. My blue eyes screaming through this mascara. The dress, a soft porn, a Victorian dream. And I throw everything away that I know about Sean. Everything that everyone's said. Donnie. Suki. Ali. Dev. Throw everything away that I've seen him do. Because it doesn't make sense, even to me. I want him to see me in this dress, and not just see me. I want him to fall deep into me. I want to drown inside the way he's been looking at me lately. I do. I want to drown in it. None of it makes sense.

"Toss me my phone, Mom," I say, demanding.

"Where is it? What's going on?"

"Just toss me my phone."

She slides it across the floor.

I look in the mirror and see Sean's reflection. He's holding up hats for his grandmother. Modeling them like a court jester.

I text him: *Turn around.*

A text comes back. *B? Where u at?*

I text again: *Just turn around.*

"Sean Nessel?" my mother says. "Is this for real?" But I tune her out.

Sean turns to me from across the store. I lock eyes with him.

He sees me. My pale, bare shoulders. He sees the dress. The corset. The bodice. The everything. His face lights up. He smiles. Lifts his hands in slow motion above his head, then nervously down his face.

I close my eyes. Hand on hip. Swing my hair to the side because I don't know what to do with myself. Drape my body across a gold-mirrored table? My fingers drip over my mouth. I smile, stick out my tongue. Twirl.

He whispers in his grandmother's ear. Points over to me.

"Who is that, doll? Your boyfriend?" Blanche says.

"My daughter's boyfriend wouldn't know how to find New York City," my mother says, and though it infuriates me that she's pissing on Dev, she's not altogether wrong. "That's her boyfriend's *best friend.*"

"Scandalous," Blanche says.

I ignore them. Float over to Sean. Buzzing through the gowns. Past a table of pastel scarves. The pinks and blues and purples blending into each other.

He's still staring through me. Right into me. I can't say anything. I give him a push on his chest. He takes a step backward. Eyes light up. Saying nothing.

"What. What?"

"You."

I look down at my dress. My whole body flushed. "Aww, it's nothing. I got it out of the garbage dump."

He smiles. Shakes his head, still staring. His face so intent.

It rushes in. That we're somewhere else. A shine of light under a moving shadow somewhere.

He takes my hand and his hand feels sweaty and big in mine. And it feels perfectly normal. Yet I don't think I've ever held Sean's hand. And there we are, standing right in front of his nana.

"This is not a dress you wear to a school dance, my dear," she says. Multi-colored bangles clink halfway up her arm. She gives me an air kiss.

"Earlier I couldn't get Sean to go anywhere with me. But then you texted him. And all of a sudden he wants to go shopping. Isn't it funny how that works?" She caresses his cheek. The way she dreamily stares at him. The pride she has.

"When we're out together, I tell people I'm her boyfriend," he says. "Her young stud."

"Oh, Sean. Such a flirt. Just like your father," his

grandmother says. "Always talking about the ladies. He's my only grandson who will do this, you know. Come in and visit me and spend one-on-one time like this. And I have eight grandsons. He'll make a wonderful husband one day." She strokes his cheek. I blush. I'm not sure if she's saying this directly to me, or if she's just entertaining herself.

"Blythe." I hear my mother hissing from the other side of the room. Ignored, left in the corner with a sales associate. Not a good look for her. How could I leave her behind like that, I'm sure she's thinking.

"I have to get back to my mother," I say. The embarrassment rolling through my words.

"Here, I'll take you," he says, and leads me between the large black-tie gowns, under a massive black chandelier. I want him to push me up against the chartreuse velvet couch. Kiss my neck. Imagine his hands all over me.

"This is too crazy," I say to him, breathless.

"Nothing's crazy. It actually all makes complete sense. Finally something makes complete sense." His face closer to mine. "I'm not scared, B."

But I can barely speak.

I whisper that I have to go, and spin around, leaving him there between the gowns.

I run back to where my mother is standing. "We need to get out of here," I say, because I'm flushed, too excited. I squeeze her hand. But this is my first mistake, trusting her. She shakes me off.

"Sean Nessel? Are you kidding me?" My mother does her thing with her eyebrows. Her array of faces. "You look like a tart, Blythe. A crush on your boyfriend's best friend? I saw the way he was looking at you in that dress. You don't think that was apparent to everyone, except for maybe his grandmother who is ninety-five years old? Did you make out with him behind those dresses too?"

"Mom—Jesus. What are you doing? Stalking me from the corner of the store?"

"You just left me alone here—standing here like a fool. What was I supposed to do? Talk to the sales girl the whole time?"

Here we go. Leaving her alone. It's always about her being left alone.

"This was our shopping trip. Our time together," she says. "The only thing we barely have. That *I* barely have. And you what? You had Sean Nessel meet you here? Because don't tell me this was a coincidence."

The anger in her face. The envy. That I have everything and she has nothing. It's the way Sean looked at me; she saw that. And what does she have? My father who spends his time running away from her. Dumping her with me. Therapists and doctors. Running off to live his own life.

I slip into the dressing room to take off the dress.

"I heard his grandmother has a Chagall or maybe it's a Cézanne," my mother says outside the dressing room, her tone changing. "At the very least, maybe we can get an invitation?

Maybe she'll invite us up. Show us her art collection. We can catch a breeze on the terrace."

"This is not the time for your mania to kick in, Mother."

She swipes open the dressing room curtain. Squeezes my arm. "Don't be a shit, my darling daughter, because I know *exactly* what is going on here. I can see it in your face, and especially your nipples."

I look down. My nipples are headlights, charging through the chiffon. I conceal my chest with my arm. Whip shut the curtain.

My mother's seething explosion is not unfamiliar to me. Half of it mumbled and garbled in mania. This is how we converse when she's not so heavily medicated. She flips out, says nasty things. I say nasty things back. She cries. She holes herself up in her bedroom for days. I apologize. Start again.

I walk out of the dressing room and hand the dress to Blanche. Kiss her on both cheeks.

"Are you taking it, my dear?"

"Of course we are," I say. "Is there any other choice?"

24

BLYTHE

Sean calls me around nine o'clock.

I see his name and I'm scared to pick it up. What his voice will sound like. What I want to say to him after today at the store. That we got swept up in something. Me in that dress. Him with his grandmother. The way he held my hand.

"Where are you?" I say.

"Out for a late jog. I like running at night. It helps me think," he says.

"Where?"

I don't hear his voice. For a few seconds I think maybe he just hung up. That this is it. That it'll stop here.

"On your street."

My body jolts for a second. All of it, falling to my tummy. And further. Like I can't breathe.

"I'll be at the back fence. I'll let you in. But don't open the fence."

"Why?"

"It squeaks."

We crouch down behind my shed, our backs up against it. Our thighs touching. He's out of breath still, sweaty and dank. I don't care. I don't care at all.

"You have cute knees, B," Sean says, and touches my knee.

Just a flicker. With his fingers. His hand stays there. "How come you don't wear many skirts? Or dresses like the one you wore today?"

I lean back more, really sinking into the cold grass.

"You looked beautiful today, B."

"It's sweet that you shop with your grandmother."

"She's a trip, my grandmother. People take pictures of her on the street. Did you know that? They think she's famous. She loves it."

"She looks famous."

"Do you feel nervous right now, B?"

"Yes."

He slides his hand farther up my leg and turns to me. His soft lips on mine.

He presses his lips into me harder, kissing me stronger. His hands at the back of my head, around my neck, pulling me in, pulling me in so hard that I want to pull back. I'm just trying to catch my breath. The two of us, our foreheads touching. All of that wanting. I don't know what to do with it. "I've been thinking about you all day since we left. . . . It's why I'm running now. To get it out of my system. To get you out of my system," he says. "What are we going to do, B?"

I go to bed that night feeling guilty. I kissed Sean. I feel so close to him. So much closer than I've ever felt, and it's not just the kiss I'm thinking about now. My body shuddering from today. His words in my head. The way he tilted his head against mine. I tug down my underwear and touch myself between my thighs because it's all too much and I have to release it and let it go. I imagine him here with me.

But then I see Ali's face. Those little bangs. Ali, who looks up at me with those glowing eyes. And Dev. Who trusts me and is loyal to me. I cringe. I'm a terrible, hateful person and I don't deserve anyone. I pull up my underwear. I have to shut it all off. What am I doing anyway?

I text Donnie because I don't know where to go with all this and I hate myself.

I kissed Sean

Of course you did B

What does that mean?

It means everyone saw it coming but you

Not everyone

No not everyone . . . just me

On Monday in school, I don't know how to look at Dev. He's got his arm wrapped around me like everything is the same, but it's not. It'll never be the same. Sean and I pretend like nothing happened. I can't even look at him in the hall.

C-wing. Just me and Donnie. Smoke all around us. We're going to choke in here one day. That or set off the smoke alarm.

"How does it feel?" she says.

"How does what feel?" I exhale.

"Betrayal?" She laughs, rolling her eyes. "You are an awful person, B. But this is nothing new."

"I didn't do anything wrong, Donnie. It was just a kiss."

"I didn't say you did anything wrong. In fact, I think I've been the one to encourage you to get out of that monogamous box you're in with Dev."

Donnie flicks her cigarette onto the floor. The ashes go flying. An ember bleeds off the paper.

"He's different with me. He's softer."

"Of course he is, baby. Of course he is."

25

ALI

Sammi shows up first. Her mom drops her off, and I see them hug in the front seat of the car. She's wearing the dress from the store. With the cape. It flies behind her when she runs down the driveway. Here she comes to save the day. My eyes swollen. Welling up.

"You're crying?" she says. "You're supposed to be glad I'm here."

"I am glad."

"Then what?"

"You just look cute," I say. "Really cute." I hug her, so tightly.

Raj rides up in his parents' station wagon. Black button-down shirt. Black tie. Black jeans. His hair swept up in a pompadour.

"That's quite a limo," Sammi says.

"My parents are out for dinner. They took the Mini Cooper."

"Nice hair," I say. "How'd you get it that way?"

"Hair spray," he says, proud of himself.

Raj is smiling nervously, kind of looking away. He edges closer to me, on the porch, still not talking. He's not used to me wearing a dress. He's not used to me wearing black eyeliner. Silver glitter freckled over my eyelids. I can see it in his face, the way he keeps looking away.

"Why do you keep looking the other way?" I say.

"You look really pretty."

I laugh. It's nice. I like the attention. It's the first time in a while that I actually feel safe. Like a taste of something normal. After all those weeks of pain, maybe for a second I could feel something good.

A text from Blythe.

On my way to Cates. U coming?

I make something up.

Pops won't let me go. Too strict.

Wonder what that's like?

"Who's that?" Sammi says. "Your girlfriend?"

"She wants us to come to Cate's party."

"I'd rather eat glass," Sammi says.

"Is that what you want, Ali? To go there?" Raj says.

"We can drop her off there on the way to the dance and she can punish herself," Sammi says.

"It's not like that."

"Oh, why don't you tell us what it's like, then?"

"I don't even want to go, so why don't you both relax."

But if I don't go, what's the alternative? Texts from Blythe? Sean Nessel, thinking he got the best of me. Not that he's even thinking of me.

Not that he's ever thought of me.

Not that he ever thought of me more than as this cute girl who he could mess with.

"We don't have to go," Raj says. That concerned look on his face. His voice real low and calm. "And that's it. We don't have to do anything you don't want to do. We don't have to do anything. We don't have to go to this dance."

"No. That's not it. I want to go," I say. "I want to go with the two of you."

Sammi needed to hear this. I see it in her eyes.

"Then let's go," Sammi says, her voice lighter than before. She reaches out and squeezes my hand. "We're gonna go. And it's going to be great."

I kiss her hand. It's deserved. What I've been putting her through, I should be kissing her toes.

She dashes into the house to pee.

I think about what Raj said too. *We don't have to do anything you don't want to do.* It sends me away from this moment. I feel like I smell dirty. I feel like he's going to smell it on me.

I inch closer to him and smack him in the arm. And then I hit him again—it sends him a step back. I want to push him so much farther back. I want to repel him. Get him away from me. He should run from me. Escape me. I'm filled with awful things, things he can't imagine.

"What was that for?" he says, holding his arm.

I look away because I don't want to cry.

"That's for being such a nice guy."

26

BLYTHE

Lights twinkle through the trees at Cate's house. Dev kisses me, and we walk in. Cate's mother passes out champagne on trays in the back under a tent. Everyone's here. Dev. Sean. Suki. Plus Ray Pilcher, Chase Goldberg, and Harrison Cohen. I jump up and down in the grass, fist pumping. The guys follow because who can deny fist pumping. Me in my blush-pink, practically see-through dress and the boys in jackets and ties.

One by one, the boys form their own circle. The girls form another. I wobble in the lawn, my red heels. Cate in that purple dress. Big white sunglasses even though there's no sun. Suki in this ice-blue maxi dress.

Donnie makes an entrance. She's wearing this black flowy thing from the 1970s. The neckline plunges down her nonexistent chest and the back is open almost to her ass. Her arms are draped in sheer black wings that drip down to the floor. She looks like a cigarette with wings. Her curly hair long, the wildest I've seen it. The blue faded out. She covers her chest with the wings, like they have their own life.

"Let's see what you have on under here, princess. Give us a show."

She spins like Stevie Nicks, raising her arms in the air. The side of the dress exposes what I don't want to see: her ribs. She's so thin. She spins and spins and then stumbles. I ignore it. Go with moment. Twirl her again and we're revved up. Bouncing up and down in the grass while our parents take photos. My pink dress in the breeze.

Sean, Dev, and Chase hop up on this long wooden bench and start dancing. Sean's body bolder than I've seen it. The way he's moving his hips. His shoulders. The way he stands on that bench, like he owns it.

Rewind it all. Get back to Dev. Make it up to Ali. The buzz over my skin from the champagne. I can shift perceptions, can't I? Wasn't that the core of this whole plan in befriending Ali? To get her to forgive Sean and show her who he really is? Can't I do that? Aren't I built for that? I bring people together. Yes. Of course I do.

Maybe it's the champagne getting to me, but I could make that happen. Maybe I could make it happen tonight.

Someone passes me a second glass of champagne, and I guzzle it because it's pink like my dress and not too sweet. I close my eyes. Think of Sean. His eyes all over me that day shopping. The way he led me between all those gowns. How he had to run to my house after I saw him that day and how he kissed me like he'd never let go. It rushes at me.

Dev comes up from behind me and swipes my hair to the side. Kisses my neck.

"Hey, beautiful."

I collapse into him.

I climb into the limo after Dev. He pulls my legs out from under my dress, sliding me next to him, kissing my neck. I let him do it, just run his hands up and down my body the way he wants. I'm so buzzed it doesn't matter.

Sean looks up at me as he ducks in the limo. I drift off, imagine sitting on his lap. Curling up with him. I have to look away, so I turn to Dev. "You," I say, tracing his lips. He smiles. "You too, B. You too." I have to keep it this way. It's just a fleeting desire that I can push down. I know I can.

Donnie crawls in and slides next to me. She's super messy, pressing all the buttons and dancing in her seat with her eyes closed. We're all messy. Champagne on an empty stomach will do that.

Suki's parents and Cate's parents, Dev's mother, Sean's parents—they all wave as the limo pulls away from Cate's house.

I hear someone scream, "Be safe!"

We scream at the driver to open the sunroof. I want to fly away in the wind. Take my hair down and throw it around.

Passing around a bottle of rosé. "It matches B's dress," Donnie screams, and the driver yells that he's going to pull over if we don't calm the fuck down.

He's screaming at us like that. This big sweaty white dude. "CALM THE FUCK DOWN."

We all start chanting: "Calm the fuck down, calm the fuck down. Big man who's driving says calm the fuck down."

Every time he says, "I'm not fucking kidding, you spoiled brats," we scream back, repeating him.

"This guy is like the villain in Scooby-Doo," Suki says.

"If it hadn't been for you meddling kids!" I yell.

Cate and Chase go at it. Nothing matters anymore. Everyone chants. "Tongue, tongue, tongue." And she still hasn't taken off those white sunglasses.

Sean crawls over, next to Dev, and he leans over him to talk to me. He doesn't know what he's doing. I shake my head. My heart pounding. This isn't the time. Not here. Not now.

"This is about Ali."

"Oh," I say. "What about her? She's great. She's awesome. Everything's fine."

"Nessel, you gotta chill about this girl, man," Dev says.

"She glares at me in the hallway," he says, slurring.

"Nessel. You're paranoid. She's not going to do anything," Dev keeps saying. It's like we're talking to a wall.

I reach over and stroke my hand on his cheek. "I'm going to make everything better. You watch. Everything is going to be all better. We'll find her when we get to the dance. You'll see her tonight, and it'll all go away. It's going to be great. I promise you. I have it completely under control."

"Yeah, she wouldn't do anything, right?" Sean says, staring off. "She'd never do that to me, right?"

27

BLYTHE

We walk into the gym, and the music explodes. The fizz through my bones. That fuzzy escape. I'm not sluggish the way I usually feel when I drink champagne, but bubbly and free. I see Ali walking in and I love her so much. I'm going to repair everything. When I'm done, it'll be storybook. I can't have him, but—my little prodigy, my little Ali Greenleaf—*she* can have him.

Even if she doesn't want him, I should at least try to make it better. Don't I owe it to them both? For her to see his soft side? To see the side that I see?

ALI

"Red tights? Shut the fuck up! You are like a fashion goddess," Blythe says, attacking me the minute I walk through the dark gym. Screaming my name. *Ali Greenleaf!*

Strobe lights kick back purples and blues across the wall. All of a sudden, everything I'm wearing is neon as the music pumps with a deafening hum.

Blythe, Suki, and Donnie crowd around me.

Blythe's wearing this long, soft pink, practically see-through, strapless lace dress with bright red strappy heels. Her hair is down and wild. She's a rosy sky over an ocean. A peony in the spring. Overpowering and sweet-smelling. I'm scared that I'll never stop idolizing her. I'm scared that I'll always think she's better than me.

BLYTHE

Dev and Sean fist pump to music toward the center of the gym. Chase and Cate are way ahead of us.

I float close to Ali. Sweet, innocent Ali. I hate to see her get so mixed up in the head about things. I want to talk to her, *really* talk to her. Really give her guidance. Really show her how it can be. How she and Sean can just wash this away. I want to say so many things to her—I want to tell her the truth. That I love Sean. That underneath it all *he cares*. That it has to be a big, drunken mistake. That he didn't mean to hurt her. If she just saw him with his grandmother that day. If she saw how worried he was the night of Sophie Miller's party. That he's just a sweet, needy boy. Don't we owe boys like him forgiveness? I know it's not supposed to be that way, but I'm floating. I'm floating from too much champagne, from the music, from this dress, and I can't stop. So I sieze her hands, just to hold on; otherwise, I'm like one of those rainbow balloons in the sky, taking off.

ALI

Blythe is so wasted that she doesn't notice I'm backing away from her. She's grasping at me. I'm not used to seeing Blythe so animated. She's always so reserved and perfect. I feel uncomfortable. I want to crawl away. Donnie stands next to Blythe in this long black dress with sheer wings. Her skinny body almost translucent—the whole thing like a skeleton costume. She sways back and forth, unintentionally it seems.

I look for Sammi. She's not going to like this. Them crowding me like this. So drunk. So out of control. She's standing far behind. Outside the group. Her face in her phone.

"Where've you been tonight, Jensen?" Raj says.

"At Cate's, you silly goose," she says. More slurring. "You two bitches were supposed to come to the pre-party."

We look over at Devon and Sean Nessel, who are fist pumping with a group of soccer players. They're jumping up and down like maniacs. Raging animals ready to pounce.

Then Sean Nessel turns around and faces us. He stops jumping and nudges Devon. The two of them point to me and Raj.

Devon waves to Raj, hollering. "Re-run! Re-run!"

Raj turns to me. His voice real low. "We don't have to hang out with these guys."

I search around for Sammi. Meet her eyes. She slides in next to me.

"What's going on? We can get out of here."

But I feel paralyzed, like there are too many things

happening and I'm trapped in this weird cell that I can't get out of. And the lights. And Blythe screaming at me with too much energy.

Suki searches through her purse, a weed pen in her hand. In the school. With everyone to see.

"She's going to get busted—" Sammi says.

"Put it away, you idiot," Blythe says to her.

"It's gonna be legal everywhere soon anyway, who cares," she slurs.

These girls are too wasted and it's too public. I thought I wanted this. For Sean Nessel to see me. To be strong. I don't know what I thought I was going to do—confront him? Persuade him to fall madly in love with me? Kill him? I don't know what I wanted. I don't know what I want right now, except I don't want to be around this. I don't want to stand here waiting for Sean Nessel to stroll over. *What a cute girl you are, Ali.* I'm going to scream, or throw up, and I want to escape, but I can't move. My legs feel like heavy weights. I imagine him on top of me. Pinning my shoulder down.

BLYTHE

I look over at Sean dancing, how dreamy he looks. Lights flash across his face.

Ali. Ali. I need to focus on Ali. Make it all better with Ali.

"If you're not going to dance with me, Ali, then dance with *him*," I say.

"Who?"

I pull her hands in. "Pretend we're at a yoga retreat."

She rolls her eyes, but Ali always rolls her eyes. I don't care anyway.

"I'm not going to let go of you, Greenleaf. I'm going to make this better, don't you see? Life is about forgiveness. You have to understand that people sometimes just don't do the right thing in life. You and I know this. Don't we? I want you to be happy, Ali. And he wants so badly for you to forgive him. It's all he thinks about. If you only knew how bad he wants you to forgive him."

And I can feel him staring at me. Watching me talk to her. And I have to help him in this moment. I want to help him. And I want to help her. If she would just listen to me. If she would just give this a chance. I'm going to do that. I'm going to make it all better.

"He cried that night, Ali. Did I ever tell you that? That he cried. Actual tears after that whole thing between you two."

ALI

"Blythe, I'm here with Raj and Sammi. I don't want to—"

But Blythe doesn't shut up. I keep trying to talk, but she cuts me off. She overpowers me.

She says something about Sean Nessel crying. Sean crying. She harps on about Sean crying.

BLYTHE

"Oh, Sammi. I know *Sammi*," I say, waving her over. "Cherie's little sister. Wow, Cherie has really changed this year since going to college. Look at my dress. Do you love my dress?" I lean into Ali. Take her face in my hands. "I'm not wearing a bra. I'm wearing pasties over my nipples. Can you believe it? This top part is an actual corset. I'm Marie fucking Antoinette."

I twirl for her. I hop up and down to the music. I'm feeling so good and I want something good to happen tonight. So good that I can't escape it. Is that so wrong to ask? Is it so simple to just say that?

ALI

"My brain hurts from this," Sammi says. "I'll catch up with you later."

"You're not walking away from me," I say.

"Why? I can predict what's going to happen."

I see the hurt in Sammi's face again. I've been so distant and clammed up and now she's so uncomfortable. Her arms across her chest—she's in a Supergirl outfit. I want her to save me. But I don't know how to ask her. I don't know where to begin.

"I'm walking away. Now. I'm not leaving the dance. I won't leave without you. You can find me later once this whole thing is over."

And I let Sammi walk away. I'm too stunned to grab her hand, too paralyzed to move. I let it happen. Blythe, standing there in front of me, controlling the whole thing.

Raj turns to me. "Let's get out of here."

But I can't speak. I can't budge. I'm swollen shut here. If I move, I'll cry. I'll scream. Maybe I'll fall down. I don't know. It's safer to stand still.

BLYTHE

I slide up to Sean. "This is the moment," I whisper. "This is when you have to make your move. You have to apologize. Say you're sorry and mean it. It has to pour from your soul. Do you understand me?"

He nods.

I take his hand, his large hand, and he wraps his fingers around my fingers. Dev is right there, right behind him, just ten feet. But that's not what it's about now. It's about Ali. Sean. Making it better for him and Ali. That's all I'm doing. Helping them.

ALI

I'm looking in four places at once. It's dizzy around me. There's an echo, like the music's too loud, but that can't be it because we're not even near the music now.

Sean Nessel. The ten different faces of Sean Nessel. Him on top of me. If I hadn't had that vodka. If I hadn't talked to him that day in the hallway. If I hadn't made that stupid collage book of him.

I stare at the floor. It's the only way I can hold it together. To focus on this gray floor.

Raj is talking to me, but I can't hear him. I just shake my head. "No." I say. But I don't even know what I'm saying no to.

BLYTHE

Sean's hand in mine. Everything feels right. I'm going to make this good. I'm going to erase Ali's pain.

ALI

I look for a break in the crowd, but more people just keep meandering toward us because Blythe is the North Star. People just want to get closer to her.

I hear Donnie and Suki cackling behind me.

Blythe rushes back to me. "I have the answer to everything!"

BLYTHE

I let go of Sean to catch Ali, but she slips away, like her skin is too smooth. Oily or something. And so I vise-grip her. I'm not going to let go of her. I'm going to make everything better.

ALI

Sean Nessel's eyes target me. I look down. Back to the gray floor.

I want to escape. But Blythe clutches me like I'm on a short leash.

I tug on her dress, though there's not much there to hold on to except for the bottom of her dreess. It's like thin handkerchiefs. It's like air.

"Let go of me, Blythe."

BLYTHE

There's a yanking on my dress, as if there's a small child below me, and when I turn I see Ali. She's taken hold of my dress and is drawing me close to her. Or is she trying to push me away? Her eyes are wild. She's incensed.

"Blythe, let go of me." She spits. A monster erupts from her. Her shoulders are crouched. Her cheeks quiver. I look down, and I'm thinking, *My dress. She's going to rip my dress.* The words stick to my tongue because everything is happening so fast.

"Let go of my hand now or I'm going to kill you," Ali says.

I look down at my hand wrapped around her wrist. I didn't even know it was there.

My fingers repel from her skin.

Her contorted face glares back at me.

ALI

Kill comes out of my mouth flippantly. Racing in my chest.

I'll wrap my hands around her neck if I have to. I can feel it.

Blythe turns to me, a sharp inhale, and when she exhales it'll be fire, I know, but I don't flinch. She edges toward me so that our faces are almost touching, then peels my fingers off her dress.

BLYTHE

"You're going to *kill* me?"

"Wait, she's going to kill you?" Donnie says.

Suki cackles. "Who's going to kill you, B?"

"Ali. Greenleaf. I just heard her say she's gonna kill Blythe," Donnie says, her face lighting up.

"Ambitious, aren't you, junior?" Suki says.

They've been waiting to attack her for months. Ali's face sinks. My instinct is to protect her. Shield her from all this. But I can't. I don't even understand how this happened.

"Why would you threaten to kill me?" I screech. "And grab at my dress like that? Have you lost your fucking mind?"

"You were holding on to my hand."

"Just back off, Blythe," Raj says.

"No, I think your little friend Ali drank too much tonight, and we all know what happens when baby drinks too much, don't we?" Donnie says, taunting her.

"I was trying to help you." Every word, curt. Clear, spitting. "I want to help you—and this? And you treat me like *this*?"

"How many times have I told you not to waste your time with this one?" Donnie says, but she's preaching now. She's not making any sense. "This is how ungrateful they all are. These children."

They're all watching me.

Dev, Sean, Suki, Donnie. They expect me to say something. To have a retort.

I look Ali in the eye, and she finally looks me in the eye.

"What were you thinking?"

ALI

But I don't know how to explain it to her. The closer Sean Nessel came, how close he is now, the more boxed in I felt. That maybe he'd try to kiss me. Or get me drunk again. Or try to apologize. Something false and irrelevant. And I'd do it again. Because I don't trust myself. Isn't it why I came here?

Some stupid idea to prove him wrong? To show him I'm fine. I'm not fine.

He's still there. Standing right there, behind them as they crowd around me. As they circle the town freak. He's just waiting to pounce on me.

"I can't explain what happened. . . . I . . ."

I don't want to cry. I don't want to cry.

BLYTHE

You can't tell a girl like me that you're going to *kill her* without repercussions.

You can't do that. Not in front of these girls. Suki, Cate, and Donnie would never allow that. I would never allow that. Everything I have is built on saving face.

If I show empathy, they'll come after me. If I make excuses for her, they'll come after me.

It would make me look weak.

And I never look weak.

I give her a second more. Anything, Ali. Anything, Greenleaf. Say anything to me.

But she's in space. Like she doesn't exist. Almost like that night I saw her run out of Sophie Miller's party. So I'm going to save her from herself.

"Disappear," I say in this girly-girl baby voice, like Cinderella's fairy godmother.

28

ALI

I can't breathe. I can hardly stand. I spin around and there he is. Backing out of the crowd, floating toward me. So I run the other way down the hall, not looking back.

I tear around the corner to a set of lockers. Raj follows me, calling my name.

"Ali—talk to me."

I pace back and forth. My body not my own. How did this happen? How did I get here? Put myself here? How have I lost myself and how do I get myself back?

I crouch down on the floor. I'm scared now.

"Tell me you're okay."

"But I'm not okay, Raj. There's no okay to be found here." My voice cracking. Can't even get the words out.

"You stood up to her. Do you understand that? You stood up to Blythe in front of all her friends."

"It wasn't her I wanted to stand up to."

"What do you mean?"

I kick the locker with my poor kitten heel and the stupid tiny heel gets caught in the locker slat. I can't pull it out. I take my other shoe off and throw it at the stuck shoe. It bangs against the locker, sounding like an explosion. Then I collapse down to my knees, curl my feet under me, my red tights so bright and wild. They're tights for a confident girl. Not a girl like me. Not a messed up, damaged girl like me.

"I think I may have broken my toe."

Raj kneels next to me.

"Talk to me, Greenleaf."

"It's him, don't you understand?"

Raj is so sweet. He always has the right answers. But he's not going to have the right answers for this. I don't know if he's going to want to be around me anymore when he hears this.

"It's him. It's Sean Nessel. He did this. I'm out of control now and I can't get rid of it. I feel like I have no brain. Like someone else owns me. Like I'm going to have a nervous breakdown."

I cradle my foot in my hand. My black eyeliner drips down my face like a swarm of black ants. Messy glitter across my cheek. I can feel it.

I want to get a big giant marker and scribble all over the locker so that everyone can see.

Something happened to me.

No one would know what it means. But I would know it was there.

Something happened to me.

I know what it is, but I haven't been able to say it.

I was raped.

I can't say this out loud. I don't want to. How would I even begin? It's quiet between me and Raj for at least ten minutes.

Electronica in the background. The music pumping from the dance.

"I don't know how we're going to get out of here," I say.

"We're going to walk out."

"Everyone's going to stare."

"Not if I protect you with my invisible shield."

"What if Blythe comes looking for me?"

"I have a special invisible spray, so she'll have to stay ten feet away. And a golden lasso."

Hands over my face. Breathe. Try to breathe.

"I never told you about my sister?" he says.

I shake my head. He always has a story.

"In college last year. She was raped by someone at a frat formal."

I don't look at him when he says this. That word. That word. I want it to drift away into the clouds. I want to lock it up in the locker and get rid of it. Never see it again. But I breathe. Stare ahead. He asks me, "Should I go on?"

"Go ahead."

"She had to drop out. She had to go to the police. She switched schools. That's why she goes to NYU now and lives at home."

I look at him with wild eyes. "Was your sister *rape* raped?"

"What's *rape* raped? There's only one rape, Ali. It's not a do you like me, or do you *like me* like me."

I think of the different ways that rape could happen. I think of women who get grabbed in the subway in Manhattan or get pulled into a dark alley. Girls who get dumped on their front lawn. Not remembering the night before except for bruises and a video on social media. Isn't that rape? Is that the same kind of rape that happened to me?

"It was a guy she knew from the fraternity," Raj says. "She was really wasted. It was a pledge party. She didn't remember any of it. And a bunch of guys watched until someone pulled him off her because she was basically unconscious. She's okay now. But it's affected her. It's affected me. At first I wanted to go to her school and kill those guys. But me against a hundred frat bros?"

I imagine Raj's reaction when he heard the news about his sister for the first time. How helpless he must have felt. So helpless that he's kept this all to himself. That I'm hearing this story for the first time now. I think about how his sister felt, people watching her. Not moving while some guy had sex with her. Imagine that no one stopped it.

"That night you ran out of the party?" his voice stutters. "Did—did it go down, you know, like it went down with my sister?"

I smooth out the translucent ruffle of my black dress. It's a glacier. I am ice, black and cold. My red tights, fire. I will freeze you or I will burn you down.

I nod my head up and down. Look at his face. Right into his eyes.

Yes.

He bangs the back of his head against the locker. Then turns to the opposite side and slams the locker with his fist.

The sound of him punching the metal echoes in the empty hallway. And I've never seen him like this. In all the years I've known Raj. I've never seen him like this, and it does something to me. It makes me angry too. A feeling I haven't felt yet. Anger, stabbing into me.

29

BLYTHE

Donnie folds her arm around mine, locking us together.

"So you and your little minion got into a fight, Jensen? She's not listening to the rules?"

"I don't want to talk about it."

"Oh, we're going to talk about it."

"Oh, are we? Don't make me get loud with you, bitch. Too much has happened tonight. I need someone to solve my problems. Not make them worse."

"Fuck me gently with a chain saw. Do I look like Mother Teresa?"

"Stop it," I say. I'm not in the mood to quote *Heathers* right now.

Donnie curls her head into my shoulder. She takes the sweet approach. I can feel her heavy breath against my ear.

"Is he worth the fight?"

"*Worth the fight?* What does that mean?"

"You know what it means."

I take a quick peek around. Any person could hear her if she says it. If she opens her mouth. If she gets any messier.

"Isn't *he* what you're fighting for here? If you get Ali to forgive him. If you get her to drop whatever happened between them that night. Then you get his love. Isn't that what this is about? Otherwise, why waste your time with that *novice*? That girl. Ali. What does she know about anything? What does she know about what *we* did to secure our spot?"

I just want her to shut up. I'm tempted to slap her. She reminds me of my mother right now, the way when she's off her meds, how she rants.

"Just walk."

"To where?"

"Anywhere. I just need to sit."

Suki runs up behind us.

"You guys just left."

"What was I supposed to do? Stick around?" I say.

"In the meantime, while your little mascot was acting out, Sean went off with three sophomore girls and said he's going to do an Initiation on his own."

"What?" I say. "He's wasted. He doesn't know what he's talking about."

Donnie cackles, throws her head back. Her arms stretch out all pale and witchy. "Imagine if Sean was on a TV show— *Boys Most Wanted. Everyone wants him, but no one knows whyyyy . . . because inside he's rotting alive.*"

I step behind her. Push her forward, in the direction of the bathroom. She's talking crazy talk and I want to get away from Donnie, those black sunken eyes. The eyes of someone I don't even know.

Bathroom. A whole bunch of girls in there already. A few waiting in line, but we're the Core Four. Well, Core Three right now since Cate is off somewhere with Chase Goldberg.

We walk ahead because that's *what we do*. Donnie first. Me second. Suki last. Cram in the handicap stall. Everyone else has to wait.

"What did he say exactly, Suki? I need word for word."

"I heard him say something about how he's got three girls who are eager to get started. That he doesn't need this drama with Ali. That it's all gotten too much. He can get three girls"—she does air quotes—"'working on him' on his own."

"I'm not feeling good," Donnie says, but I ignore her because I'm trying to dissect what Suki's saying.

"Direct quote," Suki says.

"Tell her whatever you want," Donnie says. "She doesn't see him the way we see him. She sees the soft side. Isn't that right, Jensen? Sweet soft Sean, who shops with his artist-collector grandma in the city. Say that ten times fast."

Suki's face, confused. "When did you see him shopping with his grandmother?"

"Forget all that. Donnie doesn't know what she's talking about."

She wags her finger. "Oh, yes I dooooo."

Suki ignores Donnie and keeps going. "Sean was talking to everyone. To Chase and Cate. To Harrison. To Dev. Ask Dev. He was standing right there."

This is what Sean does. He rounds up the girls. And I sweep it up.

"Seriously. I'm gonna puke," Donnie says, and tries to kneel down on the floor.

Heels click in and out of the bathroom. Anyone can see what's going on with her if she falls to the ground.

"We need to sit. Get you some water, that's all."

I look at Suki and mouth to her: "Up." We prop her on to the toilet. She nods.

My body tightens up. This dress. I look down at it. If Donnie pukes, it's going to be covered in vomit.

"Whoa, whoa, whoa." She flings her arms out to the sides like a bird. "Can I tell you a secret first?"

Her neck shifts back and forth. Lips quiver and then she collapses in our arms. No grunt. No sign of distress. She's just up one second—and the next second, *whoosh*. She's deadweight.

Teachers will see. Adults will see that her face is gone from her face. She's collapsed all over herself.

"What did you take tonight? Talk to me. What did you take?" I slap at her cheeks, and she peers up from all her hair, her bones sharp and eerie. I lift her the best I can, but her body droops over my dress.

"You're fine," Suki says really loud. "You're fine. Just dehydrated. We just need to get you some water."

I nod. She's staving off the girls outside who've stopped in their clicking heels to see Donnie fall from her perch.

I don't know how we're going to get out of here. All the girls who wished they were us, wished they had our friendship, Donnie Alperstein and Blythe Jensen.

Suki and I struggle to get Donnie to sit straight. My body

wants to just collapse over her. This night. I'm so tired from this night.

Then someone, some sweet little bird, hands me a cup of water under the stall. I pass it to Donnie.

Donnie opens her eyes a little. She pulls at my hair. "Jensen, I don't know if I can make it through this. I did too much vikes. Too much vikes and that champagne."

"I'm gonna let go of you. Don't fall on your head, bitch," Suki says, and Donnie nods. She's following instructions, so I take a breath. Suki opens her clutch and pulls out a vile of her crushed up Ritalin. Suki shakes some out on her hand. Donnie opens her mouth. Drooling on Suki's hand, trying to lick Suki's palm. "No, you're going to snort it," Suki says, her voice firm. "Now inhale. Snort it up your nose."

I look over at Suki. Her eyes get crazy when she's on task. Reminds me of when we used to play soccer together. Kick that ball, Sukes. STRIKE IT.

"Snort it up your nose." Donnie laughs.

"She needs to get out of here," Suki says.

"She needs rehab," I say.

"I hear you, bitches," she says. "I say they try to make me go to rehab and I said, no, no, no." She's singing Amy Winehouse now.

We sit and wait. Donnie nodding off. I give her sips of the water. Me and Suki pushing her back against the wall to straighten her up. And then it happens. Donnie's face fills back up with pink. She's alive again. Awake. A spirit. A person. The music vibrates into the bathroom. BUM BUM BUM BUM. BUM BUM BUM BUM.

"You're both my best friends," Donnie says. "You know that, right? Not Cate. Cate is a slut."

Suki bursts out laughing. I start laughing. Relief. It's working.

Donnie stops and stands up by herself. We walk out of the bathroom quickly, not even looking in the mirror or at the idiots who are going to talk about this like wildfire tomorrow.

My mind off this emergency. One down, another one to go. Now Sean.

It's always Sean.

30

ALI

Raj drops me off at my house. Just the two of us in that old station wagon. I text Sammi to apologize for the millionth time. She forgives me because she always forgives me. How many apologies would Sammi accept? Apparently, quite a few.

I know Raj is going to tell me that I need to talk to someone. Or an even worse feeling, that he'll tell me I need to report it.

He doesn't say any of that. He just sits there. Patient. Patient Raj. How can he be so patient?

"You know sometimes I go to this jujitsu class."

"Okay. You want me to go to jujitsu with you and beat people up?" I belt out a laugh. "You don't have to have all the answers, Raj."

"I'm not pretending to."

"But you do—don't you? Don't you always know what to say?"

"One day I'm going to tell you something stupid."

"Two plus two is ten. Something like that?"

"Right. Exactly. And you're going to be so disappointed in me."

"I'll never be disappointed in you," I say.

Our gaze lingers. Like the kind of gaze that happens before you kiss someone. So I look away first. I push that feeling down. Don't let it out. Don't let the feelings show. Push it way down until you can't feel. Until it's like you're not even there.

"Raj," I say. "Did I tell you too much?"

"Never," he says. "You could never tell me too much."

Later that night I text Blythe.

I'm sorry I said that— I don't know what came over me.

It's a lie. But I need to get the apology out.

I wait for her answer back. Sit there watching my phone. Wanting her to forgive me. To understand.

But she waits a full day. Makes me pay for what I've done. Then she texts me:

Moving on

31

BLYTHE

When I get home, my mother is in her bed upstairs. Her drugs in action. There's no waking her up.

My father isn't home. He never is.

I take off my dress. The floor length part is covered in guck. Crap from it dragging across the floor. It's like I hiked through a muddy field. I don't care.

I put on my sweats and a T-shirt. All I hear is what Suki had to say about Sean. *He's got three girls who are eager to get started.*

I'm blurry-eyed from the night, but I stare into my phone. It's the only light in my room. That bright light blinding me, I scan every Instagram account of every stupid girl in our school who I can think of, anyone connected or friends with Sean. My pupils fried. Search for all the stupid bitches who would post a photo of Sean Nessel and her phenomenal hookup. There's got to be someone that stupid. Someone who wants to show off her prize.

And then I find it.

There's a picture of Sean's mouth. I can tell by his tooth. He has one crooked tooth from not wearing his retainer. It's impossible to miss. A sophomore. Hunter something. *SN,* she writes as if no one will know. As if no one is looking for those initials. The initials SN are a giveaway. If someone's bragging about a Nessel hookup, that's the first thing to look for.

Bae tired, the caption reads.

I'm sure by the morning it will be taken down. Sean will confiscate that. He doesn't like his hookups broadcast.

Stupid me. Little stupid me. Thinking that I had some kind of line attached to him. Thinking that we had some connection. Some real meaning together.

My front living room fills up with lights. It's Dev's Jeep.

I open the door. Dev walks in, his hair wet. He's showered.

"Had to rinse the stank off you, huh?" I say.

"What? No," he says. "I was a ball of sweat."

"You weren't driving Sean around to meet up with his little conquests? Pimping him out? I thought you went home with him."

He tells me that while I was taking care of Donnie, he and Sean and a bunch of freshman or sophomore girls went to some girl's house with a pool. Probably the girl who posted the photo.

"I got pushed in. Chlorine all over me and these stupid drunk girls. Someone's going to drown. They were putting this guy on a raft, and he was passed out. It was a disaster, B. You would have hated it. I heard Chase and Cate had sex in the limo, so I didn't want to go back in there. I walked home. And it was kind of nice actually. Just staring at the moon. It was so big, and then it just dipped down into the sky and disappeared. I don't even understand entirely how that happens," he says, his face full of wonder. "Do I have to really stand here in your doorway telling you this?"

Dev does not deserve a girlfriend like me. Dev does not deserve a friend like Sean.

I move out of the way, let him in. Flustered. Drunk. Stoned. Whatever he is, I know Dev is telling the truth. I know he didn't want anything to do with what Sean was doing. That he was just trying to be a loyal friend, the bro friend, the bro prince, or whatever they are. And then find his way back to me.

I tell him about Donnie. About the scene in the bathroom. Tell him what I heard. That Sean wants to rally the freshman girls and do his own Initiation. Get a bunch of blow jobs from fourteen- and fifteen-year-olds all at once.

"Before you rip Nessel apart for mentioning the Initiation, believe me he was out cold by the time we got to this girl's house. He doesn't even know what he's saying."

"We always make excuses for him, Dev. Don't we?"

Dev wipes his eyes. They're bloodshot and tired with dark circles.

"I see it as accepting his flaws."

"All the hooking up. All the girls he leaves by the wayside, like a fucking battlefield of girls—"

"A battlefield? They're not dead in the ground, B. They want to be there. These girls tonight were dragging him into the limo they had. He pulled me along because he didn't want to get caught with a bunch of minors. Nessel always covers himself. That's one thing about him that I'm always surprised about. He sees a situation, no matter how fucked up he is, far in advance. He's ten steps ahead."

I slide between my memories of Sean and I making out in my backyard, and that night after the party, the way he was crying in the car, needing me to help him fix everything. Then another moment, the way he held my hand in the hallway, always needing me.

Ten steps ahead.

Did he know how all that would make me feel? How I want to feel needed? That I want to feel like I can fix everything? Did he know that right from the start? Has he known it all along?

"It's been a long night, B. Let's just cuddle." Slides his hands around my waist. Under my sweats, behind me. He massages my shoulders, trailing his fingers up and down my back. Just caressing me.

He's so gentle and good.

And I'm a monster.

In the morning, I check the sophomore's Instagram story, the girl who Sean hooked up with, and the post is already gone.

I meet Ali on Monday outside her class just like I've been doing. I don't make one mention of the dance. She's waiting for me to say something, I know it. She's quiet now, more quiet than I've seen her.

"Will you hate me forever, because I don't know if I can take it?" she says.

"I'll only hate you for a little while," I say.

32

ALI

Everyone in school calls the school social worker Ms. Tapestry because she's got all these "taps"—her word, not mine—hanging on her walls. By taps, I mean giant purple and paisley fabrics with a trippy, psychedelic quality. If I had more problems and met her sooner, and if she were a couple of years older, I could have introduced her to my dad. Ms. Tapestry, with her long flowy skirts and collection of hot pink Buddhas, would be right up my father's alley.

This was my father's idea. That I talk to someone. I chose her because I heard she doesn't make you cry. Other therapists, that's part of their job. To pull out the tears.

"So what's going on with you, Alistair?"

I have a list of things I could theoretically talk to her about, but I don't even know where to start.

"Do you want to talk about why you think your dad wanted you to see me?"

"I've been kind of out of it lately. I think he's overreacting."

"Sometimes being out of it is a symptom of something else."

"Like a manifestation?"

She jots something down on her yellow pad. A dragon ring curls around her index finger. "Yes. Like that," she says. "So tell me about yourself. Your dad has told me a little. But I'd like to know why you think you're here."

So I start to lie. Well, not lie, but I tell her things she'd want to hear. Things that have nothing to do with Sean Nessel. "My mother hasn't lived at home in four years."

"Okay. Your father didn't mention this. That must have been very disruptive for you."

She looks up from her notepad and starts filing through her folder.

"It wasn't that disruptive, actually," I say, which, of course, is not the truth.

"No?" she says. "Can you explain?"

"My father—he's a great guy. He and my aunt help me with everything." I think of my aunt Marce dropping off Plan B. Dragging me to the gynecologist. "Plus my mother and I talk a lot. Even though she doesn't live at home."

"You see her on holidays? In the summer?"

"Right."

"That's good. So you have a strong support system."

"Yes, and friends and lots of people to talk to. Except . . ."

"Except who?"

"My friend Sammi. Who I— Things have been different for us lately."

"Why do you think that is?"

"Because I've become friends with someone she doesn't like."

"Why doesn't she like them?"

"I don't know. Maybe she's not entirely good for me."

Blythe Jensen is a drug. That's what I want to tell her. A drug I don't want to stop taking.

"Is that why you think your dad wanted you to come here? Because of this new friendship?"

I shake my leg, pump it up and down uncontrollably. I could give her countless reasons for why I'm here. I'm sure she's heard them all.

"Well, maybe I have some things to talk about. I just don't necessarily want to talk about them this second," I say, sort of satisfied with that answer.

"I'm a slow mover," she says. "We can take our time."

"Okay. Just do me one favor?" I say.

"Sure."

"Just don't tell me that I'm being too hard on myself."

"Is that how you feel sometimes, like you're too hard on yourself?"

"I feel like that a lot," I say. "Sometimes, I just want to shut my brain off."

"I know the feeling."

She agrees to not tell me that I'm being too hard on myself but wants me to do a few things that will help my brain "unwind."

She wants me to write in a journal. Spill my feelings.

At home later that night, I open a new composition book and write two words.

Sean Nessel.

I hate those two words. And I don't want to see them ever again. I scribble over them so hard that I rip through the page and throw the stupid journal across the room.

I shove my pillow to my face and scream. My body is hot and clammy. *I hate you*, I scream, my face stuffed in my pillow. *I hate you.*

An hour later. I try again. Pretend it's about someone else. A stranger. Remove myself from the equation. *How are you doing?* I write to the stranger.

Not great. I was raped.

I shut the journal.

It's enough for tonight.

33

BLYTHE

I ask Sean to meet me in the parking lot.

Donnie would scold me for it. She'd tell me how I was under his dark spell. Yes, Sean rounded up these three girls, an initiation of his own, but he was wasted. We were all wasted at the dance. Donnie in a drugged-out haze. Cate had sex in the limo. No one was in their right mind. He hooks up with girls. This is what he does. What was he supposed to be—*loyal* to me? The girl with the boyfriend she loves? His best friend? We just got caught up. That's all it was. Sean and I are friends. Close friends. That's all we are.

"You recovering from that dance?" He leans on my car window. When Sean smiles, it's almost impossible not to smile back. I want to touch his golden arm hair. His cheeks are flushed from the cold air.

"Yeah. Still a little blank."

"I wanted to talk to you. I'm glad you told me to meet you."

He slides in on the passenger side, close so I can feel his breath.

"I wanted to talk to you too."

"About the dance?"

"About the dance . . . about a lot of things. You first."

He pulls his hair back, leans his head on my seat. That innocence. Vulnerable Sean. This is the real Sean. It has to be.

"I never really talked to you about this."

"What is it? You can tell me anything," I say.

He licks his lips nervously. "I have feelings around this . . . this thing. This topic. I have *thoughts* around it."

My heart speeds up. Very briefly, I think that he may tell me he's in love with me. For that slight moment. My mind floats to the two of us in that kiss outside my house. By the shed.

"It's about the Initiation."

"Wait. What? The Initiation?"

"Yeah."

"*The Initiation?*"

"Yeah, why do you keep saying it like that?" he asks.

Just minutes ago I was convincing myself that we were all wasted. That I was acting like a jealous girlfriend. That we were all out of our minds at the dance, Donnie passing out in the bathroom stall, even. I was so sure. And now I hear it in Suki's slurry voice that night. *He can get three girls working on him on his own.* Here he is, with a straight face, bringing it up.

"I guess I'm just surprised."

"I felt weird talking to you about it because I know the girls set it up," he says.

"Actually, I was told that I was going to be the one to set it up."

"Oh, you? I didn't know that."

Bullshit. Of course he knew it. I feel my stomach, that deep pit of dread. How could he say this? How? Everyone knows I was going to be in charge.

"I know for a fact that it's always happened before Christmas. Some guys used to call it their Christmas present—"

"Wait, stop. A Christmas present?"

"Okay, fine. If you're Jewish, then it's your Hanukkah present."

"It's not supposed to be pleasurable, Sean. It was created to stop senior boys from attacking freshman girls."

In my head I start thinking about my mother when I'm listening to her on a rampage. And I sound like her. Not making any sense. *It's not supposed to be pleasurable.* Listen to how I've brainwashed myself. Lying to myself. Letting myself believe that there was a *real* agreement. That the guys can somehow be robotic and turn themselves off. Five years they've done this. For five years all these girls—or maybe not all the girls?—are walking around traumatized, believing that somehow we could *deter* sexual assaults. That somehow we could control the narrative.

And this guy. Sean. Right here in front of me.

What he did to Ali.

None of it mattered. It happened anyway.

"I know it sounds weird asking this. Or bringing this up. But a few girls brought it up the other night at the dance. A few sophomore girls who didn't get their turn."

"Didn't get their turn?"

"Why do you keep repeating everything I'm saying?" he says, with a nasty tone. "These girls, *they* brought this up to me. And I always thought it was something they were forced to do. Something that they didn't want. That's what Dev said. That's what he said you told him. But they asked me for it. *They* wanted to know when the Initiation was."

I shouldn't be so stunned. When I was a freshman, I brought it up too. I heard they had done it the year before. Anything to get the older guys to pay attention and take me seriously. I would have done anything to feel in control. That's what I was promised. That's what you get in return. You were in control of it. You were *choosing* to do it.

Except now, there's just me wanting to hurl and hit and cry until there's an empty hole that's black and scarred.

Thoughts race in like thunder. The week before the dance and how Sean had been so eager to be around me, touching me and whispering to me, *There are so many things I want to say to you*, how at the department store it felt so crazy, how he took my hand and said to me, *I'm not scared, B.* Now I can't help but wonder if he did it all to get to this moment. If he knew he had to get me on his side, not just so I could help persuade Ali to change her story but to make sure the Initiation was secure. So that he could get his Christmas present, as disgusting and vile as it sounds.

"Everything you said to me about . . . the way you feel about me. It was all a lie."

"No! I could hardly stop that night we kissed. When I ran to your house," he says, squeezing closer to me. "Look, B, you have to understand. This Initiation. It's a *natural* curiosity. Do you understand that?" He edges even closer. I can smell his breath. The Italian sandwich he had for lunch. "And if I can't have you. Do you understand what that does to me? How messed up I am about this. So I'm like, sure, you want to have an Initiation? Let's do it."

Sean. This creature. He's had everything handed to him. He deserves. He expects. He's on his throne. Taking and taking. And expecting. Expecting all the girls to kneel down. Ali Greenleaf. I brought her under my wing for him. *For him.*

"The Initiation wasn't meant for you, Sean." I'm yelling now, pushing him back.

He shifts around in his seat. His body so big, barely fitting in my tiny car. When he shifts, the whole car jiggles. That's what you get when you have a giant soccer player in your car. Who is the threat of the school. With his thick, muscular legs, his chest, his speed. We should all fear him. But I don't. So I sit up in my seat too. I can face him just as easily.

"It's no big deal. Don't make this a big deal, B."

"It's HUGE! You're asking girls to give group blow jobs to boys who are three years older than them. Some of the guys are eighteen. It's a world of difference. And to get what in return? A promise of safety? So we have to *hand ourselves* over to you to be safe?"

I see them in front of me. Flashes. Hair on their inner thighs. Muscles and knees. Smirk between each other. Amanda Shire chiding them for their laughter. Donnie staring down at the floor, ashamed.

"Hold up. Rewind. Is this about me and you? That you don't want to share me with those other girls?"

"I know you slept over at that sophomore's house after the

dance. I saw her post a photo of you on Instagram. I know how much you're with other girls—"

"And you're with Dev! So what am I supposed to do?"

"Jesus, Sean—you can get blow jobs from anyone in this school without it being humiliating for her. Without her having to sit in a room filled with guys. Without me standing over them. Screaming at you not to look. And telling them how to wrap their virginal little mouths around your dick."

But it's the game for him. It's the act of bowing down that he likes.

For a second. Just a brief second, because I can't bear to take it anymore than just a second, I think about Ali that night. Tearing down the stairs. I remember the terror in her eyes.

"So then change the Initiation, B. You have the control. So fuck it. You're right. It's stupid. Sick." His mouth smacks of anger. He flings open the car door. Slams it shut. He stands there, his big-man body and his big-man muscles and his big-man sexy hair and his big-man cheekbones. He's hypnotizing. Evil.

"I will," I say.

God forbid one of those fourteen-year-old girls tells their parents they're giving eighteen-year-olds head. And that *I* set it up? That I'm attached to rape or something worse? It's a fucking miracle that it hasn't gotten out in the past five years.

It takes everything I have, every last bit of willpower, to turn around and drive away. I don't even look in the rearview mirror. But if I know Sean well enough, it doesn't matter, because he's not looking back.

34

ALI

Picking you up in 5 mins be ready

A blaring text from Blythe.

Get me at the corner not at my house

Why? Ashamed of me? Haha

I don't respond. My dad and my aunt Marce are sitting outside by the firepit when I tell him I'm going out.

"It's just time you start coming back to the living," he says.

"I'm socializing with my friends, Dad. That's living. Isn't it?"

"Let her go. I'll hang out with her another day," Marce says. I haven't spent time with her since that day at the gynecologist. She's been trying to set up a lunch date, but I keep blowing her off. There are too many unread texts from her. Too many missed calls for her to think it's just me being busy now.

I don't mention Blythe. I don't want my father to know that I'm going out with her. He has too many questions when I go out with Blythe. I'm lying so much lately that I don't know where it begins or ends.

Blythe is smoking a cigarette when I get in the car; when she sees me, she tosses it out the window.

"I'm starting to become a chain-smoker. I just want one after the other. I went through a pack today. An entire pack.

Can you believe that I had to leave my house to buy more cigarettes?"

"Think of all the old people in those commercials who have those voice boxes they have to talk through."

"I just think of Winona Ryder with that cigarette hanging out of her mouth in *Heathers*, realizing that she just killed those two jocks. How stoic, yet how depressed she looks."

She drives a little and we say nothing. Someone has to break the silence.

"You know why I wanted to see you, right? I'm sure you heard already."

"I actually have no idea."

"Sean. It's because of Sean."

Everything has to do with Sean Nessel. It's always Sean Nessel.

"I'm sick of hearing about him. I don't want to hear his name anymore, Blythe."

Blythe rubs her eyes. Sticks her long blond hair behind her ears.

"I know what he did to you."

I feel my body getting hot. Like this car is the smallest car in the world and the metal is creeping in on me.

"I know what he did to you because the night it happened, he told me everything. He told me about the blood. He told me how you were crying. He was really scared, and I was really wasted, and I just sat there and listened to him. I didn't know you then. I didn't know a thing about you. I'm sure you were scared too. I'm sure you were terrified. I remember your face.

I saw you when I came out of the bathroom. How spooked you looked. I've been on the other side of a lot of these girls that Sean hooks up with. I've seen a lot of aftermaths."

I don't say anything. I just stare. A small speck on her dashboard. A little white smudge. Who knows how it got there. But I stare into it like it's the universe and I'd like to disappear.

"Ali?"

She's saying my name. And I have to respond. I have to.

"It wasn't just a hookup, Blythe."

I don't know what Blythe wants from me in this moment. I don't know what she wants me to say or do. If she wants me to back down. Or feel sorry for her. Understand her. But I don't care anymore.

"Why did you become my friend in the first place? To protect Sean Nessel?"

"You have to understand, Ali. It's more complicated than just saying I was protecting Sean. You don't go into it thinking this is what you're going to do. It wasn't like I was part of some extravagant cover-up. But, Sean, he's this magnetic creature. . . ."

"Oh, I'm aware, Blythe. I'm keenly aware."

"Things changed, though. We became friends. You know that," she says, on the defense. "And friendships aren't perfect, Ali. I wouldn't be sitting here with you after that shit you pulled at the dance if we weren't really friends."

"The shit *I* pulled? You were trying to drag me over to hook up with the person who . . . who raped me."

I've said it now. There's no pretending that it's not there. Blythe has a look on her face like the world has stopped. That it's all spinning around her and she can't catch it.

But for me, it's the first time in a while that things are falling into place. That I'm starting to understand myself again.

"I was trying to help you, Ali. I wasn't trying to hurt you," she's saying. "You have to believe me."

I don't let her see any reaction at all. Because it feels like she'll never let me out of this car if I don't reassure her. At least for now.

I call Sammi when I get back in the house. The first time we're really talking since I texted her after the dance. I haven't even told her that I admitted it all to Raj yet.

"I have so many apologies that I owe you; I don't know where to start."

I hear her breathing heavily. Not talking.

"Sammi? Will you talk to me? Like really talk to me?"

"Yes, Ali. Haven't I through all this? Haven't I?" She's exasperated. I get it.

"I admitted everything to Raj. I told him everything. I told Blythe everything. It's all out in the open now."

She gasps loudly and then makes this loud curdling noise.

"Sammi? Are you okay?"

"I'm crying, you idiot. Can't you hear that I'm crying?"

"I thought you were choking. I'm sorry. I'm so out of touch. I'm the worst friend."

"You've been friends with the wrong people lately. That's all. That's what has to change."

Even with everything that Blythe has done, Sammi will never understand our connection. I can't defend her, I know this. The things she's done. But Blythe's experienced the kind of pain that I have. With her mother. With the Initiation. Sammi's never experienced anything like that. Not with guys. Not with a parent.

"There are a lot of things you don't know about Blythe. She's not a robot. She's a real person. She's got layers, you know? Sometimes those layers have to be stripped away."

"I'm sure she has an awful home life. I'm sure she's very complicated, and she probably sees an expensive therapist on a daily basis. I'm sure she needs a box of tissues on her at all times. I think it's great how empathetic you are, really. It's honorable or something like that. But trust me, Ali, if you strip away Blythe's layers, you'll find a sharp dagger. She will stab you in the back if she has to. If she hasn't already."

That's not how I see it. If we're talking in metaphors, then Blythe wraps her hands around the dagger so she can protect herself.

35

BLYTHE

I drive to Dev's after I drop off Ali. I want to hide in the dark and slip inside his room. Turn the clock back. But I have to pass his parents first and I'm a terrible girlfriend. I remind myself that they're not expecting anything. Just me on a school night with my eyes swollen from crying. Another normal night.

Perfectly normal.

His mother lets me in, and I walk up the stairs, remembering what Sean said. A Christmas present. A Hanukkah present. There are so many lies.

"Your face looks puffy. Like you've been crying," Dev says. But he doesn't seem to care much. He's cold, removed. Just staring at me as I wipe tears away.

"You don't even care that I'm crying?"

"I have other thoughts on my mind."

I sit on the edge of the bed, near him, but he shifts away from me.

"Dev, what the hell is going on?"

"Nessel told me you were canceling the Initiation. Good for you."

"Canceling it?" I want to throw up. What else did Sean tell him? "Dev, I don't get to so *easily* cancel it. I told him I was backing out of it. That I wasn't going to be in charge of it."

He gets up, pacing around his room, and I don't know where

to look. I don't know how to follow him. Usually when Dev's angry it's because someone's wronged me. My mother. My father. Now he's directing that anger toward me. He knows something about me and Sean. That has to be it.

"I'm done being Sean's bitch about Ali Greenleaf," I say.

"What's that even mean?"

"It means Sean isn't my friend. He isn't your friend. He's using all of us."

It feels so good to say this out loud. Even though it started just a few weeks ago, it was so different. Sean breathless, pulling me aside in the hallway, trying to convince me that I was the only one. Sean at my house, kissing me. That we were something. All of it lies. Just to get me to do what he wanted. To get Ali to shut up. To get me on his side.

"I have a question for you," Dev says, stopping near the bed. Closer to me now. His chest rising. "Do you love Nessel?"

So there it is. Sean told him. He had to have.

"Dev—" I reach out to touch his hand, but he jolts away.

"Nessel told me you guys had a fight."

"You could say that."

"And that you might say something to me—something bad. That you might say something to me that I don't wanna hear. And I'm thinking, *Wow, what could B possibly say to me?* And I start to get a little paranoid. Because you two have been so fucking secretive talking about Ali Greenleaf. Then I think, *Wait, maybe they're not just talking about Ali Greenleaf. Maybe there's something else between them.* And, damn, how fucking stupid am I? Maybe that's why you're here tonight.

Not because of your mom. Not because of your dad. Maybe you're here for another reason. To tell me something about you and Sean."

"Dev, listen, that's not why I'm here."

But he hangs his head, stomps the floor.

"Just tell me the truth, Blythe!"

Dev's mother calls up. Wants to know if everything's okay.

"Stop yelling at me—your parents can hear us."

"So what? I already told them. You don't think I wouldn't tell them, do you? I tell them everything. They're not like your parents, B."

It stings, as much as I know he's right. This is how it works when you have people on your side. When adults look out for you. "The truth is that I love you, but I got so wrapped up feeling so sorry for him. That his life was spinning out of control. And he was so needy. Always asking me what to do. How to help him. He needed me, don't you see? And I wanted that so badly, to help him."

"Have you lost your mind? Nessel gets everything handed to him on a silver platter. He doesn't need any fucking help. Because if it wasn't you, it would have been someone else," he says, glaring at me. Of course it would have been someone else.

"Why didn't you didn't stop me that night when he was crying about her in the car, then? Why didn't you stop me?"

"Oh, it's my fault now? Jesus, Blythe. Listen to yourself."

I don't say anything. What can I say?

"Just tell me the truth. Is there something between the two of you?"

Yes. Yes. I nod. *Yes.* Because it doesn't matter anymore. My head in my hands, tears down my cheeks, stinging. I'm going to roll out of here like a ball of weeds. That's all I am.

"How, B? How could you?" His face. His eyes well up with tears.

"I promise you, Dev. Nothing happened."

But it's not the truth at all. He's been in my mind for years. I've always had him on my mind. Long before what happened with Ali.

Dev's mom knocks on the door. Dev sticks his head out. "Everything's fine, Mom. I promise. She's leaving in a minute anyway."

Leaving in a minute. To go nowhere. To sink in my own filth.

Back in my car. Outside Dev's house. My hands are trembling. I call Suki because Donnie doesn't answer.

"It's possible that I made a huge mistake."

"Wait—Blythe Jensen makes mistakes?" She makes dramatic gurgling noises. "Sorry, that was me passing out from shock. I had, like, liver failure."

"Shut up, Suki."

"What did you make a mistake about, B?"

"Everything. Everything was a mistake."

"You mean about Sean?"

"Yes. That. That and everything else," I say, the streetlight cackling over my car. My throat collapsing into what I'm about to say. I can hardly get it out. "Me and Dev. It's over."

36

ALI

I've been writing in my journal for days. Random ideas. Nothing that makes sense, but I hold on to it tight, and I thud down into Ms. Tapestry's big couch.

"Everything sucks."

"Can you be more specific?"

I think about all the things in my life that suck.

"I started writing like you told me. In a journal. And my father is asking me, like, a question every five seconds."

"It sounds like he's interested in your life—"

"Too interested."

"Writing in a journal is working for you, though?"

I shrug. I'm sick of lying. Sick of answering questions. Sick of telling the truth. I stare out the window at the soccer field, the guys practicing. I can't see faces, just red and white shirts blending in the grass. Running back and forth.

"Something out there that's interesting?"

"There's nothing interesting out there. Just assholes." Then I think of Raj. "Well, except for one person."

"Why are they assholes?"

I look away again at the field. He's number 22. The twos curve over his shoulder blades. Sean Nessel is just everywhere I turn. I can't get away from him.

Ms. Tapestry's face is blank.

"What are you thinking when people are talking to you?" I say.

"I'm not really thinking anything right now. I'm just listening."

"How can you not judge people? We all judge each other."

"That's not what a therapist does. A therapist is really more of a listener than a judger."

"So if I tell you something, you're not going to think weird things about me?"

"What would you tell me that you deem weird? Because I have a very, very high 'weird' tolerance. I'm pretty weird myself."

I think of the worst thing I could say. Something that would send a major red flag.

"Like, if I slept with every guy in the school."

She takes a deep breath and rests her notepad on her lap. I think I've pissed her off. I don't know why I'm doing this to her. She's a nice person. She's sweet, like my dad. She wants to help.

"I'd probably ask you why."

"Because I like to have sex. A *lot* of sex. I'm really, really comfortable having tons of sex."

I sit on my hands because I don't know what to do with them. I've never lied to an adult like this—or anyone like this—for no reason whatsoever.

"Oh, if you're so comfortable, then why are you sitting on your hands?" she asks. "That's usually a body language sign for feeling uncomfortable."

I pull my hands out from under my thighs.

"See over there." I point to the soccer field.

She looks up at the window and squints.

"There's a guy on the field who I hate. More than anyone else I can think of."

Because he's a bad person. Because he did awful things to me. Because my mind can't think straight now because of him.

"Do you want to tell me about it?" I shake my head. Blackness. I've turned it into blackness.

"You're having a pretty strong emotion," she says. "Maybe you want to write about it in your journal? Or what about your collages that you told me about? Maybe you can make it into art?"

"I made a whole book of him."

"What did you do with it?"

"I shredded it."

That night, I write more in my journal. More words. Scribbles. Sentences. Even if I cross them out. Even if there are words I don't want to see. No more pictures. Just words.

I have a voice. And I have a pen.

So I write. I write and write until the pen indents my thumb.

37

ALI

There are a million other places I can sit. Anywhere, really. But I'm a masochist, maybe, and I go to the field. Soccer practice. To wait for Raj. He's giving me a ride home and why should I wait in a parking lot when I can sit under a tree on the bleachers? Just because of one person?

It had been one of my favorite places to sit. Now this field is a shit storm of post-traumatic stress because that asshole Sean Nessel is in plain view.

I sling my backpack over one shoulder and tighten my stomach, wishing I had listened to my father's diatribe on meditation the other day. I've never been more nervous in my life, and the only thing that's really getting me through it is knowing that my hair looks great because the air is dry as a bone. You cannot possibly sit on the sidelines flattening your ass on cold bleachers watching the guy who attacked you on a humid day. You need to be as confident as you can, and you cannot be confident if your hair is frizzy. I hold on to this. It keeps me strong. My hair.

All of a sudden, there he is.

Sean Nessel jogging over to me. Like it's no big deal. Like we're best friends.

"Hey," he says, calling out to me. I'm up on the fourth row. Not close to him. He waves. "What's going on?"

I look over at Raj, who is packing up his gear on the other side of the field. He doesn't notice me at all, and he's too far away for me to even try to get his attention.

"I'm leaving," I say. I stand up and quickly put my stuff in my bag. "That's what's going on." I don't know what I was thinking coming here. Right here. Right where he is. I haven't seen him this close since that night. Even at the dance, he seemed so far away. Now here he is.

"Can I talk to you?" He steps onto the bottom row of metal seats like he's going to work his way up to me.

"Raj is driving me home. I don't want to keep him waiting."

I back up, almost tripping on myself. Stepping onto the fifth row. Then the sixth.

"Rerun will wait."

His commanding voice. I go back to that night. *Drink it. Follow me. Upstairs.* With Sean Nessel comes instruction. He steps onto another bleacher, getting closer to me, and my heart pounds wildly, like I might fall down.

He's on the second row now. I'm on the sixth row still, edging to the end.

"I've been wanting to apologize to you," he says. "I wasn't myself that night. You know, that night we were together."

He wasn't himself. This is the only thing that he wants to say to me. That he wasn't *himself.*

I had all sorts of revenge scenarios planned, but when you're stuck in the moment like I am now, it's very hard to get your mouth open. It's hard to say anything when you're shaking. It's hard to say anything when you feel like you might die.

"I got carried away," he says.

"Carried *away*?"

"Yeah, that's right."

"When you put your hand over my mouth, is that what you mean by 'carried away'?"

"Holy fuck," he says. "You're going to keep going on with this?"

I want to punch him. And if he wasn't almost twice the size of me—I mean, his neck is like easily the size of a tire—I would pummel him.

My voice trembles with all the words I want to say, and they tumble out of my mouth with little management by me. It's a seething power that comes over me, and I almost want to get physical with him. Grab his shirt, twist it really hard, and pull him close to me. Or just push him down into the metal bleachers. I want to see his head gush with blood.

I feel like an alien invaded my body. I never thought I'd talk to him *ever*—let alone talk to him like this. Just a few months ago I was obsessed with him. Now I feel like this empty package. Dumped and crumbled. I feel like a stupid cliché. After all, what did I expect? That he was going to all of a sudden become my boyfriend after hooking up with me one night?

He got carried away.

But something stirs in me. I take a step forward instead.

"You didn't expect me to accuse you of rape, did you?"

"Yo, I didn't rape you."

"*Yo?*" I say. "Yo?"

His face reddens. His whole body tenses. His face. His eyes. His eyes plow into me. He's angry now. I've made him very angry. "That's not the way it went."

I remember vividly how strong he was that night, how his arm held my shoulder down so I couldn't hit him, or push him off me. I almost feel like he might grab me now. We're standing only a foot apart.

I run across the bleachers to get away, crossing past him, the metal clanging as I leap over each bench. I don't know if he'll chase me. I don't care. There are too many people around. Not his style. Sean Nessel only forces the issue with too much alcohol in his system and in a dark room. In sober daylight, he's the do-gooder-all-American boy.

I turn around, and he's walking after me, calling my name. I jump off the bleachers into a pile of small pebbles. I could stone him just like in that story, "The Lottery." I could chase him with rocks, aiming for the back of his head. I could get him right between the eyes and maybe he could bleed to death. Or maim him so that his beautiful face could never, ever entice another girl into a bedroom again.

His feet stomp over the metal bleachers, and he jumps down, following me.

"Ali," he says, marching quickly after me. "You can't just use that—*that word*, Ali."

"Oh, why not?"

I turn around and see his face. Red and contorted. Like he's about to reach out to me. But I keep walking. If I don't stop walking, I have to face him. If I don't stop walking, I'm going to cry.

No, I'm not. I'm not going to cry at all.

I feel his arm wrap around the back of my arm, and I want to scream out, screech and moan, like a crazy person. I want to smack him. But I don't. Because I want to be in control. I want to be in charge.

"Let go of my arm," I say. And my face must have contorted because it reminds me of everything from that night. The way he held me down. I want to shake it out of my head because I want to make him pay right here. I don't want to back down.

He drops his hand.

"You and I got drunk together and things got out of hand."

"I yelled stop, and you put your hand over my mouth and held me down," I say. There are the words. They come out of my mouth. *My* mouth.

"You wanted to go upstairs. I didn't force you to do that."

"But you put your hand over my mouth?" Again. I'm two separate people. Someone else answering for me. "You were hurting me," I say. "That's what I was saying to you. I screamed it. I had a bruise on my shoulder. I bled all over your jacket. I was a virgin!"

Sean Nessel might not remember it at all. Isn't this the side Blythe was trying to convince me of? Sean Nessel is a nice guy. He made a mistake. He was drunk. We were both drunk. Of course, it's entirely possible that Sean Nessel is a nice guy. But I'll never get to know him that way—or ever. Because he pinned me down in a bedroom with blood streaming down my legs, and that's the only memory I'm ever going to have.

Raj finally reaches us.

"What's up?" His jaw is clenched.

"She's got the wrong idea in her head, Rerun."

"Why don't you just step back," Raj says. "You're standing too close."

"I'm trying to apologize to her, dude, so we can just get this behind us."

Sean Nessel will have no problem putting this behind him. He'll erase it from his mind. He'll convince himself that I'm some annoying junior who he thought was cute and who cried rape. *Girls are idiots. What, do I need a consent form next time I fuck some chick?*

I run off toward Raj's car in the parking lot. If I can just get to the car, everything will be okay.

Raj calls out, but all I hear are echoes—something familiar—my name. I feel like someone different now, and though hardly anything has changed—everything has changed.

Raj drives us over to Manakow Park, where there's an old swing set and hardly any kids. They're revamping all the parks in town one by one. Taking out the old swings and putting in these ugly colorful playgrounds, stupid metal climbing structures. No swings. Too dangerous, the mayor wrote in a letter that went out to all the parents. I only know about this because my father actually went to a town council meeting to complain. "How can you take swings away from kids?" he asked. But they told him that the older kids use them to hop off from a high distance. That three kids broke their ankles. That almost all the existing swings violated safety recommendations. No more swings in public playgrounds, the mayor said, and that was final.

When was the last time you were on a swing? When was the last time you kicked your legs up and down, pumped them across the wind, pulled your body back into a curve so hard that when you came down in a swan-like dive, your belly rose up, sharp? I look over at Raj, and the wind blows back his hair. His cheeks, still red from practice. His lips dry.

"I'm scared."

"You just stood up to Nessel. I don't think you have anything to be scared of."

We crisscross each other with our feet, swinging back and forth, a breeze trailing between us.

38

BLYTHE

It's after school. Loud knock on the door. Pounding.

My mother is on a new pill. Sleeping all day is the side effect. Better than her taunting me. Better than her wanting to spend time with me.

I run downstairs, swing open the door. It's Sean. Sean sweaty with his hair pulled back in this new man bun he's doing. His eyes red, as if he's been crying.

"She's going to ruin my life."

"Sean—you're getting paranoid." I push him outside, shut the door.

"No, you don't understand, B. She and Rerun. Today after practice. I went to talk to her. I apologized to her. You know. For getting so, you know, getting carried away that night." He's panting. His face in a panic. "She made me chase her across the bleachers. She's crazy, B. What the fuck am I going to do?"

I look around my neighborhood. Anyone can see us. Anyone can see the captain of the varsity soccer team falling apart on my front porch.

"Lower your voice."

"She said I raped her."

"She said those exact words?"

Every part of me tenses up, a weird tingle all over. Here

he is, standing in front of my door, like nothing happened at all. A desperate, broken-down man who I need to take care of.

"She said she was a virgin. She said all this other crap."

"Interesting. What did you say?"

He raises his voice again. "What do you think I said? I said, 'That's not the way it went.' But then Rerun tells me to get away from her and that I need to take a step back. I tower over that kid, and he's telling me to take a step back."

And where does that leave me? I'm the girl who swept in. I'm the girl who tried to be friends with Ali because Sean Nessel told me to. I'm the girl who told Ali to forget about it. To move on. That Sean is a good guy.

I flash to that night before the party. Sean's face. Salivating about Ali Greenleaf. *The way she stares at me in the hall*, he kept saying.

Every girl is a conquest. Maybe I was a conquest.

If anyone connects the dots to why I've become friends with Ali, then I become the girl who hid the information.

I become the person who tried to get her not to admit it. I tried to erase it from her mind.

If Ali tells this whole story to everyone, she is going to mess with my reputation. I was there, people will say. I knew how it went down.

Blythe Jensen knew all about the rape, and she did nothing. She just tried to protect Sean Nessel. That's what they'll say.

I knew what he did to her as she tore down the stairs, her eyes popping out of her skull as I left the bathroom. How she almost ran me over. *Leaving so soon,* I said to her. How callous. How inhumane. I pretended it wasn't happening. That Sean wasn't capable of this. Or not to this degree. That she should have known. People will talk. They'll say she was my puppy dog. That I let it happen.

And Sean? Well, Sean will be forgiven because he's every other golden athlete. Their coaches scream from the sidelines. Go all the way. Press them until it's over. Be relentless. They do not stop.

Can it be that what Amanda Shire told me that night is true? *It might seem humiliating at first, but in time you'll see that it puts you in control.* Can it?

I feel for my doorknob and slowly open it. Sean is still whimpering about how his life is ruined. I walk backward into the house.

Sean is beside himself. Hands on his knees. Saying he's going to puke.

"You'd take the moon if you could, wouldn't you? You would lasso the stars right from the sky just to brighten your little section of the soccer field while the rest of us sat in the dark."

"What are you talking about, B? Moons—what?"

"For the future, when a girl is wasted, don't have sex with her."

"Oh, Jesus, not you too. You're going against me too?" He takes my hand and pulls me toward him. "Don't you have feelings for me, B? I thought it was me and you?"

I push him back. I want to spit on him.

"You ruined your own life. You're in the process of ruining mine too."

His face crinkles up. He tries to go for my hand, but I slap him away.

"So you're not going to help me?"

I slam the door in his face.

39

ALI

The sign on the door says PRESSROOM on legal paper scribbled in thick black marker. The newspaper crew takes their shit seriously. This is where you come when you want the first copy. Thursday mornings. After drama class, I'd stand outside the pressroom door like a cultish doe-eyed moron to satiate my Sean Nessel fix for my collage book.

Now I need the school paper for another reason. I need them to tell my story.

Terrance is sitting on top of a large desk with his laptop. He turns to me, surprised.

"Haven't seen you here in a while, Greenleaf. We're all out of papers."

"I don't want a paper. I want to write for you, actually." I shift nervously.

"Well, you'd have to know how to construct a sentence," he says, dryly.

"I can do that." No flinching.

A girl with pink hair and cat-eye glasses who sits in the back corner of the room with her laptop looks up at me, blinks her eyes a few times, and then buries her head again, furiously typing.

"Talk to Savannah. She's the managing editor," Terrance says, and points to her.

So I shuffle to the back of the room and stand in front of Savannah's desk.

She ignores me for about a minute, and I turn back around to look at Terrance. He's still sitting on top of his desk, just staring at me.

Savannah then jerks her head up. Her eyes blink rapidly.

"I need someone to write about the school play," she says with this squeaky mouse-like voice. "Interested?"

"I want to write a column. Like an op-ed piece."

"Oh, she's got something *to say*, Terrance."

"You know what—I made a mistake," I say, backing toward the door. I'm nervous all of a sudden. It's too much. I don't have enough bravery in me to fight with these people.

"No, no. Don't leave," Terrance says.

He jumps off the desk with his laptop under his arm. His big boots clunk to the back of the room.

"What's your outrage, Ali?" Terrance says. "Tater tots? You hate them? They're too fattening? Or maybe it's the lettuce? You'd rather them use organic kale instead—"

"Okay, forget the kale. Maybe she wants the school to let the student body go off-campus for lunch," Savannah says.

"Maybe she just wants the dress code to change. She wants to wear flip-flops to school," Terrance says. "That's it!" The floor vibrates when he speaks.

I put my story facedown on Savannah's desk and write my email on the back, but I'm tempted to throw it out. I hate both of them. Savannah and Terrance and their stupid newspaper.

"My story is about rape," I say, and my heart races, thumps in my chest.

Savannah stops blinking. Her eyes open like a stuck record player. Terrance scratches the fuzz on his chin.

"And the school play? Sure, I'll do it. Just email me with a deadline," I say and walk out the door.

40

BLYTHE

I don't trust Ali will wait for me after class. I texted her a few times that I needed to talk to her, but her responses are just *K*. Nothing else. Now, I don't know where she is. I'm not used to being ignored, and that scares me.

I scamper out of class right when the bell rings and race down the hall, my boots stomping under me.

Ali's strolling out of her class, not even looking back.

"Ali!" I yell. It feels like the whole hallway turns around. People aren't used to seeing me chase someone. This will be their first and last time.

I get real close to her. Scorch her ear. "What the fuck is going on?"

"Nothing. Nothing at all," she says, defensive. Like she's got something to hide.

"Except Sean came to my house last night. He was a mess. So it's not nothing."

I lock arms with her. I'm the leader again. "Come with me. We need to talk."

In the stairwell. Bell rings. Hall is quiet. No one will see us here. And I want to talk to her. I don't want to bombard her. Make her feel attacked. I want to just get through to her. Convince her that I've been dragged into this. And haven't I been? Haven't I unwillingly been part of this?

"I was confused. I was . . . I was manipulated by Sean. You don't understand how social politics work. It's like a puzzle, and I haven't been as valiant as you. I've been stuck in this system for a long time."

She looks at me so carefully, studying me. A new air about her now. Something superior.

"Blythe, I'm going to write something about what happened in the school paper."

It takes my breath away. Like a brick in my chest. Everything swirling. My life in a stupid newspaper.

"You can't. You can't just do that."

"Why not?"

"Because people are going to have questions. People are going to look to me for answers. People see me in a certain way, Ali. I know you understand this."

"Ah, I see," she says, taunting. "You don't want people to judge you. You don't want people to know that you purposely became friends with me to convince me that Sean Nessel was a nice guy. The kind of guy who wouldn't do something so awful. Isn't that what you said?"

I'm not used to Ali talking to me this way. Wasn't I the one to show her how to walk through the hallway? The one to teach her how to stand? Her captain, her confidant. For just a little while, leading her through the crowded school corridors. Inviting her into C-wing. Now, her face angry and bunched. Her hands clenched. This is a different girl. Not the mousy Ali I first met. This is a girl out for blood.

"So you're just going to write about me and you think that'll be it? No consequences?"

"It's not about you, Blythe!"

"Don't say it's not about me, when I am a *big* part of this story. People are going to ask if I knew about it. They'll ask if Sean talked to me about it. If I tried to hide it when I should have reported it," I say, trying to slow my breath. Trying to get her on my side. The school paper. The archaic school paper. Who even reads newspapers anymore? But they have a website. It's the kind of story that'll go viral. I can see it now: *Popular Girl Covers Up Rape by Soccer Star.* "Ali, look. Don't you understand that he tricked me, just like he tricked you?"

"I don't believe that. Your eyes were wide open, Blythe."

"Oh my God, Ali. So you are going to just throw me under the bus, aren't you?"

"I'm going to tell the truth."

I have to convince her that this is not a story she wants to tell. Not like this.

"I thought we were friends," I say. I sound desperate. I sound fake. I wish I never said it.

She walks up two steps. She doesn't even turn around.

I have to think of something that'll stop her. Something that will make her think, to pause, just for a second. To be reasonable!

"You should know I'm not running the Initiation," I say. "I'm not stepping up. I'm backing out."

Finally Ali stops. Turns to me.

"Good. You shouldn't be anywhere near that. I'm proud of you, Blythe."

"You're fucking *proud* of me?"

"Yes. Because I know it's an uphill battle. And I know it must be hard to say no to those people. And I know how fucked up it made you," she says.

I take a step back. Once she was so broken. Now look at her. This self-assured girl. So self-assured that she's going to destroy everything in her path. Bring down the big man. And the lady. *Me.* She wants to punish me.

"I promise I'll make him apologize to you," I say. "He has to apologize to you. It's stupid that this hasn't happened already, in fact—"

"You don't understand," Ali says, seething now. Face-to-face. Turned to me. Back down the steps. "I don't want an apology from him. I don't want him *near* me. I wish you could just support me. And just be honest about how this all started. You could come clean. You were manipulated too. But you could say you made mistakes. It would be better."

"Better for who?"

She doesn't answer me.

I feel tears on my cheeks. I don't even know why.

"I'm the only person in control of my own destiny, Blythe. I'm the only one. You know that's my only option. You would never let anyone be in control of the story if this was happening to you. *Don't wait for them to get out of the way. Make the room yourself.* That's what you told me when you were talking about managing the stupid hallway. Well, guess what? This is my *life*."

I can see people looking at us from a lower staircase. I don't want to wipe the tears away from my cheeks because then it would really look like I am crying.

In C-wing. The Core Four. One cigarette after another.

"Don't tell Ali anything," I say. I instruct.

"What does that mean?" Suki says.

"It means she's writing an article for the school newspaper and talking about what happened to her."

"I don't want to say I told you so," Cate says.

"That's your response? That's the most original thing you can come up with? 'I told you so'?"

"Actually, it's kind of badass. To out Sean like that," Cate says.

"How insane would that make Sean?" Suki says, smiling, then looks away, inhales deep on her cigarette. "I kind of love it."

"I don't *kind of* love it. I really love it," Donnie says. "Dude gets what's coming to him, B. I'm sorry, but it's true. I have so much more respect for her now. I'll pass that paper around. I'll take screenshots of it and 'gram it until someone presses charges."

"I hate to bust your bubble," I say. "But will you *love it* when she goes after all of us? How we're bitches and how we're manipulators? How you basically slut-shamed her and how I orchestrated my friendship with her to cover up how Sean raped her? How we created a situation, an environment, so that she couldn't talk about it?"

Suki's face goes blank.

"But why would she do that?" Suki says.

"It's not like any of you were nice to her. You think she cares?" I say. "She wants to tell the whole story. That's what she told me. She said that I should 'come clean.' And trust me. I fucking begged her."

"You begged that bitch and she, what? She said no to you?" Donnie says.

"Yes." That's right. I knew that part would fire Donnie up. "The police could question me, do you understand this?"

"People will ask why you didn't report it," Cate says. Her eyes dumb and wide.

"No shit."

"You're part of the story," Donnie says.

"So are you, Donnie," I say. "So are you."

247

41

ALI

"Hurry up," I say to Sammi at her locker.

Sammi shoves her books in her bag.

"They don't scare me," she says. "The Core Four. What a stupid name."

"I know. I'm not scared of them. But after the thing that happened with Blythe today—I just don't want them doing anything. Any retaliation. They're like animals, those girls."

"Can I tell you what I'm afraid of?"

"What?"

She looks down at the ground. Shakes her knee. "That you'll still be friends with Blythe after all this is over."

Sammi's face drops, wary of the future, and I can see why. I can see how I just left her. And how that's been for her.

"I don't see my friendship with Blythe being the same."

"There was a real friendship?"

"Yes. I know it's hard to believe."

"No. I'm trying to understand. I am."

"There was something. We had things in common. Some stuff that's hard to explain."

There's this feeling, this sadness, when I think about Blythe. That conversation in the stairs—I haven't seen that desperation on her before. All the years I've spent watching her from afar and now I know her. And she knows me. The two of us share something so awful. Experiences with these boys, these men, who have done such horrible things. I don't know if I want to share that with Sammi. I don't know if I want to share that with anyone.

Sammi and I catch up to Raj, and the three of us walk down the hallway together, just like it used to be. For a second, for the first time in a while, I feel satisfied, like I can do anything now.

Terrance and his giant trench coat appear around the corner. Savannah by his side.

"I've been looking for you," he says, his voice booming, panting. "We read your story. It's really powerful, Ali."

Terrance has questions for me that are going to sound judgmental, he says. But he has to ask. Go ahead, I tell him.

Did I tell anyone right away? Yes. I told Sammi right away. I told Blythe. I told Raj. I even confronted Sean Nessel himself. People saw me run out of that party. Blythe saw me run out of that party. My story holds up.

"So there's a protocol—" Savannah says, and glances over at Terrance. She bites her lip.

"Because the school paper isn't its own entity. It's part of the school—"

"And you're writing about rape—"

"And underage drinking—"

"Wait, wait, wait," I say. I'm confused. The two of them. Explaining school codes and regulations and my constitutional rights. And none of it makes sense.

"Look, Ali," Terrance says. "Ms. Knox, our student adviser

and journalism teacher, has to look at it first. And if she looks at this story, she has the obligation to report it."

I'm stunned. My words can't even come out of my mouth fast enough, and I hear myself saying, "No. No. No." Backing away. I'm not listening. I can't hear them.

"Who does she have the obligation to report it to?" Sammi says, taking my hand. Bringing me back into the conversation. Holding me close to her.

"A number of people. The principal. Ali's parents. Maybe the police. Ali's a minor. It's complicated."

Time feels suspended. Everything stops.

"The *police*?" I say. Why would the police believe me? I went up there with him. I had collage books of him. I showed those books to Blythe. I feel sick all over again. Nothing will happen to Sean Nessel. People will just protect him like they always do. Just like Blythe has done.

"Forget it. I'm not doing it, then. Rip it up. Forget the whole thing."

I shake my hand free from Sammi's. My shoulders like blocks. The police showing up at my house, interviewing me about what happened and filing a report. At the police station. Questions. More questions. No way.

"You don't understand, Ali. We want to do it. We don't want to turn back," Terrance says. "So we have two options: We take over the paper, print the story, and say *fuck you* to the system. Maybe we'll win awards."

"But most likely we'll get suspended and they'll *still* call the police," Savannah says.

"Here's another option," Terrance says. "We can circumvent the school paper."

"How do we do that?" Raj says. His voice low, concerned. Like a dad. Like my dad.

Terrance swings his bag in front of him. Whips out his laptop. Opens it up on a cold radiator. Signals us to get in closer. Like we're a team. Like we're in this together. He shows us a home page. Red graffiti letters: *THE UNDERGROUND.*

"What is this?" I say.

"It's my zine." He smiles a goofy smile. Proud. It's just one page. And as he scrolls through the site, there aren't any stories. No photos. Nothing. It's just an empty page. With a really cool masthead.

"There's nothing in it," Sammi says, her voice slipping into that sarcastic thing she does. "Aren't zines supposed to have words?"

"We're just getting started," Terrance says. "It's got layers. It's going to be amazing. Once we get it off the ground."

"I have something to say," Savannah says. Her voice cracking a little, raspy. She's one of those people who seems to be in the background, despite her pink hair. Her cat-eye glasses. Her bright dresses. She's like a peacock that you don't want to go near or you'll get your face bitten off.

"I know that the zine isn't the same as the school paper. But it'll give you a voice. Because from what you wrote in this story, your attacker has a strong voice. And it seems to me, as an outsider, that there were a whole lot of people protecting him. I guess the question you have to ask yourself . . ." and she stares directly at me, her eyes welling up, because I don't know, maybe she has a story too? "Who was protecting *you*?"

No one, I think. Not Blythe. Not her obnoxious friends. Certainly not Sean Nessel.

"Think of the amount of people you could reach if it goes viral," Terrance says. He fiddles with the keyboard. His voice trailing off. "I know it's nothing now. But with your story in it, it could become something. It could become something meaningful."

There's a pause, and this time it feels important, like it's one of the biggest decisions I've ever had to make in my life.

"Are you ready to do this, Ali?" Terrance says to me. "Because if you're ready, this is going to be a goddamned tornado."

I think of Sean's hand over my mouth and his horrible, disgusting excuse: *I got carried away.*

I think of the blood between my legs.

I think of the bruise I had on my shoulder for a week.

I think of my father and how I'm going to explain this to him.

Everything in my body is telling me to walk away right now. To forget the article. To tell them it was a mistake. But I close my eyes. Think back to that night. Me crying on the floor. And I want everyone to know.

"I'm ready," I say.

42

"Ask Me If I Care"

by Alistair Greenleaf

It was like any other day. I was smoking in the C-wing bathroom at school when I noticed another student, Reggie. All I said was, "How ya doing?" and she proceeded to tell me how she was raped.

"Raped?" I said.

"Oh, yeah. We were both drunk at this party. I willingly went up to a bedroom with him. No doubt, I was into it at first. But then I said no, because I got scared and didn't want to go any further. Plus I was drunk and confused. And he, well, I guess I was just a body. An object."

Do I want to know this? I thought. Do I care? Why did I ask her how she was doing?

It's a simple question, just one to make the time go by when you're smoking in the handicapped bathroom, crammed in with a bunch of other girls. Four other girls were there. The kind of girls who stare down at you. Who judge you for breathing. The kind of girls who protect each other at all costs.

"There was one girl who knew about it," Reggie said. "She knew it all."

"How did she know?" I asked.

"Because the guy, you know, my rapist, told her. It was her job to persuade me not to tell. And she even had her own experience as a freshman. But her assault was sanctioned, whatever that means," Reggie said.

Now I know all this, this tale of sexual assault, and I don't want to know it!

I want to un-know it! I was just being friendly. I didn't expect her to reveal her personal life. I didn't expect her to talk about rape.

I feel bad for this girl. Rape is almost impossible to prove. The most popular kid in school? His best female friend? Their word against hers? Isn't this the exact reason why statistics show that most sexual assaults aren't reported?

Still, is this information I need to be privy to?

People walk up and down the hallways of our school and ask at least twenty times a day, "Hey, how you doin'?" It brightens their day and makes it seem like you're actually interested in their existence.

I was just trying to smoke, y'all.

"I was a virgin before this whole thing started, just a girl enamored with this boy. Made a collage book of him and everything. I'm sure it wasn't his intention to rape me, but when I said no—and I said no loudly and clearly—he put his hand over my mouth, pinned my shoulder down to the floor," she said.

I noticed the bruises on her upper arm peeking out. The marks where he must have held her down.

Oh God, why do I deserve this grueling tale? Why do I have to be left with the responsibility of knowing this?

Because I asked her how she was doing.

Have I learned my lesson? Will I take a chance and ask someone how they're doing, or will I simply nod and turn away?

The latter will probably avoid any type of unwanted conversation, but it will take me a while to get out of the old habit.

"Anyway, no one is going to believe me because he'll just say 'She wanted to do it . . .' or 'I can get any girl I want, why would I rape someone?'"

No, a simple hi will do just fine.

43

BLYTHE

It's been a few days since I spoke to Ali. Hoping she'll change her mind. That maybe she has. The two of us passing each other in the hallway like clouds. A nod. An acknowledgment. Hardly anything.

Suki sees it first on Instagram.

"There's something going around. Something about Ali," she says.

"Like what?"

"Something about Sean. Something about you."

"I told you she was going to do that school paper thing," I say. "We already knew this."

"No, B. Something else. In some trash blog," she says. Her face weighted down. Serious. "You don't even know the half of it."

In C-wing stall. Donnie, Suki, Cate, and I read Ali's article. It's published on a website. Something ridiculous called the *Underground.* Anything that can be accessed by anyone is not "underground," but that's beside the point.

"She's fucked our whole senior year," Donnie says.

"Oh, stop. Who's going to read this article? This thing? Some stupid article from a newspaper dork?" Cate says.

"Tap through to see the list of likes," I say.

"This morning it was practically nothing. Like twenty. Maybe thirty," Suki says.

We refresh Instagram. Suki's mouth open. Her hand to her lips as she scrolls down the list. And scrolls. And scrolls. "I don't know. It's a lot. It's over a thousand maybe."

I grab her phone out of her hand. "Over a thousand? Who the hell is liking this thing?"

I scroll down through the list. All the people, none of them any faces or profiles I even recognize.

"If the school finds out about this," Cate says.

"And she had to go and mention C-wing, didn't she?" Donnie says.

"She had to say there was one girl who *knew* about it. *She knew it all*. What a bitch. I didn't know about it *all*. That's not even remotely true," I say.

And I *didn't* know about it all. Did I have an idea? Yes. Did I know something bad happened? Yes. But wasn't it more complicated than that? And who was I supposed to believe? Sean, who I've known for practically my whole life, or Ali, who I never spoke to once until that night? I wanted to help Ali. I wanted to make it . . . less public. I wanted to be by her side through this. Not out the whole situation on social media.

"She could have had allies," Donnie says. "But she had to go and mention all of us."

"Give me a break, Donnie. You hated her. You thought she wormed her way in here."

"She did, Jensen. She was your little charity case. But I

could have backed her up if she had done this differently. I could have done some damage to Nessel without her even asking me. Any of us—" She looks at Suki. "Any of us would have done this for her. But you wanted to keep her close like a little mama birdie. You wanted her right there, stuffed under your wing. And now she's written something that's going viral that's going to be damaging to you."

I think of Ali and her little face. How she was always confused, squinting at me like a little nothing. Donnie's right. Ali's a baby bird. A little swallow. I took her into my world with *my friends* and she liked it. She can't deny that she liked it. That she liked being around me.

We were really friends. Weren't we?

Weren't we?

I think back to that night when Sean cried.

That girl made a mess of my jacket. She bled everywhere.

You know I would never hurt anyone. You know I wouldn't do anything to anyone.

His words drowned everything out. All I heard was his side. All I knew was *his* want. *His* pain. *His* fear. And what's been the outcome? My friendship with Ali is over. Dev broke up with me. All to absolve Sean.

But she wouldn't listen to me. The other day in the stairwell. I tried! I told her I was backing out of the Initiation. That I wasn't going to be in charge of it. And what was her response? *I'm proud of you.* Then she goes and paints me as an evil witch who tried to cover it up.

"Don't you remember how it was in the beginning, B? You

were the one who tried to convince her that Nessel was this great guy. The kind of guy who *would never do such a thing*," Donnie says.

"I tried to get her to see Sean's side. That was all. I never told her not to tell anyone."

"Yeah, and that seemed to go well."

Donnie grabs the phone from Suki. "Let's dissect this shit." She reads it like she's some Shakespearean actress.

"*There was one girl who knew about it. She knew it all. How did she know? Because the guy, you know, my rapist, told her. It was her job to persuade me not to tell.*'"

"That's called obstruction of justice, B. She's trying to get you arrested," Donnie says.

"You're being paranoid," I say. But wasn't that the same thought I had? That the police would want to question me?

"Maybe she wants some notoriety," Suki says.

"Maybe she just wanted to blow the top off everything, which I would totally back," Cate says. "I just don't know why she had to mention us."

"She didn't exactly mention *us*," Donnie says. "She mentioned Blythe. And worse, she told *Blythe's* story. Without your permission. She wrote about the Initiation, basically." Donnie reads from the paper again. "'*She even had her own experience as a freshman. But her assault was sanctioned.*' She outed you, B. Do you understand that?"

"Who gives her the right to say that?" Cate says. "She went up there with Nessel like a little fucking lapdog."

"She was half dead when B found her," Suki says.

"How did you lose control of this girl, Jensen?" Donnie smacks the gum in her mouth. Blowing oversize billowing bubbles. Waiting for answers, waiting for me to take charge. The three of them. Their eyes heavy on me.

I unravel from all my Ali Greenleaf empathy. I loosen from that friendship that we had. Raging now.

They're going to come for C-wing next. We toss our cigarettes in the toilet. Maybe for the last time. Attached to a bathroom. Isn't that strange? How can you be attached to a bathroom? But this is the end of it.

I whisper to Suki as we're walking out, "Remember everything I said before about letting go of this?"

She nods her head.

"It was a temporary lapse of reason. She can't do this to me. To us. This isn't going to be a war. This is going to be revenge."

44

ALI

In school it feels like everyone is watching me and I can't think straight. All my teachers and their words droning together. I thought it would feel better to write this. But it feels worse.

Terrance nudges me in physics. "The article is blowing up," he says, his face bright and smiling. I think about Blythe and if she's read it. I wonder what she and her friends are thinking. If the police are going to find out. I wonder if Sean Nessel's read it yet, what his reaction will be when he does. I spend most of class staring at the Instagram post, my phone tucked under my desk. I know I wanted this. I know this was my idea. But I didn't know how it would feel after. To be so vulnerable. To feel pulled in two directions like this. So ashamed and also so proud.

I drift off as Mr. Chui talks about balanced and unbalanced forces. I think about me and Blythe. He draws a boulder on the board. A little stick person pushes the rock on one side and another stick person pushes the rock on the other. I remember how Blythe squeezed my wrist at the dance. How she wouldn't let me go. And how I jerked away from her. My force, greater than hers. I always thought she was stronger. Blythe Jensen the mighty.

But it was me. I was the one. I had more strength than she did after all.

Sammi meets me at my locker before lunch. I get weepy when I see her. Like when I was a kid and I'd fall on the playground. I'd brush myself off. Hold back the tears. Pick the gravel out of my knee. Until my mother came, her worried face asking what happened, and I'd crumple in her arms.

"No, no, no. Don't fall apart now," Sammi says, wiping tears away. "You're a warrior. A goddess. Look what you did." She strokes my hair, brings me close to her. My face wet. The shoulder of her T-shirt soaked. "Look how many girls are going to look up to you. Look at what you opened up here. You outed him, dude. You're a fucking legend. Don't you feel so good? So strong?"

And I do feel it. As scared as I am, I can feel it. But I'm hesitant. "I'm not really there yet," I say. It's not about Sean Nessel. He's not the one I'm worried about. It's about her.

Because I know the blowback from Blythe is coming.

45

BLYTHE

This isn't even about Sean. This is about outing the C-wing bathroom and ruining our safe space. This is about calling me out as the girl who tried to persuade her not to tell. Wasn't I more than that? Wasn't I her friend? For all I've done for her.

This is going to be an exercise of public humiliation.

The game is: Like. Dislike. Rate.

Cate posts a photo of Donnie in her stories and over her face it says this:

Like: your reactions and emotions hahaha and you're, like, one of my besties and I lover you.

Dislike: nothing, of course

Rate: 378645272

Then she posts a picture of Ali and over her face it says this:

Like: the way you blow smoke rings because you have such a round mouth, good for sucking (lol lol)

Dislike: what a liar you are.

Rate: -4

A few hours later she deletes it. Then something new. A photo of Ali with the word *LIAR* over it. Then another photo from another account. *USER.*

A fourth photo. Of the article. The text reads: *WHEN YOU STAB YOUR BFF IN THE BACK.*

A fifth photo of the article. *WHEN YOU FLAT-OUT LIE.*

Donnie opens another account. Calls it "Greenleaf the Stalker." She posts endless photos of dead birds in black-and-white. Donnie thinks it adds a goth touch. She says it's a work of art. She tags Ali over and over.

It makes me uncomfortable. I can hear Ali's voice in my head. *What's wrong with you? How could you?*

I tell this to Donnie. That it's enough already with the dead birds.

"You're a fucking loser, Jensen," she says. "What we are doing to this girl is nothing compared to what she did to you. Did you see how many people read that thing? What she did to you is going to stick. Do you understand that? You're always going to be the girl who tried to get her not to tell. What we're doing to her is run-of-the-mill harassment. She can delete it. She can stop going on Instagram. It's dead birds. It could be so much worse, and you know it. She doesn't even have to see it. But she'll *know* about it. Because people will tell her. And she deserves to be uncomfortable. She deserves a little prodding. That's all this is. Don't think of it any deeper than that."

I have to keep reminding myself that. It's not deep. It's just a little bit of a lashing. That she brought this on herself. That she didn't have to involve me at all.

I hate feeling so conflicted. I'm not used to feeling so conflicted. I'd usually run to Dev, snuggle in to him. Listen to him tell me that everything is okay, even if it's robotic, even if it's a line he learned to say. But now I don't have Dev. I've lost him too.

This goes on for a few days. I keep waiting to hear something from Ali. I wait for her to text me to make it stop. But nothing. Not one thing. Not one apology. Not one *I wish you would understand.* Not even a mention about Dev, which I know she must have heard about. I see her in the hall, and she looks down. Refuses to even acknowledge that I'm there.

And it makes me want to strangle her. I used to think that her coldness had to do with what happened to her. But now I see that's just who she is. A cold bitch. Uncaring. Self-centered.

I want to make her squirm. I see her in the hallway and stare at her. Walking with Sammi and Raj like they're so tight. Like *I* ruined her life. Me.

A few days later, Suki makes a hate page. She's only going to leave it up for six hours. Not long enough for Instagram to flag it. They usually take forty-eight hours to take something down and send out a warning. Someone might snap a screenshot and show it to the school, but what can the school do? If it wasn't done during school hours, they don't want to have anything to do with it.

"This is a punishment, that's all," Suki says to me. "Quick and simple."

"If she goes to the police, they can get me on witness tampering, you guys," I say. I've watched *Law & Order: SVU.*

"If they were making a case against you, they would have brought you in already," Cate says. "You're being paranoid, B. She's not going to the police. Not about you at least."

She breathes into me. She wants so bad to please.

The hate page has three photos. One of Ali with a huge dick attached to her. Another with Sammi standing behind a blown-up photo of Ali. There are burning bushes in the background. They're maybe the dumbest photos I've ever seen. But Ali will be upset. Anyone would be upset. The worst is the third. Suki found a photo of Ali on my phone and stretched her mouth out with an app. Made her look like the Joker. Posted across it. *Liar. Backstabber. Jealous bitch.*

"If Ali Greenleaf kills herself," Donnie says, "we are all in deep shit."

"That's not funny, Donnie."

"Wah-wah." Donnie being her evil self. "It was just a joke."

Ali will never speak to me again after this. If she just called me once. Just begged me to end it. If she just threw the goddamned white flag and took me out of the whole story.

"So evil," I say. "Do it."

They want to come up with a grand plan for Friday night.

"Let's send the SWAT team to her house," Suki says. "Say she's suicidal and we can't get in the door."

"No, something to really punish her. Something more humiliating," Cate says.

"Words against words," Donnie says.

"Isn't the social media takedown enough?" I say.

I regret saying this immediately.

"It's sweet to see you so caring, B," Suki says.

"I'm always caring, bitch."

She carefully tucks one of her perfectly straight strands of hair behind her ear. Smooths down her sweet little green top.

"It's like a chess game. We don't want to be pawns," Suki says. "Haven't you said that to me a million times, B? Haven't you?"

Friday night. Cate's driving. We pull up to Donnie's house once it's dark. Donnie looks like shit. "Gas attack. Allergies. I don't know what's wrong with me," she tells us. But she's slurry. I can tell it's Vicodin.

"Someone at the school is going to eventually read that stupid article and shut us down. C-wing is probably my fondest memory of high school," Cate says, and opens the bottle of vodka she stole from her house. Takes a swig. Her face scrunches up. She passes it on.

"C-wing is my *childhood*," Donnie says.

"A secret club. A place we could escape from all the crap that goes on during the day," I say.

I take a swig of the vodka. The burn comes fast. I pass it on to Suki. Her little sips. Four of them. Then she passes it to Donnie.

Suki opens the window and sticks her head out. Her straight long brown hair blowing through the wind. "This is for you, C-wing!" she screams while throwing up her fingers in a peace sign as we drive.

We huddle in the wind outside Ali's house between cars.

The street is dark. She lives on one of those streets with bad lighting.

Cate goes first. White spray paint on the street just in front of the car. *Ali Greenleaf likes it up the ass.* Suki writes in hot pink on the sidewalk. *Ali Greenleaf sucks cocks.*

Donnie jumps out in front of the car so she's in the middle of the street. *Ali Greenleaf is a fucking liar.*

"Get out of the street, Donnie," I say.

"She's gonna get caught, B." Cate's whole face looks like a squished marshmallow.

"I'm going to inject you with Xanax if you don't shut up," I tell Cate.

The spray paint is so loud. The *zizzz* of it. She's writing more. Letting it all pour out. *Slut. Bitch. Liar. Phony. Stalker. Psycho.*

"This was supposed to be a quick thing. One to two minutes. We have to get out of here," Suki says. She's starting to make me nervous. *If we get caught. If we get caught.*

But that rush. That rush when you're doing something so wrong. There's a surge of it through my body. I'm breathless from it.

"How does it feel to destroy a friendship, Jensen?" Donnie says.

And I see now. How happy it's made her. Suddenly, I feel a wave of sadness. How Dev would react to this. He'd be disgusted. He'd be happy that he had broken up with me. Donnie struts back to the car. We hide behind it all together.

"Classic Jensen. Takes a rookie under her wing and then tears her wings off when the girl isn't looking."

"You're fucking evil, Donnie."

"Jensen's going to have to send her SAT scores to San Quentin instead of Stanford," Donnie whispers, smirking.

"We should get out of here," I say. But Donnie wants to do one more thing.

She stares at the house with this empty look and crawls across the grass like a Navy SEAL.

"Not close to the house, you idiot," Suki whispers. "She's got a death wish, B."

"Donnie, get back here," I say, seething.

"Just one little thing."

A light flicks on across the street. Donnie whips her head around. Her face scared now, seeing that light, and she scrambles back to the car. I open the door, wave her in, and lightly shut it behind her. Cate and Suki are already in the front. Ready to go.

"Press on the gas, Cate. Make the car go, Cate."

"I'm doing it. I'm doing it," she says, her voice cracking.

The car is, thankfully, all electric. There's no sound as she drives off.

Once we're far from the house, once it all sinks in that we're safe, that we're not going to get caught, Suki lets it all out. "I feel such a sense of accomplishment!" she yells into the night. It's that adrenaline rush. It should be a freeing feeling like after stealing a pack of gum from a store. Or like the time I stole those jeans without the security tag. You hold it all in, waiting, waiting, and then it comes so fast. At least that's what should happen.

What do I feel? I feel a void. Empty. Numb.

46

ALI

I wake up at three A.M. dreaming of bats flying out of a cavern. My mother is standing in front of the entrance inviting me in.

I sit up in my bed. It's been a week of harassment from the Core Four. From Blythe's little crew of minions. Tormenting me on social media to no end. I just keep blocking and blocking. Sammi reported one of their hate pages to Instagram.

But one goes down and another goes up. Fake account after fake account, messaging me that I've stabbed a girl in the back. That I'm not a true friend. That I'm a slut. A liar.

I ignore them. I stop going on social media altogether. Delete it from my phone. But I think about it nonstop, how much Blythe hates me. Maybe she was right. I didn't have to mention her in the article, did I? But how could I leave her out? She tried to get me to erase it all. She was trying to get me to see that he was a good person. That he just made a mistake. And that I should live with that mistake forever.

Sean Nessel *will* forget. One day someone will ask him about it and he won't even know what they're talking about. Not me. I'll always remember. And I'll always remember that Blythe was part of it.

Maybe I'm a terrible person. I can't decide.

* * *

My room is dark, the light from my laptop a blue glow. I'm searching for plane tickets to Albuquerque because I want to see my mother. I don't know if my dad's going to understand this. It's not a scheduled trip, but I feel trapped here by Blythe and her friends, Sean Nessel, even my father. Especially him, how he's been looking at me lately, like he wants me to say more and like I have so much to hide. I thought writing the article would help make me feel better, but it's still in me, all the hiding and secrets and shame. There's this nagging need for my mother. Or maybe it's just a nagging need to escape.

I reconcile it. I have to.

I walk into my father's room. Edge onto the side of his bed and whisper for him to wake up. He rubs his face and squints into the white fluorescent glow of my computer. The bed creaks in harmony.

"This better be something incredible," he says.

"I want to see her."

"Who?"

"Mom." He sits up in bed and scratches the fuzz around his chin.

"You have plans to go over spring break, honey."

"No. I mean, now. Over Thanksgiving break," I say, and I know that this could hurt him because *he* should be enough. But I spit it out. "I want to see her, Dad. I need to be around her right now."

I see it in his face. The wheels moving. He takes my computer and slips his reading glasses on to look at the prices. He does the rest quickly. On his phone. Calling my mother at one o'clock in the morning. I can hear her voice from the phone, worried. *Yes, she's saying, Yes, of course, send her out here.*

I have two connecting flights. I'm flying all day Monday. But I don't care how long it takes.

Saturday morning.

My father goes outside to get the paper and that's when he sees it. The hot pink spray paint in front of our house. The white spray paint on the street.

He's sitting downstairs waiting for me. I come down bleary-eyed and tired from too many bad dreams.

"If I could only get you out of here sooner," he says.

My neighbor has a power-washer and she's already getting the *Ali Greenleaf sucks cocks* off the sidewalk and the street. It comes off in tiny strips. Like it had never even been there.

It's like I knew. I knew they were coming for me.

That dream was a premonition. I don't believe in dreams as premonitions generally, but this one I can't deny. That I felt it. Maybe I felt Blythe's guilt.

Blythe didn't write those things, I'm sure. But she approved of it. She orchestrated it. She stood by watching. They wouldn't do anything so destructive without her.

This is what happens when you get the wrath of Blythe Jensen.

I feel sick. I'm tempted to call her. *How could you?* Part of me, and I know this is sick, but part of me understands why Blythe did it.

I couldn't just let you get away with disobeying me, could I?
Isn't that what she'd say to me?
How could I not, Ali? How could I not?

Monday. I'm flying over the desert outside Albuquerque, New Mexico. It's always a jolt flying over the desert each year. Brush, settled dust, and patches of green.

My mother is wearing a long pink skirt with bells and cowboy boots when she picks me up at the airport. Her hands stretch open, and she rests her fingers across my cheeks. "Let me look at you." Then she wraps her arms around my body. We stand in this long hug as people grab their luggage. Her bells jingle as I shift.

I climb into her car, a small used four-door. "One day I'll get the white Jeep," she says. This is what she always says. There's always an unfulfilled dream with her.

We bump along the highway for two hours through the desert with the windows open because that's how long it takes to get from Albuquerque to Truth or Consequences. The mountains that seem to line the horizon here no matter where you look are striped with ragged colors of red and yellows. Some of them are flat on top like a crew cut. Miles and miles of bramble.

My mother lives in this little peach house with a pink door. The peeling paint looks worse in the glare of the sun. The crystal blue sky. Big and wondrous. Yellow-and-white-striped fabric blocking her yard from the street hangs outside on a twig fence, blowing in the wind. Little pots of cacti and desert plants surround the front of the house.

"It's very dry, Ali. You have to drink a lot of water."

"You say this every time, Mom."

She takes my hand and leads me inside. There are all sorts of pillows strewn about. Silky, cozy-looking pillows. I sit on my knees and then stretch out.

She comes closer and caresses my head. I look up at her. Her soft hair. The way her mouth curls up when she smiles. Her deep-set brown eyes. It's like a mirror of myself.

47

BLYTHE

In school on Monday with Suki and Cate.

A girl whispers as she passes us. *Ali Greenleaf*, she whispers. Then another girl next to her, glaring at me. Faces I never noticed before. They've always been here but never looked at me like this. Not with such contempt.

Everyone is talking about the article she wrote. You can hear them talking in class. Everyone knows it's Sean. That Ali and Sean were in the kitchen at that party before they even went upstairs. They all know that I was the girl who tried to persuade her not to tell. That I was the girl who, in a stupid, drunken evening, spray-painted trash in front of her house. No one says a word, but they all know.

I cut drama class and head to Donnie's locker.

"We messed up. We were too sloppy. They're all staring at us," I say.

"They always stare at us, B."

"Not like this. They're staring at us now like they want to hurt us. Like they want to attack. Like they hate us."

"They probably always hated us. This is nothing new."

Raj comes down the hallway. Coming right for me. His face pinched, his jaw clenched. "How can you live with yourself, Blythe?"

"I was just a friend to her," I say.

"You weren't a friend to her. Jesus, is that what you think?" he says. "She went to New Mexico, did you know that? She ran away because she couldn't be here."

"Wait a second. To be with her mother? That's so—that's not like her."

"How would you know what *anything* about her is like, Blythe? You don't know a thing about Ali."

"You have it all wrong. It's more complicated than that," I say, whispering now. "I knew her. I know her. And what about what she did to me? What about what she wrote in that article. What's breaking the internet now?"

"You're pathetic," he says, and walks away. He turns his back and just goes.

"See? See what I mean?" I say to Donnie.

"How could you not have expected this, Jensen?" she says. "Of course people are going to act like this." She stares at me hard. "They don't understand. Why should they? They don't know what it is to be like us."

Us. I don't even know what that means anymore. Who are we together? Destructive and angry and resentful. Like stones. So shut off from emotions that we have no feelings of repercussion? I've done so much damage that I've pushed Ali to run to her mother. Her *mother*? The woman in the desert with the crystals and the hot springs and the AA meetings? I look up at the hot fluorescent glow from the ceiling and my eyes well up. Can't breathe. Like everything has changed right in front of me and I've lost control of it.

What have I done? *What have I done?*

Donnie takes my hands. Her forehead to my head.

"It's going to be okay, B," she says.

"No, it's not," I say. "The police are going to come after us for our little stunt. They're going to question me after they read Ali's article. We're on a sinking fucking ship. We're like the *Titanic* right now. I'm Jack and you're Rose. Just let me fucking go so I can float away in the icy tundra and die my deserving death."

She's got her hands on my shoulders now. Draws me in.

"You are Blythe fucking Jensen. You don't do self-pity. I'm not going to tell you that you're Jack. We're not drowning. We're not sinking. You're not floating on a door somewhere in the Atlantic Ocean."

"Donnie, there's probably going to be a team of police officers at my house tonight."

"Maybe you'll get lucky. Maybe she won't have even called the police. My guess, from what you told me about Ali, is that she just wanted to write her little story and now she wants to be left alone. My guess is that she's not going to do a thing because it would have been done by now."

I take a deep breath. Maybe Donnie's right. Maybe it would have happened already.

"Now we're even. She knows now that dragging you into this was wrong. Let's just leave it at that. It's over." She hugs me tight, and it feels so good. Even though her body is so thin and she feels like she's wasting away, this right now feels like me and her back together again like it was. And for a minute I feel safe.

A woman calls my name. I turn around and it's Ms. Tapestry, the school social worker. I don't even know her real name. That's what everyone calls her.

"Hi, Blythe. I'd like you to come to my office. Can you do that right now?"

"I have science . . ."

"Just tell me which teacher, and I'll get you a note."

My mind floats a million miles a minute. *Ali Greenleaf sucks cocks.*

"I have a science test that I can't miss," I say. A lie. More lies. Lies on top of lies.

"Oh—okay, well, then we can do the period after. Fourth period. Sound good?"

I nod. I don't have a choice.

"I'm going to invite your other friends too, but first I want to talk to you."

"Which friends?"

"Oh, you know, the Core Four. That's your crew, isn't it?" she says, and points to Donnie. "Donnie Alperstein, right?"

"How do you know my name?" Donnie says, defensive.

"Everyone knows you girls. Everyone."

So this is how they're going to do it. They're not going to call the police. They're going to get one of us—me, the band leader—to admit how I covered up the whole thing with Sean to the school social worker.

Ms. Tapestry is being so nice to me. Probably wants to rip my eyes out. But being fake is her job.

"I want to talk to you about what's going on with Ali Greenleaf," Ms. Tap says. She tells me to call her that: Ms. Tap.

"I already have a therapist," I say. "I've been seeing her since I was eleven."

"Okay, that's wonderful. But this isn't a traditional therapy session; this is more like talking. Because there are some problems going on in the school—you've obviously heard about some of them, like the graffiti in front of Ali Greenleaf's house, the article that's being passed around on a student's blog—and I need to talk to all my girls to find out what's happening."

I want to be defensive. I want to say that all these things happened off school property, and that she has no jurisdiction over me. But saying anything will blow my cool. I need to pretend I'm a dumb popular girl. A girl so high above it all that I have no interest in high school drama.

"So I'm one of your girls? I didn't know."

"Every girl in this school is one of my girls."

She stares at me like she's going to cut me up and feed me to the wolves. I am *so* not one of her girls. She's mama bear to the underlings. To girls like Ali. Not to girls like me.

She asks me a lot of questions about Ali. And I say nothing.

I picture Ali's face. Her brown frizzy hair. How she pouts when she's upset. How her eyes peek out from under her bangs now that her hair has grown out more. How she doesn't even need to wear eyeliner and her hazel eyes sparkle. Those long black eyelashes. "Blythe. I want to tell you that there's an official bullying specialist in the school. So you can talk to her, or you can talk to me. I will tell you this. She has different rules than I do."

I nod. I freeze up. I'm tempted to just tell her everything. Confess everything. But I have to continue this face. This apathetic face. Because this has nothing to do with me. I have to keep repeating that. Cycling it in my mind.

"She also doesn't have much of a sense of humor," she says. "So how about this? How about we schedule another session after Thanksgiving break? We can bring your therapist in here as well if that makes you more comfortable?"

No, I tell her. I'll be fine. She can ask me anything she wants. I have nothing to hide.

That night, I have an emergency session with my real therapist. I don't talk to her about what we did in front of Ali's house. I can't admit to that. I can't tell her. So I go for something easier. I talk about Dev.

"I didn't tell Dev that Sean and I kissed," I say. "We've broken up, and he's still going to hate me even more than he already does."

"So let's explore why you might make a choice like that."

Sean and the long con. So much else has happened between then and now that I almost forgot about it.

The one thing I had with Dev was trust. It's what drew me to him. It's why I stood on the side of that soccer field all that time cheering him on. Kissing his sweaty face when it was over. I miss his texts at night before bed. How close he sat next to me. How I could rub my head against him. How he listened to me. How he wanted to protect me.

I hate myself for losing him.

"People expect me to be with Dev. I expect *myself* to be with Dev. I have prom dresses picked out. There are expectations," I say.

"You keep saying expectations, which is interesting to me. What about love? What about mutual respect? I want to hear the part of you that feels torn up over breaking up with Dev."

"Wait—I don't get it. You want to hear me cry?"

"No, Blythe. I want to hear you speak about empathy. I want to hear you speak about sadness. There's a lot of acting out in your world. And there's a difference between acting out and talking out. I want to hear you say either you're going to miss Dev. Or that you did this with Sean because unconsciously you were already done with your relationship with Dev. I want to hear *feelings*."

She shifts in her chair. Moves her silvery hair off her face. She must have been so beautiful at one point in her life. And I see something else in her. This tearful look that Ali used to give me. This *poor Blythe* look. And I hate it. I'm so angry at it because everything feels so overridden with lies. Lies from me. My friends. From Ali. My parents. Sean. There are so many lies. I couldn't swat them away if I tried.

"I TALKED TO ALI— I told her things! She wouldn't listen to me!" Shaking now. Screaming. "She didn't really care about me. She used me."

She gets up and slowly approaches me so that she's standing behind me. Rests her hand on the back of my neck. Full palm. She tells me to breathe. She tells me to close my eyes.

"What's going on with you right now? In this moment."

I imagine a jungle with floating trees that reach high above me. Winds that I can barely walk through. Silvery trees. Thin limbs swaying over my head. Birds squawking, though they're not happy. They're struggling. Something is coming.

"Like I'm lost in a forest and I can't find my way out."

"The first thing you have to do is ask for help, and then receive it."

"I don't know how to do that," I say. Tears pouring down my face now. She always makes me like this. Cry and cry until I can't get anything else out of my mind. "I've been relying on myself for too long. I've been taking care of my mother for too long. I feel so alone."

She sits down in the ottoman in front of my seat and I open my eyes to her. She's staring right back at me. Her eyes bulgy, concerned, like they're feeling so much sorrow for me.

"You're so hard on yourself, Blythe. You know that? You don't have to be so hard."

"Is there any other way?"

48

ALI

My phone has only three bars in Truth or Consequences.

I text Raj and Sammi a selfie of me in the fuchsia hammock in the dusty backyard. The yellow-and-white-striped fabric blowing in the wind behind me. The sun just about to go down.

Sammi sends hearts and smiles.

It's such spotty reception out here. No bars now. And when you can't talk on your phone and you're stuck in the desert, you gaze into space. The stars are bright and enormous out here, sparkling satellites, nothing that I've ever seen before.

I want to write things down. I want to carve it into the ground with a branch from the sage bush. I want someone to read my story years from now.

I want to tell my mother everything that happened. What it feels like to have a man on top of you who won't let you go. Will I want to be with anyone ever again? Crickets chirping. Classical music streaming from someone's trailer down the road. All of it, desert sounds. My own breath hot, and my face wet from tears.

I'm homesick. I'm everything-sick. I don't want to be anywhere.

My mother appears like a vision through the curtains.

"You can't sleep out here, honey. Too many wild animals."

I quickly rub the tears away. I don't want her to see me, even in the dim light of the lantern.

"Ali? Are you crying?"

"No."

She curls around behind me, leaning into the hammock.

"When you were little, I used to do this thing to your back," and she tickles her fingers up and down my spine. "Spiders going up. Spiders going down."

My body melts as she does this. It's kind of the best feeling ever.

"Do the crack-an-egg," I say.

I close my eyes, and my mother lightly hits her fist at the top of my head, spilling her fingers across my hair and neck and down my back.

"Crack an egg on your head, let the yolk trickle down," she whispers.

In the morning, my mother and I bike over to Riverbend Hot Springs because everyone bikes in Truth or Consequences. No helmets required. I wear sweats and a bright green trucker cap that looks like it's from 1975. My mother owns a collection of hats.

We pass an orange van that's been parked there for five years. It's very T or C. People sometimes drive an orange van here and then just never leave. It's the kind of place people come to drop out of reality. People like my mother.

We ride into the parking lot, and the sign is bright blue, the same color as the sky behind the mountains. At Riverbend, the woman at the front desk is sweet and cheerful with braids in her hair and tanned cheeks. There's a sign on the door that says LEAVE WITH A SMILE.

I want to smash that sign.

I woke up angry and I can't shake it. I want to stamp on things. Even the little yellow flowers that follow the footpath to the front office. I want to bully those who have bullied me. I want to make everyone pay for it.

It's a rocky little climb down to the pool. It faces the river and mountains and we have it to ourselves.

I'm in my T-shirt and bra and undies and we dip down into the pool. The water is hot, as in 103 degrees. My shoulders release into the water. I lean my head back on the rock and stare ahead at the mountains across the river.

My mom reaches out with her foot and touches mine under the water.

"Your feet used to be so tiny."

"They're bigger now. I'm a big girl."

"Your dad told me what happened at the house, Ali. The graffiti. You gonna talk to me about it?"

But I don't say anything and my mother sinks down into the pool. Her lips surface at the water's edge. *Blub, blub, blub.* Her curls flatten out around her face.

I hoist my body up out of the water and perch on the wall. Stare at my mom. Blubbing in the pool. Taking the heat. Sammi's mom braids her hair before breakfast. She doesn't have to ask her dad to drive her to the store to get tampons.

Her mother knows exactly what she needs. And it's just there in the cabinet or next to the toilet. Magic. Sometimes Sammi will walk into her house and see her mom sprawled out on the couch and Sammi will spread herself across her mother's body. Like they're the same person.

My throat tightens, and I want to hold back all the tears that are fighting to break through, but I can't. I splash the water on my face so that they'll blend in. Doesn't matter. I can't stop crying. I hate it. I want to shut myself off. My mother lifts herself up, her skin pink from the heat, then reaches out and touches my hand.

"I could have used you around the past couple of months," I say.

"I'm just a phone call away; you know that, honey." But she sounds like a commercial.

"So you're just going to pretend like everything is great because you live in this weird little town where everyone lives in run-down houses and people blast classical music from their trailers and no one has enough money to fix an orange van on the street? It's always sunny here, right? Everything's just perfectly fine."

"Ali, what's going on?"

"I'm being real, that's what's going on."

My feet are going to explode in this water; it's so hot. I tug them out, yet I'm still panting. Steam rises into the air.

"Ali, drink water."

"Stop telling me what to do."

"I don't want you to dehydrate."

"This is not about me dehydrating! Stop focusing on me dehydrating!" I want her to see right through me so I don't have to say a word. "Because I'm the one who walks around without a mother. I'm the one who every day only has a dad to come home to. I'm the one who can't go to the mother-daughter events. I'm the one doing all this without you."

My mother takes a deep breath. Closes her eyes. "Ali, you booked a flight in the middle of the night to come here. What's happening right now? Talk to me. I feel so in the dark. Your father said there was a lot of stuff happening, but 'stuff' can mean many things. I want to hear it from you. I want you to talk to me, Ali."

"Talk to you? What else do you want me to say?"

She reaches her hand out to me and I swat it away. I would like to hit her. Hard. Harder. Like in the face. Or in the chest. But what kind of person hits her mother?

Only someone as angry and disturbed as me. Only someone as broken as me. Someone who gets raped by a guy she was totally in love with. Someone who betrays a group of girls like Blythe and her friends, who were nothing but nice to me.

Okay, so they were mostly mean. But sometimes nice!

"You don't know what's going on with my life at all," I say, and it pours out. People in other pools stare at us. And I can't stop it. My arms twist into a crazy, enraged concoction. "You have no idea what it feels like not to be able to run to you. That I can't even tell you that a boy—"

"A boy what?"

But I'm silent.

"He what?"

I twist around in all sorts of pained movements—hands to forehead, slapping palms on rock, splashing feet in water. I want to tell her so bad. I want to purge it. I'm so tired from carrying it around. It hurts. The pit of my stomach deep down; I can't hold it there anymore. It's been trapped for so long and it wants to come out. It wants to be birthed and gutted and expelled, and I can't even close my mouth fast enough before it comes out without me even having control of it.

"I didn't want to have sex with him. Even though I did. But then I didn't."

"Then you didn't?" she says. Her face trembling. Her eyes wide. Waiting for me to say it. And I don't want to say it. I don't want to say it at all.

She's staring at me still. Waiting for me. Her face. "What, honey?" She takes my hand. "Tell me, baby."

So I say it. I finally say it.

And after I say it, I glance down at the rocky bank of the Rio Grande, but the river itself isn't fast moving. It's shallow, I know, because I've been tubing in it before and I scraped my ankle across the bottom. I want to jump into it. Because now I've said it out loud. Now that I've told my mother, where will I go? Back to her tiny peach house that's falling apart? Back to the hammock?

I want to throw up.

My face in my hands. Her arm snakes around me. Her thigh next to mine. The heat. Too much heat. She hands me a cup of cold water. "Please, honey. I'm begging you. Drink."

"I want to run away," I say. "I want to run away and never come back."

"I know about running away, honey," she says. Her voice quavering. "It doesn't work. I promise you it doesn't." She whimpers an awful sound of defeat. Whispering over and over. "I'm so sorry, Ali. I love you so much, Ali. You're going to be okay, Ali. You're so strong, Ali. I'm so proud of you, Ali. We're going to get through this, Ali."

And I feel like she's talking to someone else. Someone who's not me anymore.

Down the street. I can barely walk, but I trudge through the gravel road. My bike holding me up. The sun behind us. The dust in front. Walking through it like it's nothing, like it's part of us. All that unforgiving sunshine. Not one cloud. Just the glaring sun and the blue forever. We go slow, and I tell her what happened. How it happened. About Sean Nessel. About Blythe. About the article I wrote in the *Underground.*

Back in her house, I don't know how long later. She's a good listener. She tells me she's been working on that. Listening. She rubs my temples with lavender. She strokes my hair. She kisses my tears. We sit there tangled for a while, saying nothing. She's soft. My mother is so soft.

Sometimes when I'm watching her, I'm watching myself. Her eyes. Her chin. The shape of her jaw. I have so many of my dad's mannerisms. But I'm all her.

49

BLYTHE

Wednesday, the day before Thanksgiving. All the college freshmen are coming home to rule the town. Everyone will meet up at the Sweep, the dive bar that doesn't card. The dive bar where people make out inside the antique phone booth. The place where the forty-year-old alcoholics line the barstools, in their Danzig and Megadeth T-shirts thinking it's 1996 or whenever they were seniors. When the pores on their faces were smaller. When their cheeks were less reddened. The women are worse. They glare at us with such hate. I'm surprised they don't call the cops. Most of us are underage.

I don't see Dev anywhere. Maybe he's with Sean; though the last time I spoke to Dev, it sounded like he hated both of us. I know we broke up, but I didn't expect him to cut me off completely. He won't even answer my phone calls. I find myself wanting to talk to him every day, the only rational person in my life, and now he's just gone. It's brutal. And it's all my doing.

Cate and I walk in. Donnie and Suki are catching up later.

Past the bartender, in the corner of the room, I see Amanda Shire.

A friend of hers, Satya Ferris, her *Cate*, her henchman or henchwoman, whatever, sits next to her. Obviously Satya never lost her freshman fifteen because she doesn't look like the anorexic girl I knew when I was a freshman. The girl who echoed Amanda Shire's sentiments. The girl who told me to listen up. The girl who said I should smile.

Most people see Amanda as a mythical creature. When she comes home it's like they bring out the parade floats. Amanda Shire. Sitting and flipping her hair at a dive bar full of underage kids. Maybe it was just me who saw her as a mythical creature. The weird things I noticed. Her hairless skin. Her soft blond eyelashes. How she had no trace of anything out of place ever. Even when she sat cross-legged in a bikini at Bry Jacobson's pool party. Her skin, under there, near the outline of her bikini bottom, near perfect. No shade or stubble. No red dots like I have. No ingrown hairs.

"Amanda Shire."

Her face lights up. She jumps too quickly.

"Lil sis." Air-kiss.

"What are you doing here?" I say, air-kiss back.

"I guess I just want to see who will show up. But I don't even know anyone anymore."

"That's because you've aged out of the Sweep," I say.

She side-eyes me. "You've gotten ambitious, Blythe."

I've become you, I want to say.

"Remember all those times riding for pizza instead of going to the gym at the end of school in Billy Casten's car? Remember Bry's pool parties? Remember Kramer? You were the cute little mascot. So eager to please. Such a beautiful girl so early on." She sips her drink. She orders a round of shots and passes them to me and Cate. I drink it, the alcohol burning the back of my throat like it always does. But I want to keep up with her. I want her to know that I'm not really behind her the way she thinks I am. I'm way ahead.

She passes me another shot. It goes down easier this time. My mind fills with more rage. Something easy-going and moody plays on the jukebox—the whole music collection is from the 1980s. That jukebox is like a treasure chest. It's on automatic. The owner doesn't want anyone touching it. It's the nicest thing in this place.

The words beat out like soft rockets.

My body fuzzy from the shots. I stare at her. She doesn't even look at me. Just through me. Over me. Looking for anyone. Opportunist. She's just waiting for someone to arrive. My neck stiffens. My hands squirm. All of it right here in my throat.

"I'm not leading the Initiation this year."

"What did you say?"

"I'm not leading the Initiation," I say, repeating myself, but louder this time.

"Oh, no?" Her face pinches. Her forehead stuck in irritated lines. "Then who is?"

"Hopefully no one," I say. "Hopefully not a freaking soul."

She hops off her barstool and slides in close to me. I can feel Cate next to me, her body moving in too. Her arm to my arm.

"You don't even know what goes on in half these schools in the country, do you? And I'm not talking about sexual predators who you read about in the news. I'm talking about guys you know who just ignore all the signals and pretend like everything they've ever learned means nothing. And then they feel bad the next day. They feel oh. So. Bad." She and Satya make these little pouty faces.

"You're still in high school," Satya says. "You don't even know."

"Don't you get it, Blythe? This Initiation, it was a social experiment. It's not perfect. But it worked. It worked for a reason. You don't know what it was like before we started doing it. Girls were afraid to go to parties. And I'm not talking frat parties. I'm talking *high school* parties. A girl was raped with a fucking toilet plunger," she says. "Do you not understand, Blythe? We did that to help girls . . . we helped *you*."

I snort—too loud, but I don't care. I've already done too much to turn around from here. All the humiliation from that night as a freshman turning into anger.

"You helped girls by shoving dicks in our mouths?"

She comes closer, breathes in my face. Her breath full of tequila and whatever else she drank.

"First of all, lower your voice."

"First of all, I'm not one of your sorority sisters."

I see Donnie and Suki walk in.

"Everyone wants something from you, Blythe. You might as well give it to them in advance, because that's when you have the control. Not at a party when you're wasted. Not when you're in some room with a guy all by yourself and you don't even know what's happening. When you're doing it to *them*. That's when you have the power. Don't you get it?"

"What's going on?" Donnie says, interrupting. Her body taking up space between me and Amanda.

"Your friend Blythe has gotten some things wrong."

"I doubt it," Donnie says.

"I'm not doing the Initiation. No one's doing it. It's over," I say. "That's what's happening."

"If this is going to be a thing?" Amanda says.

"There's no thing," Cate says.

"Oh, Blythe." She whispers my name like she's casting a spell over it. "Do you know he lost his virginity to me?" Amanda grabs my hand, jerks me toward her.

"What?"

"Sean. He was my little angel for a whole year. My little bitch."

Donnie pulls my other arm, trying to get me out of here.

"You and Sean?"

"That's right," she says. "Just ask him all about it."

"Amanda," someone says.

I stare dumbly, watching Amanda turn her head. It's Bry Jacobson. The infamous pool party guy.

"Bry!" Amanda squeals, brushes past me, knocking me into the bar, and jumps into Bry's arms. "I'm so glad you rescued me."

"Yeah, no one does the Sweep anymore. Everyone's jailbait here."

I feel Donnie's hand tighten as she drags me through the crowd. People stare, their faces full of hate.

Donnie turns to me just before we get outside. "How are

you going to possibly end it, B? You know these younger girls. You know they want to be part of it. They don't understand until afterward how bad it is. You cut your head off as the ringleader and someone else will sprout up in your place. You know this."

"There are ways," I say.

Dev is in the parking lot when we walk out. Surprising all of us.

"What are you doing here?" I say.

His eyes look bloodshot and puffy. Like he's been crying. His usual spark, his usual cheery face, all of it gone.

"I need to talk to you," he says.

Donnie, Cate, and Suki tell me they're going to meet me at the car. No one wants to get in the middle of this.

His face is turned inside out. "I'm so messed up in the head, B. I'm so messed up right now."

"You broke up with me, Dev. You think you're the messed up one?"

"Why did you have to start this shit between you and Nessel, huh, B?"

"Wait—I . . . I didn't start anything."

"You started it by fighting with him and tearing everything we had apart. And then the two of you? I thought we were like this." He curls up his three fingers. "And now—I can't even go out with my best friend because I don't know who he is. I don't have a girlfriend. Somehow I'm the only innocent person here, and I lost both of you. I don't want to talk to anyone. I don't want to go out. I don't want to eat. I can't sleep.

My head feels like it's going to explode. Like I'm going to die. I'm totally alone."

I get closer to him, and I can smell the sadness. His despair. It reeks through him. I just want to touch him. Hold him. But he keeps backing away from me.

"And you know what —it all trails back to you, B. Connect the dots, and it all goes right to you." He's pointing at me, angry and mean, and underneath, I can see it. He's so hurt. Wounded. "How could you do this to me, B? How could you?"

"That day at your house. You told me it was over. You haven't answered any of my texts. My calls. I've tried. I've tried so hard to reach out to you. To make it up to you." I touch his face. His scruffy face. "I didn't want this, Dev. I still don't want this. I need you. Do you understand how I need you?"

I feel sick to my stomach. I have to press my hand against the car to hold myself up. I bend down to the ground. Maybe I'll puke. Maybe it'll all come up and wash out of me.

People are staring. Some girl chants "fight, fight, fight" under her breath as she walks past with her phone out, recording the whole thing. Everything's so different now. All of us, like prey. Dev opens the door and gets in his Jeep but then stops. He turns around, searching for something in the parking lot, but nothing is there. There's just an empty, wanton feeling of dismay and sadness. Garbage piles. Old cars. Gum stuck to the ripped-up gravel.

"What am I to you?" he says. His foot out of the Jeep. One limb that I think he's giving to me. And I reach for his thigh. Rest my hand on it. Stroke his knee.

"You're the most supportive person I've ever met," I say.

"So I'm your safety blanket? That's what I am?"

"Dev—"

"Did something happen between you and Nessel?"

And I realize in this moment that whatever I say isn't going to change anything between me and Dev. He'll always wonder if something happened between me and Sean. But it wasn't just a kiss. It was the connection, however brief, that makes me more guilty. I have to tell him. I have to say it. I can't blame Sean. I can't blame Ali. I can't blame anyone but myself.

I nod my head.

"I'm a bad person, Dev. I'm rotten to the core. An awful person."

"You weren't always this way."

"Yes, I was. You just didn't see that part of me."

"I saw other things. I saw beautiful things."

The tears explode in his eyes. I reach for him, but he retracts, like I'm an illness.

He pounds his fist on the wheel. Turns the ignition in his Jeep, backs into reverse, and peels away. And just like that he's gone.

50

A L I

I'm back in the hammock again. The glow of the pink neon sign from the motel across the way lights up the street. I haven't wanted to look at my phone. Fearful of more retribution. Or I don't know what.

But I turn it on. I have forty-six new DMs. They file into my phone with a fury. Also, a text from Terrance that says: *I SENT YOU AN EMAIL; READ IT.*

Hey, Ali! How's Truth or Consequences? Is it like Truth or Dare? (My lame attempt at a joke.) Get ready to sit down. Your article went viral on Twitter. Shared over 9,000 times. The *Underground* is going to become a real paper. Like an online paper. With more articles than just three. Maybe comments too. (I don't know if I want everyone's opinions, but whatever. That's why I'm the editor! I get to shut the comments off when I want.)

There are a lot of people talking, Ali. I heard what happened at your house. But your article did something. A lot of people are really upset. And not just in our school. You've reached people. They heard you. I hope you know that.

Anyway, I have some other news. There are tons of other girls writing to us about how they had the same shitty experience. They want to talk to you. They want to hear more from you. And I want to hear more from you! I think you're a rock star. You should probably also look at the comments on the *Underground*'s Instagram feed. They're really supportive.

See you when you get back.

—T

I scan all the comments on Instagram where he posted it.

This sounds real.

I wish she would out the guy.

She had bruises on her arms just like me.

She sounds scared. I understand. I see his face every time I go to my school.

He said "she wanted to do it"—I've totally heard that.

This sounds like my life, and now I don't know what to do.

I'll never be over it.

I call my mom over. Show her everything. Give her my phone, shaking. The air is so still tonight. I can hear myself breathe. She pulls me out of the hammock. Brings me inside. My hand in hers.

We sit down together, sink into her sofa. She's close to me. Stroking my arm. My fingers. Her sniffle, choking up.

We read through comments and more comments and more. Hundreds of stories from hundreds of girls my age. Women my mom's age.

It's the first time that I really miss my dad. He's always around, so I never have to miss him. But he reacts. When he sees this, he's going to emote. He's going to be upset. I'm not ready for that yet. My mother is more quiet. She's what you'd call an *active listener*. My father is more like an *active interrupter*.

It feels like hours. My mom and I sifting through sexual assault articles. Organizations. Websites. Survivor groups. Countless affirmations. An overflow of relief washes over me. That I'm not alone. I didn't know how much was out there. I didn't know.

We end up on a website filled with photos of women holding up signs. They've all been raped. And their signs are quotes from their attacker.

Attacker.

I never thought of Sean Nessel like that. As an attacker. But he attacked me. I was attacked.

These girls and women (and a few men). Different body shapes and sizes. They cover their faces. Their signs are handwritten. The cruel and careless words they hold.

I think of what my attacker said to me.

How are we gonna clean all this shit up?

I scroll down through some of the signs. The words blare out like bloody screams.

One woman with long blond hair and a peaceful smile. She

holds a large sign with perfect handwriting. You can only see her smile. It's a lot like Blythe's.

I don't want to think about Blythe.

The girl's sign says: *Sorry about that. We're cool though, right?*

Her caption underneath: *What my attacker said after I told him that I had said no.*

I scroll down to another woman with super-short hair and tiny glasses. She's wearing overalls and has a smiley-face T-shirt on. She looks young and kind of reminds me of Sammi.

Her sign says: *Oh, hey, I remember you.*

Her caption underneath: *What my attacker said when I went up to him at school two days after he forced himself on me in a bathroom at a party. We were both drunk and I couldn't stop him.*

"We don't have to keep going, Ali. This is a lot, honey."

"I don't want to stop." I want to read them and read them until my eyes burn out. Until their words are seared into my mind. Until I've read every single one of them.

"I know. But how many of these can you read in one night? I don't want you to— You're so fragile. I don't think you realize how fragile you are." I turn toward my mother, who is crying. "You don't have to stop. I'm just saying to take a break. Give yourself time to digest this."

"I feel like if I don't read it all now, it's going to disappear. That I have to just infuse it into me. Does that make any sense?"

"Ali," she says, a deep sadness in her voice. "This isn't going anywhere."

I always wished my mother was more like Sammi's mother. Cooking and cleaning around the house and listening to old records. Making lasagna on Sunday night. My mother's a person. A human. With flaws. She's real. She's herself. She lives in a peach-colored shack in the middle of the desert.

I think of Blythe again. One day she'll be sitting alone, wondering what happened to the real friendships in her life. What happened to the Devons and the Donnies and the Sukis and the Sean Nessels. She'll wonder why it was so hard for her to please all of them. Why what she gave them wasn't enough.

"I'd like to come back to New Jersey with you if you want me to," my mom says.

But that's not what I want.

I want to be one of those girls with the sign.

I want to be the girl who says what's been done to me. To record my story. Without anyone holding my hand. Just me. And my sign. My story. My words.

I lean into her, my head on her chest, and she strokes my hair. "I just want to be whatever you need from me right now," she says.

But this is all I really need right now. Just this.

51

BLYTHE

I'm headachy and feel like I'm going to puke. But Donnie wants to go up to the old cliffs. She says it'll get my mind off things. And she's meeting someone up there. A new friend named Dylan. Donnie's secret life.

She curls her fingers like she's a witch. She's wearing these long silver rings; they look like body armor against her slight hands.

"I have a crystal ball. I know everything."

This is the moment I miss Ali. This is the moment I wish I was friends with someone normal. Someone like her. Someone who doesn't search out drama. But I destroyed that friendship with Ali. I destroyed my relationship with Dev. I destroy everything.

The four of us go in Cate's car. The Core Four.

"We're all together," Cate says, singing. But it drifts off into the night.

We crawl under the gate to hike up to the old cliffs. My shoes slip over the rocky path. This dirty place, with all its boulders and its shaky ground and its cliffs, used to be the place to hang out. Under the dark lights we could be whoever we wanted to be. Now it's gated with trespassing signs. Much smaller crowd. Hardly anyone wants to attempt the climb after some kid broke his leg last year.

Donnie pulls my hand, leads me up the hill. Dylan, she keeps saying. She wants me to meet Dylan. Dylan's waiting for her on the edge. And that's where Donnie wants to be. On the edge.

She sits cross-legged on a boulder in front of Dylan, who is too skinny and too ratty-looking. Long dirty hair and brown moccasin boots. He probably gets her Vicodin. I don't bother to ask.

I slide up next to Donnie. Curl into her. Like we used to at parties. It's been a long time since it was like that. Pretend like we're here together. Alone.

"Everything's changed so much, Don. Why has it changed so much?"

"Because we're human. We evolve. You don't see that, B? You want everything to be the same. You want to be a Polaroid? You want to be a trophy? A stuffed deer on a wall? People have to experiment. We have to open our hearts to new ways of thinking."

There's a little packet of crushed-up vikes in her palm.

"I'm not doing that," I say.

"Why? You've done everything else like it before. If you do it, you'll see the way the stars line up. And we can do it together. Me and you together forever, B. You'll forget about all the other stuff with Dev tonight. It'll make all the bad stuff go away."

"I'm not sticking that shit up my nose."

"You've swallowed it before. It's just a different high, snorting it."

I push her hand away.

She rolls her eyes and closes her hand, shoves the packet back in her jacket pocket. Zips it up to her chin.

I want things to be the way they used to be. How we used to fantasize about throwing people in the black hole, the joke we used to have when we were little. People who were mean to us went into the black hole. They'd disappear in there, fly in a circle, their arms raised and desperate.

"Don't you just have a vape pen? Can't you keep it light?"

But Dylan says that vape trash will kill you. And Dylan has two joints. Because Dylan likes it old-school. He'll only smoke flower, he says. I hate people like Dylan. I don't know how Donnie can stand him.

I try to catch her attention, her face; I just want to see her. Make eye contact to signal that I'm done here. That we're done here. But she's somewhere else, her dark curls shielding her face. Then she hops up, stumbling, claps her hands to a cheer we made up freshman year.

"Five-six-seven-eight! Roll-a-joint! Roll-roll-a joint!" Then she spins. Shaking my arms. Trying to get me to sing along. "How-you-think-you-roll-that-joint? Come on, B, sing it with me. Roll-a-joint! Roll-roll-a-joint!"

I laugh and look away. I just want to get out of here. That's all I want to do.

But Dylan rolls the joint and passes it along. There's a circle of us now. Cate. Two of Dylan's friends.

Me, Suki, and Cate look at one another. Shake our heads. None of us takes a hit from it. Who knows what's in it. Dylan pulls something out of his pocket, then squishes himself between me and Donnie. And they hover over it together, snorting it up their noses.

Suki gives me a look. She shakes her head. Mouths *Let's go*.

Donnie's eyes get soft and hazy. She tosses her head back. Tired, euphoric? I don't know anymore.

"They're all gonna OD and we're going to have to drag them down this mountain to a hospital," Cate says, whispering. "This is like a very bad Lifetime movie."

She's right. Cate is totally right. They're all going to die.

I know Donnie's here, and I know she's my best friend and I'd do anything for her. But I'm not staying.

Donnie crawls over to us, her jeans dragging through the dirt. Her brand-new white sneakers, filthy. Her hands in the gravel like she's some wild creature. Then she looks back at Dylan, still on all fours. He's more wasted now than I had realized.

"Sometimes you have to start something to get things started," he slurs, and I don't even know what that means.

"You should just tell him everything, B. That's what I do. I just tell him everything," Donnie says. She's practically salivating. I lower myself down to her.

"I want to take you home with me. I don't want you to do anything crazy."

But Dylan's talking louder now. In the center of us. Babbling about the moon and stars. He won't shut up. Then he blurts out: "I read Ali Greenleaf's story online. That girl goes to your school."

My hands feel numb, like all the blood is rushing to my fingertips. Like the night was awful already. And now it's just delved into hell.

"You're high. You don't know what the fuck you're talking about," I say.

"But you know I do," Dylan says, too confident. "I know all about it."

"He doesn't know shit, B. Look at him. He's in space," Cate says. "Let's get Donnie and get out of here."

"Some girl got raped and you guys tried to take her down," he says. "I read it. I know it's about you."

I give him the finger.

Donnie grabs my leg. She's still in the dirt. "We shouldn't have done what we did. I told him all about it."

"She's wasted again, B. Don't listen to her," Suki says. "How many times have we gotten you out of a mess this year, Donnie? You always go too far. Just shut up."

"Stand up," I say, grabbing at Donnie's arms, but she's hitting me away, fighting me. "We're taking you home. Stand up."

"Remember when it just used to be us, B?" Donnie is saying, stroking my thighs. Kneeling below me. "Remember when it was just me and you? And none of these hangers-on . . ." she says, holding on to my thighs, because if she doesn't she'll fall. I take her arms. Support her. "Why did you need anyone else but me? Why did you need Sean? The way you followed him down that hole? And who did it lead you to? Ali Greenleaf? And then you followed her, crushed on her, and let go of me.

Couldn't you have liked me the way you loved Ali?"

My hands over her cheeks. Pleading with her, her thin body still kneeling in the ground. "I love you, Donnie. What are you talking about? I love you. That's why I'm here. That's why I'm begging you to come home with me."

She raises her body up slowly, painfully, holding on to my hands, like she has weights on her shoulders. One foot in front of the other. Her hands out. Balance.

And like a snap, a quick snap. She's got no floor. "Catch her, catch her," Cate is screaming. Donnie's face pale and greenish. She's on the ground face forward in the dirt. All her beautiful curls floating. I shake her, screaming her name.

"What is she doing, B? Turn her over!" Cate screaming. Like *I* know. Like *I'm* in charge here.

"Don't turn her over," Dylan says, but it's more like a whisper from a ghost. He's sitting in the dirt. His head rocking between his knees. "That's how Jimi Hendrix died. Choked on his own puke. Just leave her. I'll take the princess home. She's just nodded out. Prop her on her side."

I've done pretty awful things in my life. But I've never left my best friend with her face in the dirt in the middle of the night.

"How are we going to get her down, B?" Suki says. Her face struggling for an answer. "She's gonna die, B."

I hiss for her to shut up.

"Suki, you're going to take her head and shoulders, and Cate, you're going to take the middle. I've got her feet and legs."

We hoist her up, and she's so bony yet so heavy. Suki screaming in Donnie's face. She's still breathing. She's still there. My face is wet with tears. We're shaking her as we make our way down the hill.

"All we need to do is get to the car. That's it. We just need to get to the car."

We stretch her out in the back seat of the car, pulling and unfolding her limp body. All of us breathing heavy. Checking her pulse like Nurse Chiltarn taught us in health class.

"This seems like a long time for her to be out, B," Cate says, panting. "This just seems like a really long time."

Suki leans over Donnie's face and shakes her. Hard. "Wake up, Donnie! Wake up, Donnie, you idiot!" Then right in her face, her mouth so close to hers. "We are taking you to the hospital! Can you hear me!"

Donnie opens her eyes.

"You're not taking me to the hospital," she says. Coughing, her eyes blinking as if she's trying to focus but she can't.

Suki starts crying. Really crying. Rolls off Donnie and crawls backward out of the car. Sits on a rock.

My eyes are closed. Listening to the hum of Suki's cries. She's in the car now. Up front. Shotgun like she always wants. I'm in the back with Donnie on my lap and I feel us moving. The windows are open. Like it's any other night. Like it's the four of us just cruising.

But everything is different now. We all know this. That none of it's the same.

"Take me somewhere easy. I just want to go somewhere easy," Donnie whispers.

If only there was such a place.

I fold over her chest. Surrender to the night. Suki twists her body back to me and reaches her hand out to grab mine.

"You know when you just have no more left?" Donnie says, licking her dry lips.

"Yes," I whisper.

"It's like that."

"I know," I say. "I know."

52

ALI

It's on the plane back to New Jersey that I decide to report what happened to me. I don't know what clicked. I think it was the thought of Sean Nessel getting his Christmas presents and feeling relieved, like the worst part of his life was finally behind him and how did he get so lucky to escape it? I imagine him sitting there like a child who got everything he wanted from Santa and how maybe he'd go off to college and do the same thing to other girls that he did to me. How easy it would be for him.

That's when I decided that I didn't want to make things easy for him. I saw way deep into the future, where one day someone like Sean Nessel would exist as a powerful figure, in charge, making decisions. Where his past would completely escape him. Where rumors would be dismissed as teenage antics because nothing was actually on the record. This doesn't mean that this is the right choice for everyone. But right now, this feels right to me.

That night. Home with my dad. I explain it all to him. My nose wrinkles from the smell of my words. Ever have that happen to you? Your words stink so bad that you can smell it— It's like that awful rotten-egg stink.

My father whimpers an awful sound of defeat. He looks

around the room. Sits on his hands. Scrubs his hair. He is not ready to process this. I try to hold it together for him. My tears would just make it worse. I'm going to be okay, Daddy, I want to tell him.

I show him the article. I want him to see how people responded to me, all the supportive comments.

"You wrote this?"

"Thank Sheila the She Woman," I say. "I went Deep Throat."

He laughs until he cries. My dad rests his head on my shoulder and leaves it there like that for a minute. "I don't want to let you go. Ever."

Everything is going to change.

53

ALI

Your dad calls the police station, and they say they can come to your house in about a half an hour.

Two women. One is named Phyllis. Phyllis looks like a mom. She has that mom haircut, short on the sides, slightly longer in the back. Phyllis is from the county's Rape Crisis Center. The other is Detective Bolero. She's from the Special Victims Unit, yes, as in SVU, and you almost bust out laughing because it makes you sound like you're on television.

These women don't laugh, and they don't think your self-deprecating jokes are funny.

Detective Bolero is nice enough, her voice calm and low, and she asks you questions while you sit there with your dad. You become someone else. Someone else who has to tell your story to strangers. About your crush. About drinking at a party with a boy you don't even know.

You have your notepad with you. They ask you what you're writing, and you say you're a journalist. That you want to document this. They tell you it's good to write things down, but they don't really mean it, do they?

Now Phyllis talks. That's when your dad walks out of the room. Phyllis is so sorry this happened to you.

"Can you help me understand what you're able to remember about your experience?" Phyllis asks.

You don't feel like you're able to tell her any of it. You don't want to tell her any of it, ever.

But you do. That's why they're here.

"Tell me what you need, Ali," she says.

Yet you can't. You keep thinking about what Sean Nessel said to you on the field a few weeks ago.

So that's what you tell her. Not about that night. Not about what happened in that room. You tell Phyllis that on the field, in the bleachers, you confronted him.

"What did he say?"

"He said he was sorry for getting carried away."

"That must have been a really traumatic moment for you."

You close your eyes. You don't want to do this. You're away now. That's all you want to concentrate on now. Being far away.

Phyllis hands you a tissue. She wants to know if you feel safe in school. If you feel threatened. But surprisingly, you don't.

That's when you tell her about that night. And Phyllis tells you she believes you.

Your dad walks the detective and Phyllis to the door and you tremble. It's a vibration that you only feel from the inside, and you hear a low ringing in your ears. You close your eyes to get it to stop, but it's still there, humming away across your arms, up at the back of your skull. Your father says something to you, tells you what might happen next, but you don't hear a word he says. He takes your hand. But you don't want to hold hands.

You don't want anyone to speak to you. To touch you.

54

ALI

The next day. I'm scared to go to school, but I'm also scared to stay home. My dad wants to homeschool me. He wants to lock me in a room and keep me safe forever. I practically have to beg him to let me go.

At school, Sammi right next to me, I open my locker door and about ten notes topple out. They float to the ground like valentines. I look around the hallway. I guess they're notes from Blythe and the Core Four, more slut-shaming left over from before I went to T or C.

But then I open the first one.

> *Ali,*
>
> *I was raped by a junior at another school just a few months ago. He told me if I would just relax, I would enjoy it. I've been walking around holding it in for so long. I'm not sure if your article is real or not, but either way, it doesn't matter. It gave me the courage to talk about this. Thank you for that. Thank you, thank you, thank you, and I'm sorry that you had to go through your experience just so I could talk about mine.*
>
> *—Rachel, a freshman*

I look around the hallway, clutching the note in my hand. There are faces everywhere, people I've never even noticed before, who now are staring at me for long periods of time. Like they want to talk to me and bare their soul. Or want to hit me in the face.

I pick up all the notes. And I don't know what to do with them. There are too many to read, Sammi says. It's too overwhelming and not healthy and I don't need that right now.

"I have to read them," I say. "They wrote to me in confidence."

"Let me do it, then. I'll read them all. One by one. I promise."

It's later that night and Sammi calls me. She read through them all. But there's one that she wants to tell me about. It took her by surprise. It's from Blythe.

"I was going to chuck it in the garbage, you understand that, right?"

"I do."

"But I thought it was the right thing to tell you. She sounds sincere. Though who knows with her. I still hate her, you know that, right?"

"I know," I say. And then she reads it to me.

Dear Ali,

I know you might rip this up once you realize it's me. I might rip it up too if I were you.

There's no forgiving me for what I've done. I made some really bad choices. Choices! How absurd for me to use that word, choice. I did awful things. I did things that I can't excuse.

I don't know if you'll ever forgive me, but I'm deeply, deeply sorry.

You were one of the truest friends I've ever had.

I'm so moved by what you wrote that I think I wanted to lash out at you for it. I was so embarrassed about my part in it. So ashamed that I was manipulated by him too. I lost control, and I never lose control. My therapist says that I was angry at myself for trusting him, for trying to take care of him, and I wanted to take that out on you. (I know it's ridiculous to mention my therapist in this apology letter, but if I'm going to come clean, I have to give her credit.) I was so jealous of your ability to stand up for yourself. I've only been able to do that by pulling other people down. Isn't that tragic?

Anyway, I'm writing to tell you my story because I saw that other people were writing you too. I saw them putting notes in your locker. So many girls! And I asked them what they were doing.

Sharing stories, they told me.

I have a story too.

It's about the Initiation.

I'd like to go public with it. Maybe something for the Underground? Maybe something that would call attention to it? So it could finally stop. Maybe you could help me figure out how to do that. I'm not much of a writer. I wouldn't know the first thing to say.

Maybe we can talk.

Maybe I can apologize to you. You don't have to forgive me.

—B

55

BLYTHE

I know Ali's schedule, so I sit outside her last period class. Everything feels blurry. The whole thing like a bad dream.

I keep thinking about what my therapist said. That I wasn't present in my life. That my ego took over. But mostly it was rage, she said. That I've had rage buried for years. About my mom, my dad. About the Initiation. Sean. I have to work on my rage.

Donnie says Ali's never going to forgive me, and why should she? Why does she need me as a friend after what I did to her? But I have to see for myself. I have to try at least. I have to *at least* see Ali's face. Donnie won't have much to say for the next three months anyway since after that last incident at the cliffs, her mother sent her to rehab. Who knows if she'll even come back to school.

Me, Suki, and Cate decided to quit drinking even if it's just for a month. I need to get clear. I need to understand myself. To grab hold of my life.

Ali's last out the door. And then she sees me.

Everyone walks past me. Because that's what people do now. They pass me like I'm a ghost. Like I don't exist. Maybe I like it. Maybe I don't want to be the center of attention. I don't want people to admire me. I don't want people to bow down to me. I'm not a good person. They all know this about me already. They sneer. And I take it. It's part of my punishment.

Ali walks over to me. I don't even have to chase her.

"How was Truth or Consequences?" I say.

"What do you want, Blythe?" she says, sharp and cold.

"I fucked up," I say. "I was so mad at you. I was so angry. So jealous of how strong you were. How strong you are. I wanted you to hurt the way I was hurting. I was hurt for irrational reasons. I thought you owed me an explanation. I thought you owed me coverage. I didn't think about you. I only thought about myself."

"It took my neighbor two hours to power-wash that shit off my sidewalk."

She hovers over me. Like she may kick me. And I'd deserve it.

"I understand if you never trust me again. I'm not a good person—and I'm not saying this because I want you to be, like, 'No, B, you're a good person. You're a great person, B—'"

"For one, I've never called you 'B.'"

"True. True."

"And I would never let you off the hook like that."

My face just melts a bit. I can feel it, isn't that odd? It just falling down, my mouth turning into a deep pout. The corners of my lips tightening.

"I don't know what to do." I cover my face with my hands. "I'm so embarrassed for the way I acted. I'm so ashamed."

I can't even look at Ali. I can't lift my hands up without all that horror.

"I can't make this better for you," she says.

"I don't expect you to."

I wipe my wet face. She stares at me carefully. Waiting.

"I think your story is worth telling if you want to tell it. You mentioned that in your letter. About the Initiation. You can talk to Terrance. Pitch it to him for the *Underground*. But it's not going to be easy. Because people are going to look at you."

"They already look at me, Ali." I pause. I want to hold on to this moment. I have so much more to say to her. About Sean. About Donnie. About Dev. About how awful I feel. How low and detached I feel. That maybe they should put me in an institution after this. Maybe they will. "Can I walk with you?"

Ali's mouth just opens. She can't contain the irony. And she finally smiles. Not a real smile. More like a smirk.

"I have rules to you walking with me."

"I'm sure you do," I say, smiling. The first time in weeks. Smiling because of Ali. She really does make me smile. "I'm sure you do."

The hallways after school have this lingering stink of bodies, all of us crammed in here day after day. But if you stay long enough, about an hour after everyone leaves, there's this fresh breeze that sneaks through as people open and shut the doors.

The few people who are left stare at the two of us together. I am a pariah.

I pretend there's an arrow on the floor, a neon arrow that says *start here*, and I follow that. Hold my head up. Keep my posture up. That's all I can do.

56

ALI

It's right before winter break. A dusting of snow on the ground. Everything so white and crisp. Blythe walks into Ms. Tap's sexual assault group with me.

There are about ten girls in the room and they glare at Blythe. They are not happy Blythe is here. Anyone can see that. They don't care that she did community service for spray-painting my sidewalk. She and Suki and Cate. They don't care that she spoke to the police about Sean Nessel. That she's being cooperative in the investigation. That she's going to testify in front of a grand jury even though he gets to walk around free on bail until the investigation goes in front of a judge. Raj thinks he's going to have to go to community college because no school will take him now. I say he takes a gap year. Makes it look intentional.

Blythe has come completely clean. After her article in the *Underground* went viral, she told the police all about the Initiation. I heard she went into the police station by herself. No parents. No friends. Just her and a lawyer.

Amanda Shire was charged with endangering the welfare of a child, a sexual hazing ritual, and a conspiracy to commit aggravated criminal sexual contact. But it doesn't seem fair that a girl, a woman now, should take the fall for all that.

Even someone like Amanda Shire. She didn't do this on her own. The Initiation might have been her brainchild, but she needed help implementing it.

At first, people didn't even seem outraged about the Initiation. They said, *It was so long ago.* That girls like Blythe and Donnie agreed to be in that room with those boys. No one held their heads down. No one chained them up. No one sat on top of them. It wasn't a gang rape. Alex Kramer, the guy Blythe was paired with, saw it as a hookup. That's what he told people. Nothing more. He's planning to go to law school now, someone told Blythe. This kind of thing will ruin his life. Someone said that to her without irony.

But then a reporter at *The Star-Ledger* who read Blythe's article in the *Underground* wrote a front-page story about the Initiation. That fourteen-year-old girls were giving oral sex to eighteen-year-old athletes. That eighteen-year-old girls orchestrated it. There was an emergency school board meeting. Just the other day, I saw an article about it on CNN.com. *Dateline* is doing a story now. A letter went out from the superintendent.

Still, people want Blythe to pay. These girls in Ms. Tap's group watch her carefully. Their eyes heavy, staring at her. They don't understand how I could even talk to her after what she did. How I could forgive her. And I don't forgive her. I don't see it that way.

"Thanks for letting me sit next to you," she whispers.

So much of what she and I have been through feels so

far away. Maybe we were different people then. Maybe now, we're more stripped down. Like we're meeting each other for the first time.

I look at her and wonder if I know Blythe. Really know her. I don't, of course. The Blythe I knew wouldn't have sat in this room. A room full of girls with stories to tell. A girl whose cousin molested her at six years old. A girl whose boyfriend held her down. A girl who woke up naked not knowing what happened. There's a girl from last year's Initiation here too. There will be more girls like Blythe here.

Ms. Tap wants to see me after the session. Blythe walks out by herself. She waves to me. I wave back. There's nothing more than that.

Ms. Tap takes my hand. "Ali, I just want you to know that this is one of the proudest moments of my life, being around you. That knowing you has changed me so much." She starts to cry. She makes that weird guffaw sound when you're trying to suck in tears.

It hurts to hug her, because no one wants to be *the girl who changed everyone*. It's too much weight. I would have liked to be the girl who did nothing all year. The invisible girl. The girl with a collage book filled with pictures of a boy she didn't know shoved under her bed.

On the wall, a shadow. It's like someone is making bunny ears in a film projector, except this is more triangular and pointy. It floats back and forth like a chime. It's three little paper planes hanging from the ceiling.

I reach up and touch one of the wings of the plane. It dangles back and forth in this easy way in this innocent place with paper planes and goofy stuff that childhoods are made of.

In the hallway outside Ms. Tap's room, Sammi sits on the floor, leaning against the wall, waiting for me.

"I saw Blythe walk out."

"We don't have to talk about her."

"No, I think it's good if she can be real." Sammi waits. Thinks about this. "Can Blythe Jensen be real?"

"I don't know. Honestly. I don't know."

I look through the rectangular windows out onto the soccer field. The season is long over.

"It's hard for me not to still hate her."

"I know," I say. "Do you mind if I don't hate her?"

I know this sounds weird to Sammi. I know this would sound weird to anyone after what she did. But something in Blythe changed.

"Oh, I know you can't hate her," Sammi says, laughing. "Maybe you'll love her, hate her. But you'll never just *hate* her, hate her. I've accepted that already."

I want to say a lot more. Defend myself. Defend Blythe.

But I don't want to talk about Blythe anymore. I want to clear her from my head. Stop dreaming about her, what it was like when we were so tight. What it meant to me. How she made me feel.

I lock my arm in Sammi's the way we used to when we first came to high school in the ninth grade.

We walk past the gym. The basketball players and their squeaking sneakers over the court. Past the gym door until we can't even hear them. Just an echo of their voices. And as we walk farther away, through the big doors leading out to the parking lot, Sammi unlocks her arm from mine and throws her arm over my shoulder. It's a gray day, but that doesn't really matter because some days are just like that.

RESOURCES

If you or someone you know has been sexually assaulted:

National Sexual Assault Hotline
800-656-HOPE (4673)
Trained staff members are available 24/7.

Rape, Abuse & Incest National Network (RAINN)
www.rainn.org

National Sexual Violence Resource Center (NSVRC)
www.nsvrc.org

#MeToo Movement's Healing Resource Library
metoomvmt.org/healing-resources-library
Find resources and organizations near you.

#GirlsToo
girlsinc.org/girls-too
Girls Inc. provides safe spaces for girls to speak out about their experiences.

If you or someone you know has substance abuse issues:

SAMHSA's National Helpline
1-800-662-HELP (4357)
www.samhsa.gov/find-help/national-helpline

This is a free, confidential, 24/7, 365-day-a-year treatment referral and information service (in English and Spanish) for individuals and families facing mental and/or substance use disorders.

Shatterproof
www.shatterproof.org
Shatterproof is a national nonprofit organization dedicated to reversing the addiction crisis in America.

If you or someone you know is struggling with depression or anxiety:

National Alliance on Mental Illness (NAMI)
nami.org
NAMI provides advocacy, education, support, and public awareness so that all individuals and families affected by mental illness can build better lives.

Crisis Text Line
www.crisistextline.org
Text from anywhere in the United States, Canada, or the United Kingdom to connect with a trained crisis counselor. Every texter is connected with a crisis counselor, a real-life human being trained to bring texters from a hot moment to a cool calm through active listening and collaborative problem solving.

AUTHOR'S NOTE

I was on my way to attend Rebecca Traister's event at the New York Public Library for her book *Good and Mad: The Revolutionary Power of Women's Anger* when I found out that Razorbill was interested in publishing my book.

Only five days earlier, Christine Blasey Ford testified about being sexually assaulted at a high school party by a young, popular, very smart, and very drunk Brett Kavanaugh. The hearing was still fresh in my mind and had affected me as it had many women across the country. I was outraged.

I watched Justice Kavanaugh and his spitting anger and defense and was shaken by the similarities to the rapist in my book, the "beatific" Sean Nessel. The characteristics fit a certain type: privileged, arrogant, sexist bullies and predators.

But it was the moment Dr. Blasey said that Justice Kavanaugh had covered her mouth, held her down, and tried to pull her clothes off in a bedroom upstairs at a party that I realized Sean Nessel was eerily similar to Brett Kavanaugh. I could see Sean Nessel on a similar path forty years from now, angry and confrontational, in denial, actively lying about his past, and on his way to becoming a Supreme Court justice.

When asked what Dr. Blasey remembered most about the assault, she said this: "Indelible in the hippocampus is the laughter, the uproarious laughter between the two. They're having fun at my expense."

It's important to know that not every sexual assault survivor remembers all the details. Traumatic memories can be fragmented and fuzzy, with survivors vividly remembering certain images, but not, for instance, the time of day.

I had started writing *Something Happened to Ali Greenleaf* about twenty years ago. It began as a short story about a girl who was raped by the most popular boy in school. After the incident, she took a shower and held her feelings in, telling no one. I had never really understood why I wrote it. *This isn't me*, I'd tell writers in workshops who'd read it. I'd assure them, *Oh, no. Not me.*

It took me years to realize that this story was an outlet for my own experiences that were too difficult to talk about or too painful to understand.

I lost my virginity to a boy in my college dorm room who refused to let me go until I told him, "Fine, just get it over with." I've never forgotten how I told him the blood he saw was just my period and how I escaped to the bathroom, trying to wipe it all off. I've never forgotten how that boy, the same year, raped my friend while she was incapacitated on psychedelic mushrooms.

I'll never forget walking into a room at a high school party where an intoxicated friend was sprawled out in a dark bedroom, unconscious, as seven boys stood around her, groping her body. How one of those boys shamed me for being a "party pooper" when I stepped in and dragged her out of there. How a tailor taking in my prom dress went in for a feel on my breast. How, when I was sick with the flu at nineteen years old, a male doctor told me that I needed to take my bra off because it was the only way he could really listen to my heartbeat.

Here are the statistics: Younger people are at a higher risk of sexual assault. Females ages sixteen to nineteen are four times more likely than the general population to be victims of rape, attempted rape, or sexual assault.[1]

I was a high school senior in 1989 when the Glen Ridge, New Jersey, rape case hit the news, living just a few towns away. (For the record, I now live in Glen Ridge.) A young woman with an intellectual disability was gang-raped in a basement by a group of high school athletes. The victim was called a slut. Many educators and students sided with the athletes. A female friend of one of the perpetrators even tried to convince the victim not to testify. That detail always stuck with me because it was the worst kind of betrayal. Eventually that story morphed into Blythe Jensen.

When I first wrote this story, Ali Greenleaf didn't have a voice. She was raped and the story ended. But as I grew—and as my understanding of myself developed from years and years of working with a very good therapist, as I understood rape culture, as I understood that this behavior didn't happen in a bubble—the story grew.

I've written for publications including *The New York Times*, *The Atlantic*, *Marie Claire*, *Lenny Letter*, *The New York Times Magazine*, and more. And in many ways, I approached this book like a journalist: I researched, I fact-checked, I interviewed experts, I pored over articles and journals. I worked with an authenticity reader who gave valuable insight and feedback. Even with all of this research and my desire to get

---

1 Department of Justice, Office of Justice Programs, Bureau of Justice Statistics, Sex Offenses and Offenders (1997).

things right, there still might be mistakes that are my own. I also know that despite my best efforts, some people will still feel that this story isn't fully accurate to their experiences.

I hope reading *Something Happened to Ali Greenleaf* will have opened your mind to the complexities of sexual assault. I hope it gives you insight into what the act of surviving looks like. But as much as this book is about female rage and the aftermath of sexual assault, it's also about the beauty of female friendships, as well as their worrisome dynamics. These girls often treat each other in the way teenage girls aren't *supposed* to treat each other. Girls today are expected to have evolved beyond the mean-girl trope. But it's important to show that while, yes, teenage girls can be compassionate and forgiving, they can also be complicated and dark. And sometimes menacing.

Lastly, if you've jumped ahead to read this note because you are wondering, *What kind of person wrote this book?* and *What is her backstory?* and you feel too overwhelmed to dive back in . . . then close the book. Stop reading. Give yourself some time for it to settle. Seriously, I will not take offense.

Ali and Blythe find a way to heal through writing. It's how I've found a way to heal too. For me, writing is breathing. Writing is meditating. Writing is the map that leads me outside of my mind. Writing can also feel, as the New York journalist Sid Zion once told me, like being boiled with a pot of hot dogs. So, look, writing is not always the answer, and it can be incredibly frustrating, but it can get you to understand yourself, and it can be an incredible release.

Even if you just write something down in a journal and chuck it in the trash. Put those words on the paper and leave them there. Don't look back. Sometimes that's enough. So do that, will you? Grab a journal and write.

Hayley

ACKNOWLEDGMENTS

First and foremost, I want to thank my parents, Amy Krischer and Norman Krischer, for always supporting me, for being my biggest fans, for always embracing my creativity and my eccentricities. I love you both with all of my heart.

To my agent, Emily Sylvan Kim, who believed in me since the beginning, never wavering. Not once. I will forever be indebted to your belief in me, your honesty, and your sage advice.

To Julie Rosenberg, for being not just an editor, but my partner in all of this. I feel like we've been dual therapists for my characters—you have such an empathetic soul for all of them, understanding them with such great compassion and treating them as if they're your own. I'm so grateful for all that you do and for giving me this opportunity.

To the Razorbill and Penguin Teen team, Casey McIntyre, Alex Sanchez, Gretchen Durning, Jayne Ziemba, Wendy Dopkin, Marinda Valenti, Abigail Powers, Liz Lunn, Tessa Meischeid, and Bri Lockhart. Writing a book is solitary until it is not, and having a team like all of you is a writer's dream.

Thank you to my cover designer, Samira Iravani, and to Monica Loya for your original artwork. You brought Ali to life and I cannot thank you enough.

The female friendships are the most important relationships in this book for very good reason. I had the most loyal best friends in high school, who rallied around me and got me through some of the worst times of my life. Without them,

I probably wouldn't be here, and I certainly wouldn't have this book. Thank you, Jessica Sherman, Amy Griffiths, Irene Stamos, and Liz Adams, for reading my first-ever YA book when we were seventeen, for watching *Heathers* with me over and over, and for embracing my specific level of crazy. Thank you, Liz, for being my own personal Sammi, for rescuing me from too many situations to count and counseling me through practically every crisis in my life.

I also have to thank my girl gang, Beth Block, Sara Kaye, and Miriam Rosenberg, my anchors, my traveling partners, my therapists, my spiritual leaders, and for holding me tight and never letting me go.

My sister-in-law Melissa Adler, my creative brainstorming partner. Like Oprah Winfrey said about Gayle King: Melissa, *taka*, you are my mother and my sister. You are the friend that everybody deserves.

My therapist, Iris Ascher (because every writer has to thank her therapist). Iris, you gave me vision and insight; you blessed me with boundaries and taught me self-worth.

To my brother David Krischer and my sister-in-law Brandi Morris. I'm so lucky to have your wisdom, your friendship, your heart, and your understanding.

Thank you to *all* of the Adlers and Solomons, for being my tribe, with Mel and Eileen at the helm. Thank you for making me feel loved in this big boisterous family that you've created. I'm so grateful.

A tremendous amount of research went into this book. Special thanks to Bernard Lefkowitz, author of *Our Guys*, a detailed account of the Glen Ridge rape case, which was instrumental to the writing of this book.

Thank you to Grace Brown, the photographer behind Project Unbreakable, a photography project aiming to give a voice to survivors of sexual assault, domestic violence, and child abuse.

Thank you to all of my readers, Nicole Cooley, Jodi Brooks, Ruby Brooks, and Miriam Novogrodsky. To my teachers at Lesley University, where I got my MFA in creative writing, Hester Kaplan, Michael Lowenthal, and Laurie Foos, for encouraging me and putting so much into my work.

To Jami Attenberg, for creating #1000wordsofsummer. Jami, I was in a low place when I started your challenge in the summer of 2018. I thought I had no future as a fiction writer. Your challenge lifted me from a bad place and got me to look at my writing differently. Do yourself a favor and follow Jami's #1000wordsofsummer—it's inspiring and will turn your writing around and, as Jami says, you will have 14,000 new words after two weeks. What could be bad?

Most of all I would like to thank my children, Jake and Elke. I would be nothing without you. You both have changed me and enlightened me, more than you will ever know.

And to my husband, Andy, my shining star. Thank you for your honesty, for your compassion, for your love, for being absolutely the weirdest person I know, for making me laugh even at the most inappropriate times, and for being the best and most thorough reader any writer could ever ask for. I love you.

Finally, I want to thank the young Hayley. The girl who wrote and wrote and wrote because breathing is writing and she had to write to live. Thank you for not giving up on yourself. Thank you for persisting despite the hundreds upon hundreds of rejections. Thank you for pushing through the anxiety and the fear, the depression and the loneliness. Look at you now, girl. Look at you now.